AUGUST IS A GOOD TIME FOR KILLING

And Other Blood-Curdling Stories
of Murder in the East

AUGUST IS A GOOD TIME FOR KILLING

And Other Blood-Curdling Stories of
Murder in the East

Edited by

Billie Sue Mosiman
and Martin H. Greenberg

RUTLEDGE HILL PRESS®
Nashville, Tennessee

Published in Nashville, Tennessee, by Rutledge Hill Press®, Inc., 211 Seventh Avenue North, Nashville, Tennessee 37219. Distributed in Canada by H. B. Fenn & Company, Ltd., 34 Nixon Road, Bolton, Ontario, L7E 1W2. Distributed in Australia by The Five Mile Press Pty. Ltd., 22 Summit Road, Noble Park, Victoria 3174. Distributed in New Zealand by Tandem Press, 2 Rugby Road, Birkenhead, Auckland 10. Distributed in the United Kingdom by Verulam Publishing, Ltd., 152a Park Street Lane, Park Street, St. Albans, Hertfordshire AL2 2AU.

Cover and book design by Harriette Bateman.
Typography by E. T. Lowe, Nashville, Tennessee.

Library of Congress Cataloging-in-Publication Data

August is a good time for killing, and other blood-curdling stories of murder in the East / edited by Billie Sue Mosiman and Martin H. Greenberg.
    p. cm.
   ISBN 1–55853–576–4
    1. Detective and mystery stories, American—East (U.S.).
2. Murder—East (U.S.)—Fiction.   I. Mosiman, Billie Sue.
II. Greenberg, Martin Harry.
PS648.D4A94   1998
813'.0872083274—dc21   98–4796
                                            CIP

Printed in the United States of America

1 2 3 4 5 6 7 8 9 — 03 02 01 00 99 98

CONTENTS

INTRODUCTION

The East Coast is a region of the country with some of the oldest cities and settlements in the United States. If we think about it that way, we'll realize that the history of our nation's crime has its oldest roots along the Atlantic Seaboard. From the corridor of power in the nation's capital, north through the metropolis of New York City, to Maine's inhospitable coast, decades of mysteries have been set in many of America's oldest cities.

In this volume we present stories by some of the most talented authors in the mystery field. In "Enduring as Dust," Bruce Holland Rogers gives us a fine tale in which the narrator says, "In a government agency, a mystery, any mystery, is a potential bomb. If you're not sure of what something is, then you must assume that it's going to blow up in your face if you mess with it." We get a sense of how enduring things are, not only government agencies and their protocols, but the whole nature of how the world works.

In Charles Ardai's "Nobody Wins," set in New York, we find a gangster softened by grief and loneliness. He contacts a private eye to look for his lost lover. There is pathos, and final justice in the outcome of this unusual story.

In John Lutz's "The Real Shape of the Coast," the setting is a Virginia institution for the criminally insane and the detectives are the inmates in one bungalow where a patient is found dead on the beach. Lutz is the master of labyrinthine twists and this story enhances his solid reputation.

These exceptional tales of crime are all set along the eastern coast, where murder might be subtle or perplexing—but is always entertaining and always true to the quirks of the region.

Find an easy chair, pull over the good reading lamp, curl up, and immerse yourself in this collection of East Coast murders. You'll know with certainty you spent that time in the company of master storytellers.

Billie Sue Mosiman
1997

AUGUST IS A GOOD TIME FOR KILLING

And Other Blood-Curdling Stories
of Murder in the East

Rex Miller's other short fiction has appeared in such anthologies as Forbidden Acts, Stalkers, *and* I, P.I. *His stories often leave readers wondering if everything is as it appears, even after the final twist is revealed. "Dead Standstill" is no exception.*

Dead Standstill

Rex Miller

On a sweater-chilly robin's-egg-blue-sky Tuesday morning in the second week of May, Nancy Hamilton was flat on her back, freezing where her sweater and shirt had worked up and exposed her skin to the cold plastic sheet, trying to make the family spa stop making those tortured, dying noises.

"I mean it," she whispered. "I'm going to *murder* you," she threatened the gargling thing. The innards of the fiberglass and wood four-person hot tub gurgled and burbled and moaned in response, sounding as if it was about to give up the ghost on its own.

Gentle efforts to reason with it had failed. Imprecations hadn't worked. She'd worked her way up to murderous threats.

What was it Mike used to say about how things wear down? Something about how you can't repeal the second law of thermodynamics. Alas, the great handyman was no more. Mike was history. Things had worn down. Their marriage, for instance.

Exasperated, she slammed the access door to the monster shut, and of course the hot tub motor immediately quit making the hideous noise and began purring contentedly. The old angry door slam—the oldest trick in the service manual.

"Un-be-liev-able." She laughed, pulling her shirt down and tucking it in, rearranging her sweater, and walking through the master bedroom and into the bathroom to wash the gook off her hands, proud of having single-handedly changed the spa filter.

When she turned on the faucet, the hot water heater made a moaning, gurgling noise.

If Mike was here, *he'd* be tending to all this stuff. Changing the filter, checking the frammis—whatever it was. This was man's work. She identified the sexist thought and rejected it.

In the kitchen there was a list of everything that was falling apart, going wrong, running down, breaking. She would go in and write *bathroom faucet* at the bottom of the list, and when she got hold of Mr. Emmert, their plumber, he could take care of everything at one time.

She missed having a man in the house. She missed the kids. And more than she cared to admit to herself at the moment, she missed Mike.

She couldn't face an attack of the guilts right now, and she decided some fresh air would do her a lot of good, so she got an old windbreaker and a scarf out of the closet and went out into the yard.

It was chilly, but the ten foot high cedar fence that closed off a large section of their yard, now Nancy's flower garden, managed to block off most of the cold wind.

As if it had tuned in on her mood, a bright yellow male goldfinch swooped down for a seed pit stop, landing virtually at arm's length from her. Amazingly unafraid as it availed itself of the feeder. She stood still for a minute or so enjoying the beautiful bird; then she walked over to one of the benches and sat down to relax and enjoy her yard.

It was a never-ending show at this time of the year. She sat, transfixed, as a dumb sparrow ran a hummingbird off the swinging feeder. Glossy grackles soared overhead registering their opinion. A male cardinal carefully cracked a seed and carried it away to his nesting mate. She always put seed out for her birds, and was inevitably rewarded by a serenade of song and a chorus of cheerful chirps.

She'd fed birds when they lived in the rental houses, too, but it hadn't been the same. These were *her* birds. *Her* yard. Once it had been their yard. But it hadn't worked out.

At thirty-eight, Nancy was petite, five feet two and a half inches tall, pretty, smart. A year ago she would have described herself as a housewife. The year before that a housewife and mother. But all that had changed.

In the two year interim, the accident had taken Davey, Nora had run away, and Mike had fallen in love.

It was a love affair with someone awesome in her wiles; a woman with whom Nancy Hamilton could not compete. Mike had fallen for the white lady. Cocaine. Or maybe cocaine and money in equal parts—what difference did it make now? He was gone from her.

It had all started when Dixie, Mike's aunt, had passed away and left Mike the money. Ninety-seven thousand and change. Such a godsend, they'd thought. And who would ever have imagined Dixie would have saved up all that money—all those hundreds and fifties hoarded away in a closet shoebox?

Until then the dream of building their own home had been out of reach. But when you added the ninety-seven thou to their certificates of deposit, it was just enough to do it. The first thing they did was send away for some blueprints. And even before the bank had transferred the funds, Mike was talking with a local contractor about the nineteen hundred square foot dream house they'd thought about for so many years.

Mike could never settle for anything ordinary. He had to be a big shot. They couldn't build on a lot in town. No. He was tired of living in those "boring tract houses in the city," so they bought a twenty acre country site beyond the city limits. That was just the beginning of their problems with the house: no city water.

The hard water had been a major problem at first. There was such an unusually high mineral content you couldn't drink the water, you couldn't wash your clothing in it—you could barely stand to bathe in it. But then there was the damn *pool.*

Mike had to have a pool. He insisted on it. It was all he really wanted, he said. You can have your courtyard and your garden, your sewing room, your spa, your plants, your built-ins, your kitchen. "But I get my pool." An outdoor, Olympic-size, below-ground, deluxe pool complete with all the gadgets and goodies the pool people said you couldn't live without.

Now Mike's pool was no more. It was a few feet away, long since filled with earth, covered in thick PVC, bordered in tubing and concrete, then topped with a layer of pea gravel.

She was just getting so she could look at the ring of gravel without feeling a stab of pain in her chest. Soon, she had been told, the heartache for Davey, their beauty of a six-year-old son, would fade and she'd find she wasn't missing him so awfully. "In time, whole days will pass and you won't think about the day your child drowned. A day, maybe even two, will go by without you blaming yourself for his death," someone had told her.

She'd just gone to answer the stupid telephone, she thought, glancing at the cordless hunk of hard plastic she carried with her everywhere now, her little Linus blanket. When Nancy had come back—not forty-five seconds later—their beautiful child was face down in the pool. The horror and numbing shock of it was still such that she had to close her eyes and breathe deeply to rid herself of the images.

Losing Davey had been the beginning of the marriage's disintegration.

Mike's social proclivity, as she called it, for drugs went into high gear. She supposed his dealing dated back to about that same time, and she knew he was moving a lot of narcotics so that he could keep up with his new country club buddies.

He quit his good job at Missouri Chemical, and he and his rich friends would suddenly disappear for long weekends "to Atlantic City on business," or "just down to the Mardi Gras to see this guy." And she didn't let herself think about all the women.

They fell like dominoes. Nora was next. Her beautiful, headstrong teenager. Small like Mama. Five feet tall and ninety-five pounds soaking wet, but with the hair and face and curves to make men of all ages stop dead in their tracks.

Nora had a good brain, she was sweet-tempered, athletic, interested in everything—her whole life was in front of her. But when they lost Davey, and then her dad left, too—that blew it. Within a few months she'd dropped out of school—an honor student in her senior year—and was dating this horrible sleazebag who had a small town garage and Hollywood dreams.

Nancy and Nora had never been the best at communication to begin with, and Nora blamed her for the breakup of the marriage. It was now Nancy's fault that her father, as well as her little brother, was gone. Pleas to stay in school fell on deaf ears. Gentle suggestions about Tony, her longhaired, sleazy beau, met blind eyes. A few months later Nora was gone. Nancy got a postcard, heartbreakingly without a salutation, that said, "I wanted to tell you don't worry about me. I'm fine. Tony and I are living in Colorado. We have a place in the mountains. Nora."

Not even "Love, Nora." No return address, naturally. Nancy forced the family woes from her mind and tried to concentrate on the flowers.

The ringed stone courtyard was visually pleasing, and it was bordered in landscape timbers that contained nearly three hundred feet of flowers and blooming shrubs—white and purple delphiniums, pale lavender hosta, yellow and white coreopsis, yellow shasta daisies, red and pink dahlias, Chinese holly, lavender and blue-spired veronica, purple hyacinth, white candytuft, blue geraniums and playcoden, royal robe violets—and everything was blooming now. If only it didn't turn too cold. She shivered a little, thinking about predictions for a May frost.

But the sound of the wind through the trees was an orchestral background to the birdsong. Maybe she could just sit out here smelling the honeysuckle and listening to the birds and everything bad would go away.

The interior court was a riot of pink and white weigela, Persian lilacs that were so overpoweringly fragrant they were all you could think about when you smelled them, hot pink crepe myrtle, tulips in every color of the rainbow, maroon columbines, lavender wisteria clustered among the Siberian squill, cinnamon and ostrich ferns, Spanish needle yuccas that survived *anything.*

Even the weeds were gorgeous. She loved the yellow sheepshire that grew around the reddish-orange climbing honeysuckle. Not as fragrant as its wilder, seductively-scented cousin, but the feathered friends loved it and the blooming cardinal shrubs and lilacs gave you all the aroma you could handle and then some.

Someday, she thought, I'll come out here and look at all the pretty flowers, and the ring of gravel will not look like Davey's grave.

"Hi, Mr. Clendennon, thank you for returning my call," she said into the phone.

"Well, I'm sorry it took so long, but I've been wiring a house for Elmer Carr over at Willow Point. So, you know, I been gettin' home late." It had taken nearly three weeks to get the electrician on the telephone.

"Oh, no problem," she said, lying. "I wonder if I could get you to fix my doorbell and my telephone?"

"Whatsa matter with 'em, Mrs. Hamilton?"

"The doorbell rings all the time and there's nobody there. It just goes off—day and night, you know? I thought it was kids playing pranks at first. And then the phone will ring and you pick it up and it's dead."

"Well, the phone and the doorbell don't have anything to do with each other, so—" He let it trail off.

"Couldn't the wires be crossed somehow?" she asked without thinking. Jim Clendennon gave her a five minute answer, but finally she got a commitment out of him to come over and look at the door-bell. He said he was "not empowered" to work on phones. Gave her another five minutes on AT&T and Ma Bell and Western Electric and General Electric and various other companies. Apparently getting the telephone to work right was now an affair of state.

She'd had Richie Lanning look at it. He had taken it apart after extracting her promise that she wouldn't "tell," and he'd even gone outside and shown her how you could tap her phone from the box on the side of the house, which was of very little interest to Nancy at the moment, thank you very kindly, but he was a friend of the family and she'd been polite.

The phone still rang at all hours with nobody on the other end, and the doorbell routinely went off at least a couple of times during every twenty-four-hour period, particularly unnerving in the middle of the night, as it was one of those that played a little chimey tune.

The consensus was that the culprit was either (a) a CB base sta-tion (CB base stations now got all the flak formerly reserved for ham radio operators in general—the public now knew the phrase "CB *base station!*"), (b) a garage door opener "on the same harmonic frequency" (as *what?*), (c) power tools down the road at a neighbor's house (in the middle of the night?). Or none of the above.

Having obtained a guarantee from Mr. Clendennon, acknowl-edged master electrician of the entire tri-state area, and also the high-est priced, she picked up the dreaded instrument and phoned her girlfriend Sondra Reynolds.

"It's me."

"You going?"

"I don't think so."

"Oh," Sondra whined, "you chicken."

"I know." She copped a plea of temporary fat thighs and told her she'd take her up on the invitation next time. A float trip. She'd sur-veyed herself in the cutout job in her bedroom mirror. The thighs were still okay. She just couldn't leave the house right now with all that was going on.

There was another call she was going to have to make soon, but she couldn't face that one today. With Nancy no longer putting in a four-day week at school, and the bi-monthly stipend from Mike now coming infrequently, the last of the checking account money was dwindling to nothing. Sondra told her she should get a lawyer and "sock it to him." But lawyers were anathema to Nancy after the endless problems they'd had with the house.

In fact, one of the reasons the float trip was out was that when she and Mike and Nora had gone away for two days, just a weekend at the lake, they'd returned to find their patio awash in water. It seemed the foundation had been built too low, and heavy weekend rains had seeped into the paneled, closed-in patio, the standing, blowing rain water soaking the carpeting and the baseboards.

The irony was that when they'd come into the money Mike insisted she quit her teaching job, arguing that she needed to "concentrate on the house." That she'd done. Since Davey's tragic drowning, it seemed that it had become her entire life. But she had to wrench her mind back to the work at hand. There was nothing to be gained stewing about her errant teenager in the Colorado mountains, or her doper of a husband.

That night Nancy Hamilton had a horrible dream of Davey's drowning, a nightmare in which she kept hearing a child screaming and choking, and when she sat up wide-eyed and fully awake at two ten A.M., the noise hadn't gone away. She heard a kind of "loud, gargling horror in the pipes," or so she described it to Red Emmert, after having literally shouted at Mrs. Emmert to put him on the phone or she'd be over to camp on their doorstep.

Mr. Emmert was there at seven, visibly irritated, but at least he'd come. Perhaps, to be fair, he was so snowed under he only worked on emergencies. Well, this was one of those. She told him about the many problems with the plumbing, the spa, the bathroom faucet, on and on. And of course nothing acted up while the plumber was there. He replaced a couple of washers and was gone inside fifteen minutes, leaving Nancy to consider the fact that she'd dreamed the whole thing.

Three days later she was taking a shower and suddenly all the cold water was off and the hot water was boiling out of the plumbing, scalding her, she was screaming, fighting to get out from under the shower. Again, Emmert came out, and again he could find nothing wrong.

"Miz Hamilton," he said, kindly, "I know you been through a lot and that with the little boy, you know, and I, uh, I think maybe, uh—" and she finished the sentence for him.

"I know what you're thinking. I guess maybe you're right." And she didn't protest. Let it go at that. Maybe the trouble was of her own making.

But the next morning she looked out the living room window and was chilled with fear at what she saw. Every other flower and small plant in the garden was either dead or dying. Her precious flowers! Even the large shrubs were suddenly beginning to look brown. She worked in the garden all day, watering, spading, mulching, but she couldn't kid herself about it. Something was wrong. She double-checked with the weather station, but there was no way the nights had been cool enough to cause this. Something had come up out of the ground and killed everything in the courtyard.

The following night she dreamt again, although she could not recall the specifics of the dream. Only that when she awoke shortly after one A.M. she heard not so much a gargling horror as a loud and unnerving bubbling noise in the plumbing.

This time she was taking no chances. She got the small tape recorder from the study, made sure it had two fresh batteries in it, and taped ten minutes of the noise coming out of the pipes.

"Hello," Mrs. Emmert said in her irascible snarl.

"Mrs. Emmert, this is Nancy Hamilton again."

"You gotta stop calling in the middle of the night like this. My husband gotta get his rest."

Nancy knew one of the Emmert kids from school. The girl was just like her mother: lazy, fat, petulant, mean-spirited, and hypochondriachal.

"Mrs. Emmert, just listen." She hit *Play* on the recorder, and a loud but undecipherable gargle spit into the phone.

But when Red Emmert showed up she didn't need the recording—the noise was still bubbling away. It had grown louder, if anything.

"Well, I can tell you what *this* is," he said. "But this isn't the way you described the noise before."

"No," she explained, "I know. But it wasn't making this noise before. What the heck is it?"

"I'll tell you exactly what it is. It's a high water table. We got the same thing in some of the houses in town." He explained to her what a high water table was and how it could cause the bubbling phenomenon.

"But what can we do to stop it?"

"You cain't do nothing to stop it. Not till that water level drops back down."

"But won't this tear up the pipes and everything?"

"Nah. It won't hurt nothin'. Just don't run no more water than you have to."

That night the faucets began dripping. The pipes had stopped bubbling temporarily, but all the faucets in the house were leaking water—the newly washered hardware! Drip . . . drip . . . drip . . . *drip* . . . *drip* . . . DRIP . . . DRIP!

It was an irregular and maddening noise that woke her about four with a really loud and metallic ping . . . *ping* . . . PING; an increasingly loud noise coming from the direction of the kitchen. Almost as if someone was *making* the noise, like hammering on the kitchen pipes with a ballpeen hammer . . . *ping* . . . PING! BANG! Wait a minute. The noises were too loud for any dripping water. Suddenly Nancy was aware that these were man-made and she was frantic, fumbling first for the revolver she kept under the bed and then dialing the sheriff's office on the bedroom phone. A bored dispatcher telling her "we'll send somebody," trying to ask her a lot of questions and the pounding getting louder and louder.

She slammed the phone down on the idiot and, holding the weapon shakily in front of her, began to make her way down the darkened hallway between the master bedroom and the living room adjoining the kitchen.

Should she turn the lights on and scare away the intruder?

Just as she was going around the corner, the noise stopped and Nancy froze, and it was at that moment of insight she remembered that sometime after the problems with Mike had begun, she'd become afraid of the loaded firearm under their bed, and she'd removed the bullets. She could see the bullet box very clearly in her mind, a green and yellow box of Remington .38 Special "Plus P's." Very deadly, silver bullets just like the guy with the mask used. The one small problem—they didn't happen to be in the gun she was holding.

She was still standing there like a statue in marble, *Woman in Bathrobe Holding Empty Gun,* when the sheriff's vehicle crunched up in the driveway and she heard his loud banging on the front door. Nancy knew even as she answered the door, turning on the lights and breathing again, that there would be no one outside.

A week later and she was soaking in the tub and "rusty red-brown stuff began coming out of the plumbing." She shut off the faucets but not before something that smelled like excrement had seeped into the bath with her. She leaped out of the tub, then tried to wash it out and wash herself off with the shower, but more of the same. The smell was beyond anything imaginable.

She ran outside into the courtyard, nude, opened a garden hose, and miraculously it did not spew filth and she was able to rinse herself off.

By mid-afternoon she'd dried her body, dried her tears, and had two full-scale knock-down drag-out screaming matches with Red Emmert's wife. So it was a combative woman who snatched the phone from the receiver on its first ring and, instead of her usual warm "hello," uttered a tight "Yes?"

She was floored to hear the once-familiar baritone say, "Nancy, it's me."

"Mike?"

"Sorry to bother you, but I need some tax stuff. You got a couple seconds?" He seemed curt and even colder than usual.

"All right," she replied, keeping her voice in an equally flat tone.

"I need to come over and borrow our last joint return. Do you still have all our returns in the metal file box?"

"Yeah. As far as I know. Mike, listen, we've got real problems. I need to see you about the house." With the word "house" the flood-gates burst, and suddenly she was telling him about all the problems. About what a nightmare the house had become. About money worries. Letting it all flow into the telephone.

"I don't know what to do. The place is costing a fortune. I can't afford to keep paying plumbers. Mr. Clendennon is going to send me a big bill. The medical insurance is due. I've got Red Emmert's wife ready to kill me. I can't get him out here. I—"

"Emmert is about a hundred years old, number one. Call that guy Ducas—you know who I mean?"

"No."

"He does industrial work, mostly. I'll get hold of him and have him come out. You gonna be home in the morning?"

"Sure."

"Okay," he said. She extracted a promise from him to come out in the morning and try to help with the house. She would give him the tax records then. They could discuss her money problems.

True to his word, Mike was there bright and early, and the new plumber showed up soon after. The men agreed that the culprit was the septic tank.

"Red Emmert called that one right, Mrs. Hamilton," Ducas assured her. "You've got a real high water table out here. You can dig down about a foot and you hit bubbling water. That's what happened—that water is messing up the lines and that. It's got into the drain lines and I 'spect caused the crack in the septic tank, which leaked that sewage into your plumbing somehow—see?"

Mike knew of a guy who would help fix the tank and sink new drain lines. After Mr. Ducas was gone, she told him all about the noises, the false alarms, one thing after another, and he just stood there looking at her like she'd lost her mind. Listening to her run through her catalogue of household woes with undisguised irritation.

"You know, this is really great." He started to read her off but managed to bite his tongue and just shook his head. He seemed like a stranger with a familiar face. Once so tanned and handsome, he was pallid and unshaven. Her once fastidious husband appeared disheveled, his movements nervous and exaggerated. Nancy wondered if she had changed as much in his eyes.

"It's not my fault the house is coming down around my ears," she said in a soft and what she hoped was an unchallenging voice. "I can't afford to keep it up. And even when I go back to work, which I'm going to have to do immediately, Mike, I'm not going to be earning the kind of money this place is going to take. We've got to sell the house." He looked at her like she was crazy.

"This is a rotten time to sell." He talked about soft housing starts and a lot of things she didn't understand. But he said, "I guess I can ask around. See how difficult it would be to get a buyer for the place." Soon he was gone and Nancy was once again alone with the house.

The following two days were uneventful. Then, late at night, Nancy caught herself listening for a telltale squeak of floor in carpeted, reinforced flooring that she *knew* could yield no sound. Listening for the boiling, bubbling, mean essence of this ground that would spew up in the pipes as she lay in bed, unprotected and alone. She knew what she was doing to herself.

She knew so much about this house—she could stare at a pattern of flowers in her handpicked, hard-won wallpaper and see the sheetrocker's product, or the insulation that she and her man had helped to stuff carefully between the framework of the two-bys. See the house naked under its coat of many colors. She knew this baby, bad and good. And she knew there was a presence here besides herself.

Finally, when she fell asleep, deeply, she dreamed the worst nightmare yet. And in the dream she saw light catch on gold and saw it to be the hand of a man. A golden band on the hand of a man, she dreamed, musically.

Dreamed of a woman in a mirror. Soft, shoulder-length hair. Large and expressive eyes in a pretty, oval face. Good cheekbones. Nice nose. Small and well made. Wiry toughness under velvety smooth skin. Sturdiness of upper leg, slimness of ankle.

"Sometimes I forget how beautiful you are," a man whispers from so many months ago. Baby-talk nicknames. Giggled pillow secrets. A remembered foreplay to lovemaking. An aftermath of angry recriminations, talk of money and coke. "Have the goodness to lower your voice." They are not alone in the house.

She dreams of the little child. A boy so small, his tiny body wet and slickly smooth. Nancy will never forget the touch of his icy skin. She fights not to remember this so clearly in the vivid and painful dream, and as it segues to another incident, she still shivers from the screaming injustice of it, shakes from the extraordinary depth of abject grief.

She dreams she is awake and eyes like saucers stare into the luminous face of the bedroom clock. A noise.

This dream that knows no logic, no chronology, no mercy, has her wide awake and listening to the drip-drippppp—*ping*—PING! She is moving silently through the house, her footsteps deadened by seven thousand dollars' worth of wall-to-wall turquoise shag. Hammering from the kitchen.

Frozen, fighting not to breathe, she waits for the frighteningly irregular pounding to resume. BBBAAAAMMMMMM! A grenade-loud concussive explosion pounds against her senses and she springs for the nearest weapon.

Hand clutching gun. Where are the bullets? CALL THEM CARTRIDGES. THE BULLETS ARE THE PART ON THE END, a man's voice growls from the past. Her shoulders shake as she sobs in her sleep, passing the leaded glass tiger who is so beautiful by day, but whose image in the vista of the nighttime garden is menacing beyond expression. A man's hulking shadow fills the hallway and she says, in a voice like a hard, clenched fist, *I have a gun . . .*

*   *   *

"Mike. I can't take it any more," she tells him. On the phone at the crack of dawn. She will not listen to soft housing starts, plumbing repairs, high water tables. "We've got to sell it," she screams into the phone, forcing back the tears that will soon come. "I can't take another night of sleeping pills, plugs in my ears, the house crying out to me, phones and doorbells ringing. Things leaking and dripping and breaking. I CAN'T TAKE IT ANY MORE!"

There are weeks Nancy never let herself think about again. Mike found a guy who could take the house off their hands—someone he'd met out at the club—she knew him vaguely and had never liked him. But it was the offer that was so ridiculous—fifty thousand dollars. It was a quarter of a million dollar house, conservatively, not counting the acreage.

Bad weeks. Savage time of illness and depression. They ended up closing the deal. When the smoke had cleared, she was left with less than eighteen thousand dollars, but at least she was out of the house.

Nancy and her friend Sondra had gone out to pick up her things at the house. She was in the courtyard looking at the place where Davey had drowned. The plastic around the gravel had worked itself up out of the ground and was circling the yard like ugly parts of big black serpents. Every shrub and tree had died—even the weeping mulberries in her once-romantic garden now stood barren and dry. The dead bushes resembled tumbleweeds on stalks. Weeping mulberry. Weeping peach. Weeping Nancy.

"Any problems?" Mike said to the guy from the bank.

"Nope. No problems." He hefted the attaché case in his right hand. Both of them laughed excitedly. "Does this look like problems?" He opened it.

"Jeezus!" There were stacks of beautiful portraits of Mr. Franklin. Federal Reserve note portraits. More than Mike had ever seen at one time. His buddy at the bank had a client, a big potato chip conglomerate, who decided they couldn't live without the Hamiltons' twenty acres. Mike and Nancy sold the land to a dummy corporation for fifty thousand. The corporation peddled it back through the bank for a half a million. Mike and his pal split the difference. The dummy corporation dissolved. The principals vanished. The chip people had the land. Mike and the bank guy had the money tax free. The paper trail stopped dead inside the bank! You couldn't get cleaner at the laundry.

It was also nice not to have to go play games with his ex at odd hours. Nancy had been more work than he'd thought she would be. For a while there he had thought he was going to have to start salting the well water.

Howard Pyle is an author who's appeared in anthologies such as Some Things Dark and Dangerous. *At home in either the past or the present, his prose reveals the nuances of the human condition, whether for good or evil. "Tom Chist and the Treasure Box" puts a new twist on the idea of a treasure hunt.*

Tom Chist and the Treasure Box

Howard Pyle

1

To tell about Tom Chist, and how he got his name and how he came to be living at the little settlement of Henlopen, just inside the mouth of Delaware Bay, the story must begin as far back as 1686, when a great storm swept the Atlantic coast from end to end. During the heaviest part of the hurricane a bark went ashore on the Hen-and-Chicken Shoals, just below Cape Henlopen and at the mouth of the Delaware Bay, and Tom Chist was the only soul of all those on board the ill-fated vessel who escaped alive.

This story must first be told, because it was on account of the strange and miraculous escape that happened to him at that time that he gained the name that was given to him.

Even as late as that time of the American colonies, the little scattered settlement at Henlopen, made up of English, with a few Dutch and Swedish people, was still only a spot upon the face of the great American wilderness that spread away, with swamp and forest, no man knew how far to the westward. That wilderness was not only full of wild beasts, but of Indian savages, who every fall would come in wandering tribes to spend the winter along the shores of the fresh-water lakes below Henlopen. There for four or five months they would live upon fish and clams and wild ducks and geese, chipping their arrowheads, and making their earthenware pots and pans under the lee of the sandhills and pine woods below the Capes.

Sometimes on Sundays when the Rev. Hilary Jones would be preaching in the little log church back in the woods, these half-clad red savages would come in from the cold, and sit squatting in the back part of the church, listening stolidly to the words that had no meaning for them.

But about the wreck of the bark in 1686. Such a wreck as that which then went ashore on the Hen-and-Chicken Shoals was a god-send to the poor and needy settlers in the wilderness where so few good things ever came. For the vessel went to pieces during the night, and the next morning the beach was strewn with wreckage—boxes and barrels, chests and spars, timbers and planks, a plentiful and boun-tiful harvest to be gathered up by the settlers as they chose, with no one to forbid or prevent them.

The name of the bank, as found painted on some of the water barrels and sea chests, was the *Bristol Merchant*, and she no doubt hailed from England.

As was said, the only soul who escaped alive off the wreck was Tom Chist.

A settler, a fisherman named Matt Abrahamson, and his daughter Molly, found Tom. He was washed up on the beach among the wreck-age, in a great wooden box which had been securely tied around with a rope and lashed between two spars—apparently for better protection in beating through the surf. Matt Abrahamson thought he had found something of more than usual value when he came upon this chest; but when he cut the cords and broke open the box with his broadax, he could not have been more astonished had he beheld a salamander instead of a baby of nine or ten months old lying half smothered in the blankets that covered the bottom of the chest.

Matt Abrahamson's daughter Molly had had a baby who had died a month or so before. So when she saw the little one lying there in the bottom of the chest, she cried out in a great loud voice that the Good Man had sent her another baby in place of her own.

The rain was driving before the hurricane storm in dim, slanting sheets, and so she wrapped up the baby in the man's coat she wore and ran off home without waiting to gather up any more of the wreckage.

It was Parson Jones who gave the foundling his name. When the news came to his ears of what Matt Abrahamson had found he went over to the fisherman's cabin to see the child. He examined the clothes in which the baby was dressed. They were of fine linen and handsomely stitched, and the reverend gentleman opined that the foundling's parents must have been of quality. A kerchief had been wrapped around the baby's neck and under its arms and tied behind, and in the corner, marked with very fine needlework, were the initials T.C.

"What d'ye call him, Molly?" said Parson Jones. He was standing, as he spoke, with his back to the fire, warming his palms before the blaze. The pocket of the great-coat he wore bulged out with a big case bottle of spirits which he had gathered up out of the wreck that afternoon. "What d'ye call him, Molly?"

"I'll call him Tom, after my own baby."

"That goes very well with the initial on the kerchief," said Parson Jones. "But what other name d'ye give him? Let it be something to go with the C."

"I don't know," said Molly.

"Why not call him 'Chist,' since he was born in a chist out of the sea? 'Tom Chist'—the name goes off like a flash in the pan." And so "Tom Chist" he was called and "Tom Chist" he was christened.

So much for the beginning of the history of Tom Chist. The story of Captain Kidd's treasure box does not begin until the late spring of 1699.

That was the year that the famous pirate captain, coming up from the West Indies, sailed his sloop into the Delaware Bay, where he lay for over a month waiting for news from his friends in New York.

For he had sent word to that town asking if the coast was clear for him to return home with the rich prize he had brought from the Indian seas and the coast of Africa, and meantime he lay there in the Delaware Bay waiting for a reply. Before he left he turned the whole of Tom Chist's life topsy-turvy with something that he brought ashore.

By that time Tom Chist had grown into a strong-limbed, thick-jointed boy of fourteen or fifteen years of age. It was a miserable dog's life he lived with old Matt Abrahamson, for the old fisherman was in his cups more than half the time, and when he was so there was hardly a day passed that he did not give Tom a curse or a buffet, or, as like as not, an actual beating. One would have thought that such treatment would have broken the spirit of the poor little foundling, but it had just the opposite effect upon Tom Chist, who was one of your stubborn, sturdy, stiff-willed fellows who only grow harder and more tough the more they are ill-treated. It had been a long time now since he had made any outcry or complaint at the hard usage he suffered from old Matt. At such times he would shut his teeth and bear whatever came to him, until sometimes the half-drunken old man would be driven almost mad by his stubborn silence. Maybe he would stop in the midst of the beating he was administering, and, grinding his teeth, would cry out: "Won't ye say naught? Won't ye say naught? Well, then, I'll see if I can't make ye say naught." When things had reached such a pass as this Molly would generally interfere to protect her foster son, and then she and Tom would together fight the old man until they had wrenched the stick or the strap out of his hand. Then old Matt would chase them out of doors and around and around the house for maybe half an hour, until his anger was cool, when he would go back again, and for a time the storm would be over.

Besides his foster mother, Tom Chist had a very good friend in Parson Jones, who used to come over every now and then to Abrahamson's hut upon the chance of getting a half dozen fish for breakfast. He always had a kind word or two for Tom, who during the winter evenings would go over to the good man's house to learn his letters, and to read and write and cipher a little, so that by now he was able to spell the words out of the Bible and the almanac, and knew enough to change tuppence into four ha' pennies.

This is the sort of boy Tom Chist was, and this is the sort of life he led.

In the late spring or early summer of 1699 Captain Kidd's sloop sailed into the mouth of the Delaware Bay and changed the whole fortune of his life.

And this is how you come to the story of Captain Kidd's treasure box.

2

Old Matt Abrahamson kept the flat-bottomed boat in which he went fishing some distance down the shore, and in the neighborhood of the old wreck that had been sunk on the Shoals. This was the usual fishing ground of the settlers, and here old Matt's boat generally lay drawn up on the sand.

There had been a thunderstorm that afternoon, and Tom had gone down the beach to bale out the boat in readiness for the morning's fishing.

It was full moonlight now, as he was returning, and the night sky was full of floating clouds. Now and then there was a dull flash to the

westward, and once a muttering growl of thunder, promising
storm to come.

All that day the pirate sloop had been lying just off the shore b
of the Capes, and now Tom Chist could see the sails glimmering pal-
lidly in the moonlight, spread for drying after the storm. He was walking up the shore homeward when he became aware that at some
distance ahead of him there was a ship's boat drawn up on the little
narrow beach, and a group of men clustered about it. He hurried forward with a good deal of curiosity to see who had landed, but it was
not until he had come close to them that he could distinguish who and
what they were. Then he knew that it must be a party who had come
off the pirate sloop. They had evidently just landed, and two men were
lifting out a chest from the boat. One of them was a negro, naked to
the waist, and the other was a white man in his shirt sleeves, wearing
petticoat breeches, a Monterey cap upon his head, a red bandana handkerchief around his neck, and gold earrings in his ears. He had a long,
plaited queue hanging down his back, and a great sheath knife dangling from his side. Another man, evidently the captain of the party,
stood at a little distance as they lifted the chest out of the boat. He had
a cane in one hand and a lighted lantern in the other, although the
moon was shining as bright as day. He wore jack boots and a handsome laced coat, and he had a long, drooping mustache that curled
down below his chin. He wore a fine, feathered hat, and his long black
hair hung down upon his shoulders.

All this Tom Chist could see in the moonlight that glinted and
twinkled upon the gilt buttons of his coat.

They were so busy lifting the chest from the boat that at first they
did not observe that Tom Chist had come up and was standing there. It
was the white man with the long, plaited queue and the gold earrings
that spoke to him. "Boy, what do you want here, boy?" he said, in a
rough, hoarse voice. "Where d'ye come from?" And then dropping his
end of the chest, and without giving Tom time to answer, he pointed
off down the beach, and said, "You'd better be going about your own
business, if you know what's good for you; and don't you come back,
or you'll find what you don't want waiting for you."

Tom saw in a glance that the pirates were all looking at him, and
then, without saying a word, he turned and walked away. The man
who had spoken to him followed him threateningly for some little distance, as though to see that he had gone away as he was bidden to do.
But presently he stopped, and Tom hurried on alone, until the boat and

pped away behind and lost in the moonlight
pped also, turned, and looked back whence

thing very strange in the appearance of the
ething very mysterious in their actions, and
eant, and what they were going to do. He
looking and listening. He could see noth-
only the sound of distant talking. What were they
doing on the lonely shore thus at night? Then, following a sudden
impulse, he turned and cut off across the sand hummocks, skirting
around inland, but keeping pretty close to the shore, his object being to
spy upon them, and to watch what they were about from the back of
the low sand hills that fronted the beach.

He had gone along some distance in his circuitous return when
he became aware of the sound of voices that seemed to be drawing
closer to him as he came toward the speakers. He stopped and stood listening, and instantly, as he stopped, the voices stopped also. He
crouched there silently in the bright, glimmering moonlight, surrounded by the silent stretches of sand, and the stillness seemed to press
upon him like a heavy hand. Then suddenly the sound of a man's voice
began again, and as Tom listened he could hear some one slowly
counting. "Ninety-one," the voice began, "ninety-two, ninety-three,
ninety-four, ninety-five, ninety-six, ninety-seven, ninety-eight,
ninety-nine, one hundred, one hundred and one"—the slow, monoto-
nous count coming nearer and nearer—"one hundred and two, one
hundred and three, one hundred and four," and so on in its monoto-
nous reckoning.

Suddenly he saw three heads appear above the sandhill, so close to
him that he crouched down quickly with a keen thrill, close beside the
hummock near which he stood. His first fear was that they might have
seen him in the moonlight; but they had not, and his heart rose again
as the counting voice went steadily on. "One hundred and twenty," it
was saying—"and twenty-one, and twenty-two, and twenty-three, and
twenty-four," and then he who was counting came out from behind
the little sandy rise into the white and open level of shimmering
brightness.

It was the man with the cane whom Tom had seen some time
before—the captain of the party who had landed. He carried his cane
under his arm now, and was holding his lantern close to something
that he held in his hand, and upon which he looked narrowly as he

walked with a slow and measured tread in a perfectly straight line across the sand, counting each step as he took it. "And twenty-five, and twenty-six, and twenty-seven, and twenty-eight, and twenty-nine, and thirty."

Behind him walked two other figures; one was the half-naked negro, the other the man with the plaited queue and the earrings, whom Tom had seen lifting the chest out of the boat. Now they were carrying the heavy box between them, laboring through the sand with shuffling tread as they bore it onward. As he who was counting pronounced the word "thirty," the two men set the chest down on the sand with a grunt, the white man panting and blowing and wiping his sleeve across his forehead. And immediately he who counted took out a slip of paper and marked something down upon it. They stood there for a long time, during which Tom lay behind the sand hummock watching them, and for a while the silence was uninterrupted. In the perfect stillness Tom could hear the washing of the little waves beating upon the distant beach, and once the far-away sound of a laugh from one of those who stood by the ship's boat.

One, two, three minutes passed, and then the men picked up the chest and started on again; and then again the other man began his counting. "Thirty and one, and thirty and two, and thirty and three, and thirty and four"—he walked straight across the level open, still looking intently at that which he held in his hand—"and thirty and five, and thirty and six, and thirty and seven," and so on, until the three figures disappeared in the little hollow between the two sand hills on the opposite side of the open, and still Tom could hear the sound of the counting voice in the distance.

Just as they disappeared behind the hill there was a sudden faint flash of light; and by and by, as Tom lay still listening to the counting, he heard, after a long interval, a far-away muffled rumble of distant thunder. He waited for a while, and then arose and stepped to the top of the sand hummock behind which he had been lying. He looked all about him, but there was no one else to be seen. Then he stepped down from the hummock and followed in the direction which the pirate captain and the two men carrying the chest had gone. He crept along cautiously, stopping now and then to make sure that he still heard the counting voice, and when it ceased he lay down upon the sand and waited until it began again.

Presently, so following the pirates, he saw the three figures again in the distance, and, skirting around back of a hill of sand covered with coarse sedge grass, he came to where he overlooked a little open level space gleaming white in the moonlight.

The three had been crossing the level of sand, and were now not more than twenty-five paces from him. They had again set down the chest, upon which the white man with the long queue and the gold earrings had seated to rest himself, the negro standing close beside him. The moon shone as bright as day and full upon his face. It was looking directly at Tom Chist, every line as keen cut with white lights and black shadows as though it had been carved in ivory and jet. He sat perfectly motionless, and Tom drew back with a start, almost thinking he had been discovered. He lay silent, his heart beating heavily in his throat; but there was no alarm, and presently he heard the counting begin again, and when he looked once more he saw they were going away straight across the little open. A soft, sliding hillock of sand lay directly in front of them. They did not turn aside, but went straight over it, the leader helping himself up the sandy slope with his cane, still counting and still keeping his eyes fixed upon that which he held in his hand. Then they disappeared again behind the white crest on the other side.

So Tom followed them cautiously until they had gone almost half a mile inland. When next he saw them clearly it was from a little sandy rise which looked down like the crest of a bowl upon the floor of sand below. Upon this smooth, white floor the moon beat with almost dazzling brightness.

The white man who had helped to carry the chest was now kneeling, busied at some work, though what it was Tom at first could not see. He was whittling the point of a stick into a long wooden peg, and when, by and by, he had finished what he was about, he arose and stepped to where he who seemed to be the captain had stuck his cane upright into the ground as though to mark some particular spot. He drew the cane out of the sand, thrusting the stick down in its stead. Then he drove the long peg down with a wooden mallet which the negro handed to him. The sharp rapping of the mallet upon the top of the peg sounded loud in the perfect stillness, and Tom lay watching and wondering what it all meant. The man, with quick-repeated blows, drove the peg farther and farther down into the sand until it showed only two or three inches above the surface. As he finished his work there was another faint flash of light, and by and by another smothered rumble of thunder, and Tom, as he looked out toward the westward, saw the silver rim of the round and sharply outlined thundercloud rising slowly up into the sky and pushing the other and broken drifting clouds before it.

The two white men were now stooping over the peg, the negro man watching them. Then presently the man with the cane started straight away from the peg, carrying the end of a measuring line with him, the other end of which the man with the plaited queue held against the top of the peg. When the pirate captain had reached the end of the measuring line he marked a cross upon the sand, and then again they measured out another stretch of space.

So they measured a distance five times over, and then, from where Tom lay, he could see the man with the queue drive another peg just at the foot of a sloping rise of sand that swept up beyond into a tall white dune marked sharp and clear against the night sky behind. As soon as the man with the plaited queue had driven the second peg into the ground they began measuring again, and so, still measuring, disappeared in another direction which took them in behind the sand dune where Tom no longer could see what they were doing.

The negro still sat by the chest where the two had left him, and so bright was the moonlight that from where he lay Tom could see the glint of it twinkling in the whites of his eyeballs.

Presently from behind the hill there came, for the third time, the sharp rapping sound of the mallet driving still another peg, and then after a while the two pirates emerged from behind the sloping whiteness into the space of moonlight again.

They came direct to where the chest lay, and the white man and the black man lifting it once more, they walked away across the level of open sand, and so on behind the edge of the hill and out of Tom's sight.

3

Tom Chist could no longer see what the pirates were doing, neither did he dare to cross over the open space of sand that now lay between them and him. He lay there speculating as to what they were about, and meantime the storm cloud was rising higher and higher above the horizon, with louder and louder mutterings of thunder following each dull flash from out the cloudy, cavernous depths. In the silence he could hear an occasional click as of some iron implement, and he opined that the pirates were burying the chest, though just where they were at work he could neither see nor tell.

Still he lay there watching and listening, and by and by a puff of warm air blew across the sand, and a thumping tumble of louder thunder leaped from out the belly of the storm cloud, which every minute was coming nearer and nearer. Still Tom Chist lay watching.

Suddenly, almost unexpectedly, the three figures reappeared from behind the sand hill, the pirate captain leading the way, and the negro and white man following close behind him. They had gone about halfway across the white, sandy level between the hill and the hummock behind which Tom Chist lay, when the white man stopped and bent over as though to tie his shoe.

This brought the negro a few steps in front of his companion.

That which then followed happened so suddenly, so unexpectedly, so swiftly that Tom Chist had hardly time to realize what it all meant before it was over. As the negro passed him the white man arose suddenly and silently erect, and Tom Chist saw the white moonlight glint upon the blade of a great dirk knife which he now held in his hand. He took one, two silent, catlike steps behind the unsuspecting negro. Then there was a sweeping flash of the blade in the pallid light, and a blow, the thump of which Tom could distinctly hear even from where he lay stretched out upon the sand. There was an instant echoing yell from the black man, who ran stumbling forward, who stopped, who regained his footing, and then stood for an instant as though rooted to the spot.

Tom had distinctly seen the knife enter his back, and even thought that he had seen the glint of the point as it came out from the breast.

Meantime the pirate captain had stopped, and now stood with his hand resting upon his cane looking impassively on.

Then the black man started to run. The white man stood for a while glaring after him; then he, too, started after his victim upon the run. The black man was not very far from Tom when he staggered and fell. He tried to rise, then fell forward again, and lay at length. At that instant the first edge of the cloud cut across the moon, and there was a sudden darkness; but in the silence Tom heard the sound of another blow and a groan, and then presently a voice calling to the pirate captain that it was all over.

He saw the dim form of the captain crossing the level sand, and then, as the moon sailed out from behind the cloud, he saw the white man standing over a black figure that lay motionless upon the sand.

Then Tom Chist scrambled up and ran away, plunging down into the hollow of sand that lay in the shadows below. Over the next rise he ran, and down again into the next black hollow, and so on over the sliding, shifting ground, panting and gasping. It seemed to him that he could hear footsteps following, and in the terror that possessed him he almost expected every instant to feel the cold knife blade slide between his own ribs in such a thrust from behind as he had seen given to the poor black man.

So he ran on like one in a nightmare. His feet grew heavy like lead, he panted and gasped, his breath came hot and dry in his throat. But still he ran and ran until at last he found himself in front of old Matt Abrahamson's cabin, gasping, panting, and sobbing for breath, his knees relaxed and his thighs trembling with weakness.

As he opened the door and dashed into the darkened cabin (for both Matt and Molly were long ago asleep in bed) there was a flash of light, and even as he slammed to the door behind him there was an instant peal of thunder, heavy as though a great weight had been dropped upon the roof of the sky, so that the doors and windows of the cabin rattled.

4

Then Tom Chist crept to bed, trembling, shuddering, bathed in sweat, his heart beating like a trip hammer, and his brain dizzy from that long, terror-inspired race through the soft sand in which he had striven to outstrip he knew not what pursuing horror.

For a long, long time he lay awake, trembling and chattering with nervous chills, and when he did fall asleep it was only to drop into monstrous dreams in which he once again saw ever enacted, with various grotesque variations, the tragic drama which his waking eyes had beheld the night before.

Then came the dawning of the broad, wet daylight, and before the rising of the sun Tom was up and out of doors to find the young day dripping with the rain of overnight.

His first act was to climb the nearest sand hill and to gaze out toward the offing where the pirate ship had been the day before.

It was no longer there.

Soon afterward Matt Abrahamson came out of the cabin and he called to Tom to go get a bite to eat, for it was time for them to be away fishing.

All that morning the recollection of the night before hung over Tom Chist like a great cloud of boding trouble. It filled the confined area of the little boat and spread over the entire wide spaces of sky and sea that surrounded them. Not for a moment was it lifted. Even when he was hauling in his wet and dripping line with a struggling fish at the end of it a recurrent memory of what he had seen would suddenly come upon him, and he would groan in spirit at the recollection. He looked at Matt Abrahamson's leathery face, at his lantern jaws cavernously and stolidly chewing at a tobacco leaf, and it seemed monstrous to him that the old man should be so unconscious of the black cloud that wrapped them all about.

When the boat reached the shore again he leaped scrambling to the beach, and as soon as his dinner was eaten he hurried away to find the Dominie Jones.

He ran all the way from Abrahamson's hut to the parson's house, hardly stopping once, and when he knocked at the door he was panting and sobbing for breath.

The good man was sitting on the back-kitchen doorstep smoking his long pipe of tobacco out into the sunlight, while his wife within was rattling about among the pans and dishes in preparation of their supper, of which a strong, porky smell already filled the air.

Then Tom Chist told his story, panting, hurrying, tumbling one word over another in his haste, and Parson Jones listened, breaking every now and then into an ejaculation of wonder. The light in his pipe went out and the bowl turned cold.

"And I don't see why they should have killed the poor black man," said Tom, as he finished his narrative.

"Why, that is very easy enough to understand," said the good reverend man. " 'Twas a treasure box they buried!"

In his agitation Mr. Jones had risen from his seat and was now stumping up and down, puffing at his empty tobacco pipe as though it were still alight.

"A treasure box!" cried out Tom.

"Aye, a treasure box! And that was why they killed the poor black man. He was the only one, d'ye see, besides they two who knew the place where 'twas hid, and now that they've killed him out of the way, there's nobody but themselves knows. The villains—Tut, tut, look at that now!" In his excitement the dominie had snapped the stem of his tobacco pipe in two.

"Why, then," said Tom, "if that is so, 'tis indeed a wicked, bloody treasure, and fit to bring a curse upon anybody who finds it!"

" 'Tis more like to bring a curse upon the soul who buried it," said Parson Jones, "and it may be a blessing to him who finds it. But tell me, Tom, do you think you could find that place again where 'twas hid?"

"I can't tell that," said Tom, " 'twas all in among the sand humps, d'ye see, and it was at night into the bargain. Maybe we could find the marks of their feet in the sand," he added.

" 'Tis not likely," said the reverend gentleman, "for the storm last night would have washed all that away."

"I could find the place," said Tom, "where the boat was drawn up on the beach."

"Why, then, that's something to start from, Tom," said his friend. "If we can find that, then maybe we can find whither they went from there."

"If I was certain it was a treasure box," cried out Tom Chist, "I would rake over every foot of sand betwixt here and Henlopen to find it."

" 'Twould be like hunting for a pin in a haystack," said the Rev. Hilary Jones.

As Tom walked away home, it seemed as though a ton's weight of gloom had been rolled away from his soul. The next day he and Parson Jones were to go treasure-hunting together; it seemed to Tom as though he could hardly wait for the time to come.

5

The next afternoon Parson Jones and Tom Chist started off together upon the expedition that made Tom's fortune forever. Tom carried a spade over his shoulder and the reverend gentleman walked along beside him with his cane.

As they jogged along up the beach they talked together about the only thing they could talk about—the treasure box. "And how big did you say 'twas?" quoth the good gentleman.

"About so long," said Tom Chist, measuring off upon the spade, "and about so wide, and this deep."

"And what if it should be full of money, Tom?" said the reverend gentleman, swinging his cane around and around in wide circles in the excitement of the thought, as he strode along briskly. "Suppose it should be full of money, what then?"

"By Moses!" said Tom Chist, hurrying to keep up with his friend, "I'd buy a ship for myself, I would, and I'd trade in Injy and to Chiny in my own boat, I would. Suppose the chist was all full of money, sir, and suppose we should find it; would there be enough in it, d'ye suppose, to buy a ship?"

"To be sure there would be enough, Tom; enough and to spare, and a good big lump over."

"And if I find it 'tis mine to keep, is it, and no mistake?"

"Why, to be sure it would be yours!" cried out the parson, in a loud voice. "To be sure it would be yours!" He knew nothing of the law, but the doubt of the question began at once to ferment in his brain, and he strode along in silence for a while. "Whose else would it be but yours if you find it?" he burst out. "Can you tell me that?"

"If ever I have a ship of my own," said Tom Chist, "and if ever I sail to Injy in her, I'll fetch ye back the best chist of tea, sir, that ever was fetched from Cochin Chiny."

Parson Jones burst out laughing. "Thankee, Tom," he said, "and I'll thankee again when I get my chist of tea. But tell me, Tom, didst thou ever hear of the farmer girl who counted her chickens before they were hatched?"

It was thus they talked as they hurried along up the beach together, and so came to a place at last where Tom stopped short and stood looking about him. " 'Twas just here," he said, "I saw the boat last night. I know 'twas here, for I mind me of that bit of wreck yonder, and that there was a tall stake drove in the sand just where yon stake stands."

Parson Jones put on his spectacles and went over to the stake toward which Tom pointed. As soon as he had looked at it carefully he called out: "Why, Tom, this hath been just drove down into the sand. 'Tis a brand-new stake of wood, and the pirates must have set it here themselves as a mark, just as they drove the pegs you spoke about down into the sand."

Tom came over and looked at the stake. It was a stout piece of oak nearly two inches thick; it had been shaped with some care, and the top of it had been painted red. He shook the stake and tried to move it, but it had been driven or planted so deeply into the sand that he could not stir it. "Aye, sir," he said, "it must have been set here for a mark, for I'm sure 'twas not here yesterday or the day before." He stood looking about him to see if there were other signs of the pirates' presence. At some little distance there was the corner of something white sticking up out of the sand. He could see that it was a scrap of paper, and he pointed to it, calling out: "Yonder is a piece of paper, sir. I wonder if they left that behind them?"

It was a miraculous chance that placed that paper there. There was only an inch of it showing, and if it had not been for Tom's sharp eyes, it would certainly have been overlooked and passed by. The next windstorm would have covered it up, and all that afterward happened never would have occurred. "Look, sir," he said, as he struck the sand from it, "it hath writing on it."

"Let me see it," said Parson Jones. He adjusted the spectacles a little more firmly astride of his nose as he took the paper in his hand and began conning it. "What's all this?" he said; "a whole lot of figures and nothing else." And then he read aloud, " 'Mark—S.S.W.S. by S.' What d'ye suppose that means, Tom?"

"I don't know, sir," said Tom. "But maybe we can understand it better if you read on."

" 'Tis a great lot of figures," said Parson Jones, "without a grain of meaning in them so far as I can see, unless they be sailing directions." And then he began reading again: " 'Mark S.S.W. by S. 40, 72, 91, 130, 151, 177, 202, 232, 256, 271'—d'ye see, it must be sailing directions— '299, 335, 362, 386, 415, 446, 469, 491, 522, 544, 571, 598'—what a lot of them there be—'626, 652, 676, 695, 724, 851, 876, 905, 940, 967. Peg. S.E. by E. 269 foot. Peg. S.S.W. by S. 427 foot. Peg. Dig to the west of this six foot.' "

"What's that about a peg?" exclaimed Tom. "What's that about a peg? And then there's something about digging, too!" It was as though a sudden light began shining into his brain. He felt himself growing quickly very excited. "Read that over again, sir," he cried. "Why, sir, you remember I told you they drove a peg into the sand. And don't they say to dig close to it? Read it over again, sir—read it over again!"

"Peg?" said the good gentleman. "To be sure it was about a peg. Let's look again. Yes, here it is. 'Peg. S.E. by E. 269 foot.' "

"Aye!" cried out Tom Chist again, in great excitement. "Don't you remember what I told you, sir, 269 foot? Sure that must be what I saw 'em measuring with the line."

Parson Jones had now caught the flame of excitement that was blazing up so strongly in Tom's breast. He felt as though some wonderful thing was about to happen to them. "To be sure, to be sure!" he called out, in a great big voice. "And then they measured out 427 foot south-southwest by south, and they then drove another peg, and then they buried the box six foot to the west of it. Why, Tom—why, Tom Chist! if we've read this aright, thy fortune is made."

Tom Chist stood staring straight at the old gentleman's excited face, and seeing nothing but it in all the bright infinity of sunshine. Were they, indeed, about to find the treasure chest? He felt the sun very hot upon his shoulders, and he heard the harsh, insistent jarring of a tern that hovered and circled with forked tail and sharp white wings in the sunlight just above their heads; but all the time he stood staring into the good old gentleman's face.

It was Parson Jones who first spoke. "But what do all these figures mean?" And Tom observed how the paper shook and rustled in the tremor of excitement that shook his hand. He raised the paper to the focus of his spectacles and began to read again. " 'Mark 40,72, 91—' "

"Mark?" cried out Tom, almost screaming. "Why, that must mean the stake yonder; that must be the mark." And he pointed to the oaken stick with its red tip blazing against the white shimmer of sand behind it.

"And the 40 and 72 and 91," cried the old gentleman, in a voice equally shrill—"why, that must mean the number of steps the pirate was counting when you heard him."

"To be sure that's what they mean!" cried Tom Chist. "That is it, and it can be nothing else. Oh, come, sir—come, sir; let us make haste and find it!"

"Stay! stay!" said the good gentleman, holding up his hand; and again Tom Chist noticed how it trembled and shook. His voice was steady enough, though very hoarse, but his hand shook and trembled as though with a palsy. "Stay! stay! First of all, we must follow these measurements. And 'tis a marvelous thing," he croaked after a little pause, "how this paper ever came to be here."

"Maybe it was blown here by the storm," suggested Tom Chist.

"Like enough; like enough," said Parson Jones. "Like enough, after the wretches had buried the chest and killed the poor black man, they were so buffeted and bowsed about by the storm that it was shook out of the man's pocket, and thus blew away from him without his knowing aught of it."

"But let us find the box!" cried out Tom Chist, flaming with his excitement.

"Aye, aye," said the good man; "only stay a little, my boy, until we make sure what we're about. I've got my pocket compass here, but we must have something to measure off the feet when we have found the peg. You run across to Tom Brooke's house and fetch that measuring rod he used to lay out his new byre. While you're gone I'll pace off the distance marked on the paper with my pocket compass here."

6

Tom Chist was gone for almost an hour, though he ran nearly all the way and back, upborne as on the wings of the wind. When he returned, panting, Parson Jones was nowhere to be seen, but Tom saw his footsteps leading away inland, and he followed the scuffling marks in the smooth surface across the sand humps and down into the hollows, and by and by found the good gentleman in a spot he at once knew as soon as he laid his eyes upon it.

It was the open space where the pirates had driven their first peg, and where Tom Chist had afterward seen them kill the poor black man. Tom Chist gazed around as though expecting to see some sign of the tragedy, but the space was as smooth and as undisturbed as a floor, excepting where, midway across it, Parson Jones, who was now stooping over something on the ground, had trampled it all around about.

When Tom Chist saw him he was still bending over, scraping sand away from something he had found.

It was the first peg!

Inside of half an hour they had found the second and third pegs, and Tom Chist stripped off his coat, and began digging like mad down into the sand, Parson Jones standing over him watching him. The sun was sloping well toward the west when the blade of Tom Chist's spade struck upon something hard.

If it had been his own heart that he had hit in the sand his breast could hardly have thrilled more sharply.

It was the treasure box!

Parson Jones himself leaped down into the hole, and began scraping away the sand with his hands as though he had gone crazy. At last, with some difficulty, they tugged and hauled the chest up out of the sand to the surface, where it lay covered all over with the

grit that clung to it. It was securely locked and fastened with a pad-
lock, and it took a good many blows with the blade of the spade to
burst the bolt. Parson Jones himself lifted the lid. Tom Chist leaned
forward and gazed down into the open box. He would not have
been surprised to have seen it filled full of yellow gold and bright
jewels. It was filled half full of books and papers, and half full of
canvas bags tied safely and securely around and around with cords
of string.

Parson Jones lifted out one of the bags, and it jingled as he did so.
It was full of money.

He cut the string, and with trembling, shaking hands handed the
bag to Tom, who, in an ecstasy of wonder and dizzy with delight,
poured out with swimming sight upon the coat spread on the ground
a cataract of shining silver money that rang and twinkled and jingled as
it fell in a shining heap upon the coarse cloth.

Parson Jones held up both hands into the air, and Tom stared at
what he saw, wondering whether it was all so, and whether he was
really awake. It seemed to him as though he was in a dream.

There were two-and-twenty bags in all in the chest: ten of them
full of silver money, eight of them full of gold money, three of them
full of gold dust, and one small bag with jewels wrapped up in wad
cotton and paper.

" 'Tis enough," cried out Parson Jones, "to make us both rich
men as long as we live."

The burning summer sun, though sloping in the sky, beat down
upon them as hot as fire; but neither of them noticed it. Neither did
they notice hunger nor thirst nor fatigue, but sat there as though in a
trance, with the bags of money scattered on the sand around them, a
great pile of money heaped upon the coat, and the open chest beside
them. It was an hour of sundown before Parson Jones had begun fairly
to examine the books and papers in the chest.

Of the three books, two were evidently log books of the pirates
who had been lying off the mouth of the Delaware Bay all this time.
The other book was written in Spanish, and was evidently the log
book of some captured prize.

It was then, sitting there upon the sand, the good old gentleman
reading in his high, crackling voice, that they first learned from the
bloody records in those two books who it was who had been lying
inside the Cape all this time, and that it was the famous Captain Kidd.
Every now and then the reverend gentleman would stop to exclaim,

"Oh, the bloody wretch!" or, "Oh, the desperate, cruel, villains!" and then would go on reading again a scrap here and a scrap there.

And all the while Tom Chist sat and listened, every now and then reaching out furtively and touching the heap of money still lying upon the coat.

One might be inclined to wonder why Captain Kidd had kept those bloody records. He had probably laid them away because they so incriminated many of the great people of the colony of New York that, with the books in evidence, it would have been impossible to bring the pirate to justice without dragging a dozen or more fine gentlemen into the dock along with him. If he could have kept them in his own possession they would doubtless have been a great weapon of defense to protect him from the gallows. Indeed, when Captain Kidd was finally brought to conviction and hanged, he was not accused of his piracies, but of striking a mutinous seaman upon the head with a bucket and accidentally killing him. The authorities did not dare try him for piracy. He was really hanged because he was a pirate, and we know that it was the log books that Tom Chist brought to New York that did the business for him; he was accused and convicted of manslaughter for killing of his own ship carpenter with a bucket.

So Parson Jones, sitting there in the slanting light, read through these terrible records of piracy, and Tom, with the pile of gold and silver money beside him, sat and listened to him.

What a spectacle, if anyone had come upon them! But they were alone, with the vast arch of sky empty above them and the wide white stretch of sand a desert around them. The sun sank lower and lower, until there was only time to glance through the other papers in the chest.

They were nearly all goldsmiths' bills of exchange drawn in favor of certain of the most prominent merchants of New York. Parson Jones, as he read over the names, knew of nearly all of the gentlemen by hearsay. Aye, here was this gentleman; he thought that name would be among 'em. What? Here is Mr. So-and-so. Well, if all they say is true, the villain has robbed one of his own best friends. "I wonder," he said, "why the wretch should have hidden these papers so carefully away with the other treasures, for they could do him no good?" Then, answering his own question: "Like enough because these will give him a hold over the gentlemen to whom they are drawn so that he can make a good bargain for his own neck before he gives the bills back to their owners. I tell you what it is, Tom," he continued, "it is you yourself shall go to New York and bargain for the return of these papers. 'Twill be as good as another fortune to you."

The majority of the bills were drawn in favor of one Richard Chillingsworth, Esquire. "And he is," said Parson Jones, "one of the richest men in the province of New York. You shall go to him with the news of what we have found."

"When shall I go?" said Tom Chist.

"You shall go upon the very first boat we can catch," said the parson. He had turned, still holding the bills in his hand, and was now fingering over the pile of money that yet lay tumbled out upon the coat. "I wonder, Tom," said he, "if you could spare me a score or so of these doubloons?"

"You shall have fifty score, if you choose," said Tom, bursting with gratitude and with generosity in his newly found treasure.

"You are as fine a lad as ever I saw, Tom," said the parson, "and I'll thank you to the last day of my life."

Tom scooped up a double handful of silver money. "Take it, sir," he said, "and you may have as much more as you want of it."

He poured it into the dish that the good man made of his hands, and the parson made a motion as though to empty it into his pocket. Then he stopped, as though a sudden doubt had occurred to him. "I don't know that 'tis fit for me to take this pirate money, after all," he said.

"But you are welcome to it," said Tom.

Still the parson hesitated. "Nay," he burst out, "I'll not take it; 'tis blood money." And as he spoke he chucked the whole double handful into the now empty chest, then arose and dusted the sand from his breeches. Then, with a great deal of bustling energy, he helped to tie the bags again and put them all back into the chest.

They reburied the chest in the place whence they had taken it, and then the parson folded the precious paper of directions, placed it carefully in his wallet, and his wallet in his pocket. "Tom," he said, for the twentieth time, "your fortune has been made this day."

And Tom Chist, as he rattled in his breeches pocket the half dozen doubloons he had kept out of his treasure, felt that what his friend had said was true.

As the two went back homeward across the level space of sand Tom Chist suddenly stopped stock-still and stood looking about him.

" 'Twas just here," he said, digging his heel down into the sand, "that they killed the poor black man."

"And here he lies buried for all time," said Parson Jones; and as he spoke he dug his cane down into the sand. Tom Chist shuddered. He would not have been surprised if the ferrule of the cane had struck something soft beneath that level surface. But it did not, nor was any sign of that tragedy ever seen again. For, whether the pirates had carried away what they had done and buried it elsewhere, or whether the storm in blowing the sand had completely leveled off and hidden all sign of that tragedy where it was enacted, certain it is that it never came to sight again—at least so far as Tom Chist and the Rev. Hilary Jones ever knew.

7

This is the story of the treasure box. All that remains now is to conclude the story of Tom Chist, and to tell of what came of him in the end.

He did not go back again to live with old Matt Abrahamson. Parson Jones had now taken charge of him and his fortunes, and Tom did not have to go back to the fisherman's hut.

Old Abrahamson talked a great deal about it, and would come in his cups and harangue good Parson Jones, making a vast protestation of what he would do to Tom—if he ever caught him—for running away. But Tom on all these occasions kept carefully out of his way, and nothing came of the old man's threatenings.

Tom used to go over to see his foster mother now and then, but always when the old man was away from home. And Molly Abrahamson used to warn him to keep out of her father's way. "He's in as vile a humor as ever I see, Tom," she said; "he sits sulking all day long, and 'tis my belief he'd kill ye if he caught ye."

Of course Tom said nothing, even to her, about the treasure, and he and the reverend gentleman kept the knowledge thereof to themselves. About three weeks later Parson Jones managed to get him shipped aboard of a vessel bound for New York town, and a few days later Tom Chist landed at that place. He had never been in such a town before, and he could not sufficiently wonder and marvel at the number of brick houses, at the multitude of people coming and going along the fine, hard, earthen sidewalk, at the shops and the stores where goods hung in the windows, and, most of all, the fortifications and the battery at the point, at the rows of threatening cannon, and at the scarlet-coated sentries pacing up and down the ramparts. All this was very wonderful, and so were the clustered boats riding at anchor in the harbor. It was like a new world, so different was it from the sand hills and the sedgy levels of Henlopen.

Tom Chist took up his lodgings at a coffee house near to the town hall, and thence he sent by the postboy, a letter written by Parson Jones to Master Chillingsworth. In a little while the boy returned with a message, asking Tom to come up to Mr. Chillingsworth's house that afternoon at two o'clock.

Tom went thither with a great deal of trepidation, and his heart fell away altogether when he found it a fine, grand brick house, three stories high, and with wrought-iron letters across the front.

The counting house was in the same building; but Tom, because of Mr. Jones's letter, was conducted directly into the parlor, where the great rich man was awaiting his coming. He was sitting in a leather-covered armchair, smoking a pipe of tobacco, and with a bottle of fine old Madeira close to his elbow.

Tom had not had a chance to buy a new suit of clothes yet, and so he cut no very fine figure in the rough dress he had brought with him from Henlopen. Nor did Mr. Chillingsworth seem to think very highly of his appearance, for he sat looking sideways at Tom as he smoked.

"Well, my lad," he said, "and what is this great thing you have to tell me that is so mightily wonderful? I got what's-his-name—Mr. Jones's—letter, and now I am ready to hear what you have to say."

But if he thought but little of his visitor's appearance at first, he soon changed his sentiments toward him, for Tom had not spoken twenty words when Mr. Chillingsworth's whole aspect changed. He straightened himself up in his seat, laid aside his pipe, pushed away his glass of Madeira, and bade Tom take a chair.

He listened without a word as Tom Chist told of the buried treasure, of how he had seen the poor negro murdered, and of how he and Parson Jones had recovered the chest again. Only once did Mr. Chillingsworth interrupt the narrative. "And to think," he cried, "that the villain this very day walks about New York town as though he were an honest man, ruffling it with the best of us! But if we can only get hold of these log books you speak of. Go on; tell me more of this."

When Tom Chist's narrative was ended, Mr. Chillingsworth's bearing was as different as daylight is from dark. He asked a thousand questions, all in the most polite and gracious tone imaginable, and not only urged a glass of his fine old Madeira upon Tom, but asked him to stay to supper. There was nobody to be there, he said, but his wife and daughter.

Tom, all in a panic at the very thought of the two ladies, sturdily refused to stay even for the dish of tea Mr. Chillingsworth offered him.

He did not know that he was destined to stay there as long as he should live.

"And now," said Mr. Chillingsworth, "tell me about yourself."

"I have nothing to tell, Your Honor," said Tom, "except that I was washed up out of the sea."

"Washed up out of the sea!" exclaimed Mr. Chillingsworth. "Why, how was that? Come, begin at the beginning, and tell me all."

Thereupon Tom Chist did as he was bidden, beginning at the very beginning and telling everything just as Molly Abrahamson had often told it to him. As he continued, Mr. Chillingsworth's interest changed into an appearance of stronger and stronger excitement. Suddenly he jumped up out of his chair and began to walk up and down the room.

"Stop! Stop!" he cried out at last, in the midst of something Tom was saying. "Stop! Stop! Tell me; do you know the name of the vessel that was wrecked, and from which you were washed ashore?"

"I've heard it said," said Tom Chist, " 'twas the *Bristol Merchant*."

"I knew it! I knew it!" exclaimed the great man, in a loud voice, flinging his hands up into the air. "I felt it was so the moment you began the story. But tell me this, was there nothing found with you with a mark or a name upon it?"

"There was a kerchief," said Tom, "marked with a T. and a C."

"Theodosia Chillingsworth!" cried out the merchant. "I knew it! I knew it! Heavens! To think of anything so wonderful happening as this! Boy! Boy! Dost thou know who thou art? Thou art my own brother's son. His name was Oliver Chillingsworth, and he was my partner in business, and thou art his son." Then he ran out into the entryway, shouting and calling for his wife and daughter to come. So Tom Chist—or Thomas Chillingsworth, as he now was to be called— did stay to supper, after all.

This is the story, and I hope you may like it. For Tom Chist became rich and great, as was to be supposed, and he married his pretty cousin Theodosia (who had been named for his own mother, drowned in the *Bristol Merchant*).

He did not forget his friends, but had Parson Jones brought to New York to live.

As to Molly and Matt Abrahamson, they both enjoyed a pension of ten pounds a year for as long as they lived, for now that all was well with him, Tom bore no grudge against the old fisherman for all the drubbings he had suffered.

The treasure box was brought on to New York, and if Tom Chist did not get all the money there was in it (as Parson Jones had opined he would) he got at least a good big lump of it.

And it is my belief that these log books did more to get Captain Kidd arrested in Boston town and hanged in London than anything else that was brought up against him.

Richard T. Chizmar is well known for editing the critically acclaimed dark suspense magazine Cemetery Dance. *But his fiction is establishing him as an author of the highest caliber. Recently the best of his short stories was collected in an anthology entitled* Midnight Promises. *After reading the following story, one can't help but realize that this is a writer to reckon with.*

Like Father, Like Son

Richard T. Chizmar

Father's Day was always a big deal when I was growing up. The old man loved it. Breakfast in bed. (And let me tell you, back in those days, Mom made a ham and egg omelet so big the plate could barely hold it.) Afternoon barbecue in the back yard. Horseshoes. Ball-tossing. Lots of laughter and silly stuff. And then an evening drive downtown for ice cream cones and milkshakes; all four windows rolled down, cool spring air blushing our cheeks; Dad at the wheel, singing along with the radio in that crazy voice of his, big hands swallowing up the steering wheel; Mom, sitting sideways in the passenger seat, rolling her eyes at us, feigning embarrassment.

There were three of us boys—the three stooges, Dad always called us. I was the oldest and most of the responsibilities fell on my shoulders. Come the big weekend, I was in charge of making sure the lawn was mowed, the hedges clipped, and the sidewalk swept. I was the one every year who bought the card down at Finch's Grocery Mart and made sure that Marty and Lawrence signed it. And most important, I was in charge of organizing the gifts. Of course, back when we were kids, our presents were never very expensive or fancy. Usually just something simple we'd each made in school. Individually wrapped and sealed tight with a few yards of shiny scotch tape so as to prolong the official gift opening ceremony after breakfast.

The first gift I can remember making was an ashtray in the shape of a bullfrog. Painted green, of course. Very bright green. The only frog in class with big yellow teeth, too. Dad loved it. Let out a bellow that rattled the bed frame when he pulled it from the box. Shook my tiny hand and told me how proud he was of me. And he was too; you could just tell.

Then there was the year that Marty gave the old man a wooden pipe-holder for his desktop. Sanded and polished and varnished to a fine finish, it was a thing of beauty; it really was. To this day, I think Marty could've had a successful career as a craftsman; it was that nice a job.

Lawrence, who was the youngest and the brightest, was the writer of the family and for a three-year period in his early teens, he gave the old man an "original Lawrence Finley book" each Father's Day. Each "book" was composed of five short chapters and each chapter ended with a suspenseful cliffhanger. They were typed out in dark, clear script on folded construction paper and carefully stapled down the middle. A remarkably detailed pencil sketch marked the title page of each new volume. The story itself was equally impressive: it featured the old man as an outlaw gunfighter in the Old West. Strong and brave and with a heart of gold. A Wild West Robin Hood with a six-shooter on his hip and a fast white horse named Gypsy. Of all the gifts the three of us gave him back when we were kids, I think these stories were the old man's favorite. Not that he ever would've admitted it, of course.

Years later, when all three of us were over at the university and working good part-time jobs, we each saved up and chipped in for something special: a John Deere riding mower. A brand-spanking-new one with a big red ribbon laced through the steering wheel. We surprised him with it right after breakfast that year, and he flat out couldn't believe his eyes. Neither could we; it was the first time any of us— Mom included—had ever seen the old guy speechless. Makes me smile even now just to think about it. Makes me smile even more when I remember all the times I called home from college and Mom would tell me he couldn't come to the phone right now because he was out cutting the lawn . . . again . . . for the second time that week.

Yes, sir, Father's Day was always a big deal back when I was growing up.

The drive out to Hagerstown Prison takes just under three hours on a good day. I figure the traffic to be a bit heavier than usual this morning, so I leave when it's still dark outside. I ride with the radio off and the heat on; it rained last night and the June air has a nasty little bite to it.

I drive the winding country roads faster than I should, but visiting hours have been extended because of the holiday, and I want to show up a few minutes early to get a head start on the registration forms and to check in the gifts I've brought along with me. In the back seat, I have a big bag of freshly baked chocolate chip cookies, a stack of brand-new paperbacks—westerns, mostly—and a half-dozen pouches of his favorite pipe tobacco.

The road is fairly clear and the trip takes two hours and thirty-five minutes. Plenty of time for a man to think . . . even if he doesn't want to.

When I step out onto the gravel parking lot, the morning sun is shining and the chill has vanished from the air. I can hear birds singing in the trees across the way, and I can't help wondering what they must sound like to the men locked inside these walls.

There are already a scattered handful of visitors waiting inside the lobby. Mostly young women with pale, dirty, restless children. But a few older couples, too. None of them look up at me when I take off my coat and sit down, but the hush of whispering momentarily fades to silence, then picks up again. In all my visits here, I've never once heard anyone speak in a normal tone of voice in this room—only whispers. It's always like this in the waiting room. There's an awkward kind of acceptance here. No one gawks or stares. It's like we're all charter members of the same club—each and every one of us joined together by our love for someone behind these bars and each of us sharing the same white-hot emotions of embarrassment and fear and despair that coming here brings to the surface.

My father has been here for almost three years now. And unless his case is reopened—which is very unlikely—he will remain here until the day he dies. I don't like to think about that, though. I'd rather dream about the day when he might be free again to spend his retirement years back where he belongs—back at the house with me.

But we both know that day will never come. He will never come home again . . . and still the old man claims he has no regrets. Swears he'd do it all over again in a heartbeat. After all, he tells me, I was just protecting my family.

Sometimes families just drift apart and it's almost impossible to put a finger on the reason. Age-old secrets remain secret. Hidden feelings remain hidden. Sometimes the family was never really that close in the first place, and it simply took the passage of time to bring this sad fact to light.

But you know, that's the funny thing. We never drifted apart. We remained close right up to a point and then *boom*—it was over. One day we're a family; the next day we're not. It was almost as if Marty and Lawrence had gotten together behind our backs and planned the whole terrible thing.

After college, Marty went into real estate. He married a fairly snobby woman named Jennifer (not Jenny or Jen, but Jennifer) and moved east to Annapolis and earned a six-figure income selling waterfront property to yuppies. By the time he was thirty-five, he'd had two boys of his own, divorced Jennifer after discovering that she'd been unfaithful with a co-worker, and entered into a second marriage, this time with an older woman who also worked in real estate. I've never met her, but her name is Vicki and she has a very pleasant voice and is downright friendly on the telephone (although I've only spoken with her twice).

Lawrence, who turned out to be not only the brightest but the hardest-working Finley boy, put his creative skills to profitable use— he went into advertising. He worked a back-breaking schedule and squirreled away his pennies for damn near a decade, then opened his own small agency in downtown Baltimore when he was still in his early thirties. Just a handful of years later, he was one of the field's fastest risers, appeared regularly in all the trade magazines, and oversaw an operation of some two dozen employees. Last year (and I read this in the newspaper; we haven't spoken in over five years), he opened a second office—in New York City.

But for all of their success, it quickly became apparent that Marty and Lawrence had changed. And for the worse. Sure, there were gifts and cards at Christmas and on birthdays, but that was pretty much it. Mom and Dad and I rarely spoke with the two of them—much less saw them—and whenever friends and neighbors asked, our responses were quick, our smiles forced. For a couple of years we kept trying, we honestly did, but our letters went mostly unanswered, our phone calls ignored. The whole situation made Mom and Dad furious. They'd sit around the dining room table, nibbling at their desserts and say, "If they're so ashamed of their smalltown roots and their smalltown family, then so be it. Couple of big shots is what they think they are. Good riddance to them." But I could see past their bitterness and resentment. At the end of the day, they were just like me—left feeling hurt and confused and abandoned. And it was a miserable feeling, let me tell you. Things like this might happen to other families, but for God's sake, not the Finleys.

And so just like that, we became a family of three.

And, soon after, a family of two.

Mom died in her sleep on Easter weekend 1989, and everyone—including Dad—thought it was a good thing. She'd been suffering something terrible. Lung cancer, if you can believe that. Only fifty-three years old and never smoked a day in her life.

Of course, neither Marty nor Lawrence made it home for the funeral. And if you ask me (and the state police boys *did* ask me in a roundabout way later on), Mom's death coupled with their failure to show up at the service was the final straw. Something inside the old man's mind snapped like a dried twig, and he was never the same again.

Shortly after, he began bringing home the cats. Strays, store-bought—it didn't matter a lick. Sometimes as many as two or three a month. His new family, he called them. The two of us need a family to take care of, he'd say. A family that will stay together and live under the same roof. Just wait and see.

By Christmas later that year, we were living with over twenty cats of various sizes, shapes, and colors. The old man had a name for each and every one of them. And I have to admit, he was right; we were like a family again. He must have felt it, too; he was the happiest I'd seen him in a long time.

Then, just after Easter, right after the anniversary of Mom's passing, the old man lost it and killed the Benson kid and all hell broke loose.

The drive home takes forever. It's raining again—really coming down now in thick, flapping sheets—and it's all I can to do to keep the tires on the road. I change the radio station, try to think of something cheerful, but I can't stop myself from thinking of his eyes. Sparkling with such happiness and love, pleased with my gifts, overjoyed with my presence on his special day. But then, as always, the conversation soon turns and he is asking about his family, and his eyes are transforming into something alien and frightening. Eyes so focused and intense and determined, they belong to someone decades younger; they are the eyes of the stranger who stormed out of the house and chased down the Benson kid that long-ago night.

So that's when I take his trembling hand and gently squeeze and tell him what I always tell him: that they are fine. That I am taking good care of them. That his family is safe and sound, and they are all very happy and healthy.

Before I leave he almost breaks my heart when he thanks me with fat tears streaming down his cheeks, and in a quaking voice tells me that I am the man of the family now, that I am the one responsible for their care.

It is after midnight when I pull into the mud-streaked driveway. In the shine of the headlights, I glimpse a blur of black and white fur flash past me and disappear beneath the front porch. For just one moment, I can't decide if I should laugh or cry.

As for me . . . well, I'm still here. I never did leave this town (except for college and hell, even then, I was back living in my old room ten days after graduation). I never did marry. Never had children. Never made my first million. In fact, you can still find me six days a week working the desk over at the Bradshaw County Library and every other Saturday night taking tickets at the movie theater downtown. Not very exciting, I'm afraid.

But, you know, that's okay with me. I turned forty-six a month ago today. I'm finally starting to lose a little ground—going bald on top and a little pudgy on the bottom. Started wearing glasses a while back too. The kids at the library snicker behind my back once in a while, but they're just being kids; they don't mean anything by it. And sure, I hear the whispering sometimes, I know the stories they tell— about how Old Man Finley went off his rocker and strangled little Billy Benson with his bare hands. And all because he'd set one of the old man's cats on fire.

I know they're starting to talk about me, too: about how I'm just as crazy as my old man was. Spending all that time with a house full of stinky old cats. Just like an old blue-haired spinster.

But you know what? I don't mind. Despite everything, I still like this town. I still like my life. There's just something that feels right about it. That's the best way I can explain it. It just feels *right*.

Sure there are nights—usually after drinking too many beers out on the front porch—when I lay awake in bed and stare off into the darkness and wonder what else my life might amount to. I wonder about Marty and Lawrence and why they did what they did. I wonder about Mom and what she would think about all this if she were still alive. And I can't help but wonder about the old man and those haunted eyes of his and that old green bullfrog ashtray and the evening drives for ice cream we used to take back when I was a little kid. But you know, nothing good ever comes from those thoughts. There are never any easy answers, and those nights are long and lonely and sometimes even a little scary.

But then, when I awake the next morning and feel the sunlight on my face and smell the coffee in the air and hear the purrs of my family as they gather around my ankles, I have all the answers I'll ever need.

And I'll tell you something else . . . like father, like son. I have no regrets. Not a one.

John Lutz is the creator of several of the most intriguing detective characters in modern mystery fiction. His hapless detective Alo Nudger manages to be powerless but sympathetic at the same time. His books are prime examples of how to write a mystery novel, and his short fiction can be devastatingly powerful. "The Real Shape of the Coast," a chilling tale of murder at a mental institution, is among his best works.

The Real Shape of the Coast

John Lutz

Where the slender peninsula crooks like a beckoning finger in the warm water, where the ocean waves crash in umbrellas of foam over the low-lying rocks to roll and ebb on the narrow white-sand beaches, there squats in a series of low rectangular buildings and patterns of high fences the State Institution for the Criminal Incurably Insane. There are twenty of the sharp-angled buildings, each rising bricked and hard out of sandy soil like an undeniable fact. Around each building is a ten-foot redwood fence topped by barbed wire, and these fences run to the sea's edge to continue as gossamer networks of barbed wire that stretch out to the rocks.

In each of the rectangular buildings live six men, and on days when the ocean is suitable for swimming it is part of their daily habit—indeed, part of their therapy—to go down to the beach and let the waves roll over them, or simply to lie in the purging sun and grow beautifully tan. Sometimes, just out of the grasping reach of the waves, the men might build things in the damp sand, but by evening those things would be gone. However, some very interesting things had been built in the sand.

The men in the rectangular buildings were not just marking time until their real death. In fact, the "Incurably Insane" in the institution's name was something of a misnomer; it was just that there was an absolute minimum of hope for these men. They lived in clusters of six not only for security's sake, but so that they might form a more or less permanent sensitivity group—day-in, day-out group therapy, with occasional informal gatherings supervised by young Dr. Montaign. Here under the subtle and skillful probings of Dr. Montaign the men bared their lost souls—at least, some of them did.

Cottage D was soon to be the subject of Dr. Montaign's acute interest. In fact, he was to study the occurrences there for the next year and write a series of articles to be published in influential scientific journals.

The first sign that there was something wrong at Cottage D was when one of the patients, a Mr. Rolt, was found dead on the beach one evening. He was lying on his back near the water's edge, wearing only a pair of khaki trousers. At first glance it would seem that he'd had a drowning accident, only his mouth and much of his throat turned out to be stuffed with sand and with a myriad of tiny colorful shells.

Roger Logan, who had lived in Cottage D since being found guilty of murdering his wife three years before, sat quietly watching Dr. Montaign pace the room.

"This simply won't do," the doctor was saying. "One of you has done away with Mr. Rolt, and that is exactly the sort of thing we are in here to stop."

"But it won't be investigated too thoroughly, will it?" Logan said softly. "Like when a convicted murderer is killed in a prison."

"May I remind you," a patient named Kneehoff said in his clipped voice, "that Mr. Rolt was not a murderer." Kneehoff had been a successful businessman before his confinement, and now he made excellent leather wallets and sold them by mail order. He sat now at a small table with some old letters spread before him, as if he were a chairman of the board presiding over a meeting. "I might add," he said haughtily, "that it's difficult to conduct business in an atmosphere such as this."

"I didn't say Rolt was a murderer," Logan said, "but he is—was—supposed to be in here for the rest of his life. That fact is bound to impede justice."

Kneehoff shrugged and shuffled through his letters. "He was a man of little consequence—that is, compared to the heads of giant corporations."

It was true that Mr. Rolt had been a butcher rather than a captain of industry, a butcher who had put things in the meat—some of them unmentionable. But then Kneehoff had merely run a chain of three dry-cleaning establishments.

"Perhaps you thought him inconsequential enough to murder," William Sloan, who was in for pushing his young daughter out of a fortieth-story window, said to Kneehoff. "You never did like Mr. Rolt."

Kneehoff began to splutter. "You're the killer here, Sloan! You and Logan!"

"I killed no one," Logan said quickly.

Kneehoff grinned. "You were proved guilty in a court of law—of killing your wife."

"They didn't prove it to me. I should know whether or not I'm guilty!"

"I know your case," Kneehoff said gazing dispassionately at his old letters. "You hit your wife over the head with a bottle of French Chablis wine, killing her immediately."

"I warn you," Logan said heatedly, "implying that I struck my wife with a wine bottle—and French Chablis at that—is inviting a libel suit!"

Noticeably shaken, Kneehoff became quiet and seemed to lose himself in studying the papers before him. Logan had learned long ago how to deal with him; he knew that Kneehoff's "company" could not stand a lawsuit.

"Justice must be done," Logan went on. "Mr. Rolt's murderer, a real murderer, must be caught and executed."

"Isn't that a job for the police?" Dr. Montaign asked gently.

"The police!" Logan laughed. "Look how they botched my case! No, this is a job for *us*. Living the rest of our lives with a murderer would be intolerable."

"But what about Mr. Sloan?" Dr. Montaign asked. "You're living with him."

"His is a different case," Logan snapped. "Because they found him guilty doesn't mean he is guilty. He says he doesn't remember anything about it, doesn't he?"

"What's your angle?" Brandon, the unsuccessful mystery bomber, asked. "You people have always got an angle, something in mind for yourselves. The only people you can really trust are the poor people."

"My angle is justice," Logan said firmly. "We must have justice!"

"Justice for all the people!" Brandon suddenly shouted, rising to his feet. He glanced about angrily and then sat down again.

"Justice," said old Mr. Heimer, who had been to other worlds and could listen to and hear metal, "will take care of itself. It always does, no matter where."

"They've been waiting a long time," Brandon said, his jaw jutting out beneath his dark mustache. "The poor people, I mean."

"Have the police any clues?" Logan asked Dr. Montaign.

"They know what you know," the doctor said calmly. "Mr. Rolt was killed on the beach between nine-fifteen and ten—when he shouldn't have been out of Cottage D."

Mr. Heimer raised a thin speckled hand to his lips and chuckled feebly. "Now, maybe that's justice."

"You know the penalty for leaving the building during unauthorized hours," Kneehoff said sternly to Mr. Heimer. "Not death, but confinement to your room for two days. We must have the punishment fit the crime and we must obey the rules. Any operation must have rules in order to be successful."

"That's exactly what I'm saying," Logan said. "The man who killed poor Mr. Rolt must be caught and put to death."

"The authorities are investigating," Dr. Montaign said soothingly.

"Like they investigated my case?" Logan said in a raised and angry voice. "They won't bring the criminal to justice! And I tell you we must not have a murderer here in Compound D!"

"Cottage D," Dr. Montaign corrected him.

"Perhaps Mr. Rolt was killed by something from the sea," William Sloan said thoughtfully.

"No," Brandon said, "I heard the police say there was only a single set of footprints near the body and it led from and to the cottage. It's obviously the work of an inside subversive."

"But what size footprints?" Logan asked.

"They weren't clear enough to determine the size," Dr. Montaign said. "They led to and from near the wooden stairs that come up to the rear yard, then the ground was too hard for footprints."'

"Perhaps they were Mr. Rolt's own footprints," Sloan said.

Kneehoff grunted. "Stupid! Mr. Rolt went to the beach, but he did not come back."

"Well—" Dr. Montaign rose slowly and walked to the door. "I must be going to some of the other cottages now." He smiled at Logan. "It's interesting that you're so concerned with justice," he said. A gull screamed as the doctor went out.

The five remaining patients of Cottage D sat quietly after Dr. Montaign's exit. Logan watched Kneehoff gather up his letters and give their edges a neat sharp tap on the table top before slipping them into his shirt pocket. Brandon and Mr. Heimer seemed to be in deep thought, while Sloan was peering over Kneehoff's shoulder through the open window out to the rolling sea.

"It could be that none of us is safe," Logan said suddenly. "We must get to the bottom of this ourselves."

"But we are at the bottom," Mr. Heimer said pleasantly, "all of us."

Kneehoff snorted. "Speak for yourself, old man."

"It's the crime against the poor people that should be investigated," Brandon said. "If my bomb in the Statue of Liberty had gone off . . . And I used my whole week's vacation that year going to New York."

"We'll conduct our own investigation," Logan insisted, "and we might as well start now. Everyone tell me what he knows about Mr. Rolt's murder."

"Who put you in charge?" Kneehoff asked. "And why should we investigate Rolt's murder?"

"Mr. Rolt was our friend," Sloan said.

"Anyway," Logan said, "we must have an orderly investigation. Somebody has to be in charge."

"I suppose you're right," Kneehoff said. "Yes, an orderly investigation."

Information was exchanged, and it was determined that Mr. Rolt had said he was going to bed at nine-fifteen, saying good night to Ollie, the attendant, in the TV lounge. Sloan and Brandon, the two other men in the lounge, remembered the time because the halfway commercial for "Monsters of Main Street" was on, the one where the box of detergent soars through the air and snatches everyone's shirt. Then at ten o'clock, just when the news was coming on, Ollie had gone to check the beach and discovered Mr. Rolt's body.

"So," Logan said, "the approximate time of death has been established. And I was in my room with the door open. I doubt if Mr. Rolt could have passed in the hall to go outdoors without my noticing him, so we must hypothesize that he did go to his room at nine-fifteen, and sometime between nine-fifteen and ten he left through his window."

"He knew the rules," Kneehoff said. "He wouldn't have just walked outside for everyone to see him."

"True," Logan conceded, "but it's best not to take anything for granted."

"True, true," Mr. Heimer chuckled, "take nothing for granted."

"And where were *you* between nine and ten?" Logan asked.

"I was in Dr. Montaign's office," Mr. Heimer said with a grin, "talking to the doctor about something I'd heard in the steel utility pole. I almost made him understand that all things metal are receivers, tuned to different frequencies, different worlds and vibrations."

Kneehoff, who had once held two of his accountants prisoner for five days without food, laughed.

"And where were *you?*" Logan asked.

"In my office, going over my leather-goods vouchers," Kneehoff said. Kneehoff's "office" was his room, toward the opposite end of the hall from Logan's room.

"Now," Logan said, "we get to the matter of motive. Which of us had reason to kill Mr. Rolt?"

"I don't know," Sloan said distantly. "Who'd do such a thing—fill Mr. Rolt's mouth with sand?"

"You were his closest acquaintance," Brandon said to Logan. "You always played chess with him. Who knows what you and he were plotting?"

"What about you?" Kneehoff said to Brandon. "You tried to choke Mr. Rolt just last week."

Brandon stood up angrily, his mustache bristling. "That was the week *before* last!" He turned to Logan. "And Rolt always beat Logan at chess—that's why Logan hated him."

"He didn't *always* beat me at chess," Logan said. "And I didn't hate him. The only reason he beat me at chess sometimes was because he'd upset the board if he was losing."

"You don't like to get beat at anything," Brandon said, sitting down again. "That's why you killed your wife, because she beat you at things. How middle class, to kill someone because of that."

"I didn't kill my wife," Logan said patiently. "And she didn't beat me at things. Though she was a pretty good businesswoman," he added slowly, "and a good tennis player."

"What about Kneehoff?" Sloan asked. "He was always threatening to kill Mr. Rolt."

"Because he laughed at me!" Kneehoff spat out. "Rolt was a braggart and a fool, always laughing at me because I have ambition and he didn't. He thought he was better at everything than anybody else— and you, Sloan—Rolt used to ridicule you and Heimer. There isn't one of us who didn't have a motive to eliminate a piece of scum like Rolt."

Logan was on his feet, almost screaming. "I won't have you talk about the dead like that!"

"All I was saying," Kneehoff said, smiling his superior smile at having upset Logan, "was that it won't be easy for you to discover

Rolt's murderer. He was a clever man, that murderer, cleverer than you."

Logan refused to be baited. "We'll see about that when I check the alibis," he muttered, and he left the room to walk barefoot in the surf.

On the beach the next day Sloan asked the question they had all been wondering.

"What are we going to do with the murderer if we do catch him?" he asked, his eyes fixed on a distant ship that was just an irregularity on the horizon.

"We'll extract justice," Logan said. "We'll convict and execute him—eliminate him from our society!"

"Do you think we should?" Sloan asked.

"Of course we should!" Logan snapped. "The authorities don't care who killed Mr. Rolt. The authorities are probably glad he's dead."

"I don't agree that it's a sound move," Kneehoff said, "to execute the man. I move that we don't do that."

"I don't hear anyone seconding you," Logan said. "It has to be the way I say if we are to maintain order here."

Kneehoff thought a moment, then smiled. "I agree we must maintain order at all costs," he said. "I withdraw my motion."

"Motion, hell!" Brandon said. He spat into the sand. "We ought to just find out who the killer is and liquidate him. No time for a motion—time for action!"

"Mr. Rolt would approve of that," Sloan said, letting a handful of sand run through his fingers.

Ollie the attendant came down to the beach and stood there smiling, the sea breeze rippling his white uniform. The group on the beach broke up slowly and casually, each man idling away in a different direction.

Kicking the sun-warmed sand with his bare toes, Logan approached Ollie.

"Game of chess, Mr. Logan?" Ollie asked.

"Thanks, no," Logan said. "You found Mr. Rolt's body, didn't you, Ollie?"

"Right, Mr. Logan."

"Mr. Rolt was probably killed while you and Sloan and Brandon were watching TV."

"Probably," Ollie agreed, his big face impassive.

"How come you left at ten o'clock to go down to the beach?"

Ollie turned to stare blankly at Logan with his flat eyes. "You know I always check the beach at night, Mr. Logan. Sometimes the patients lose things."

"Mr. Rolt sure lost something," Logan said. "Did the police ask you if Brandon and Sloan were in the TV room with you the whole time before the murder?"

"They did and I told them yes." Ollie lit a cigarette with one of those transparent lighters that had a fishing fly in the fluid. "You studying to be a detective, Mr. Logan?"

"No, no," Logan laughed. "I'm just interested in how the police work, after the way they messed up my case. Once they thought I was guilty I didn't have a chance."

But Ollie was no longer listening. He had turned to look out at the ocean. "Don't go out too far, Mr. Kneehoff!" he called, but Kneehoff pretended not to hear and began moving in the water parallel with the beach.

Logan walked away to join Mr. Heimer who was standing in the surf with his pants rolled above his knees.

"Find out anything from Ollie?" Mr. Heimer asked, his body balancing slightly as the retreating sea pulled the sand and shells from beneath him.

"Some things," Logan said, crossing his arms and enjoying the play of the cool surf about his legs. The two men—rather than the ocean—seemed to be moving as the tide swept in and out and shifted the sand beneath the sensitive soles of their bare feet. "It's like the ocean," Logan said, "finding out who killed Mr. Rolt. The ocean works and works on the shore, washing in and out until only the sand and rock remain—the real shape of the coast. Wash the soil away and you have bare rock; wash the lies away and you have bare truth."

"Not many can endure the truth," Mr. Heimer said, stooping to let his hand drag in an incoming wave, "even in other worlds."

Logan raised his shoulders. "Not many ever learn the truth," he said, turning and walking through the wet sand toward the beach. Amid the onwash of the wide shallow wave he seemed to be moving backward, out to sea . . .

Two days later Logan talked to Dr. Montaign, catching him alone in the TV lounge when the doctor dropped by for one of his midday visits. The room was very quiet; even the ticking of the clock seemed slow, lazy, and out of rhythm.

"I was wondering, doctor," Logan said, "about the night of Mr. Rolt's murder. Did Mr. Heimer stay very late in your office?"

"The police asked me that," Dr. Montaign said with a smile. "Mr. Heimer was in my office until ten o'clock, then I saw him come into this room and join Brandon and Sloan to watch the news."

"Was Kneehoff with them?"

"Yes, Kneehoff was in his room."

"I was in my room," Logan said, "with my door open to the hall, and I didn't see Mr. Rolt pass to go outdoors. So he must have gone out through his window. Maybe the police would like to know that."

"I'll tell them for you," Dr. Montaign said, "but they know Mr. Rolt went out through his window because his only door was locked from the inside." The doctor cocked his head at Logan, as was his habit. "I wouldn't try to be a detective," he said gently. He placed a smoothly manicured hand on Logan's shoulder. "My advice is to forget about Mr. Rolt."

"Like the police?" Logan said.

The hand patted Logan's shoulder soothingly.

After the doctor had left, Logan sat on the cool vinyl sofa and thought. Brandon, Sloan and Heimer were accounted for, and Kneehoff couldn't have left the building without Logan seeing him pass in the hall. The two men, murderer and victim, might have left together through Mr. Rolt's window—only that wouldn't explain the single set of fresh footprints to and from the body. And the police had found Mr. Rolt's footprints where he'd gone down to the beach farther from the cottage and then apparently walked up the beach through the surf to where his path and the path of the murderer crossed.

And then Logan saw the only remaining possibility—the only possible answer.

Ollie, the man who had discovered the body—Ollie alone had had the opportunity to kill! And after doing away with Mr. Rolt he must have noticed his footprints leading to and from the body; so at the wooden stairs he simply turned and walked back to the sea in another direction, then walked up the beach to make his "discovery" and alert the doctor.

Motive? Logan smiled. Anyone could have had motive enough to kill the bragging and offensive Mr. Rolt. He had been an easy man to hate.

Logan left the TV room to join the other patients on the beach, careful not to glance at the distant white-uniformed figure of Ollie painting some deck chairs at the other end of the building.

"Tonight," Logan told them dramatically, "we'll meet in the conference room after Dr. Montaign leaves and I promise to tell you who the murderer is. Then we'll decide how best to remove him from our midst."

"Only if he's guilty," Kneehoff said. "You must present convincing, positive evidence."

"I have proof," Logan said.

"Power to the people!" Brandon cried, leaping to his feet.

Laughing and shouting, they all ran like schoolboys into the waves.

The patients sat through their evening session with Dr. Montaign, answering questions mechanically and chattering irrelevantly, and Dr. Montaign sensed a certain tenseness and expectancy in them. Why were they anxious? Was it fear? Had Logan been harping to them about the murder? Why was Kneehoff not looking at his letters, and Sloan not gazing out the window?"

"I told the police," Dr. Montaign mentioned, "that I didn't expect to walk up on any more bodies on the beach."

"You?" Logan stiffened in his chair. "I thought it was Ollie who found Mr. Rolt."

"He did, really," Dr. Montaign said, cocking his head. "After Mr. Heimer left me I accompanied Ollie to check the beach so I could talk to him about some things. He was the one who saw the body first and ran ahead to find out what it was."

"And it was Mr. Rolt, his mouth stuffed with sand," Sloan murmured.

Logan's head seemed to be whirling. He had been so sure! Process of elimination. It had to be Ollie! Or were the two men, Ollie and Dr. Montaign, in it together? They had to be! But that was impossible! There had been only one set of footprints.

Kneehoff! It must have been Kneehoff all along! He must have made a secret appointment with Rolt on the beach and killed him. But Rolt had been walking alone until he met the killer, who was also alone! And *someone* had left the fresh footprints, the single set of footprints, to and from the body.

Kneehoff must have seen Rolt, slipped out through his window, intercepted him, and killed him. But Kneehoff's room didn't have a window! Only the two end rooms had windows, Rolt's room and Logan's room!

A single set of footprints—they could only be his own! *His own!*

Through a haze Logan saw Dr. Montaign glance at his watch, smile, say his good-byes, and leave. The night breeze wafted through the wide open windows of the conference room with the hushing of the surf, the surf wearing away the land to bare rock.

"Now," Kneehoff said to Logan, and the moon seemed to light his eyes, "who exactly is our man? Who killed Mr. Rolt? And what is your evidence?"

Ollie found Logan's body the next morning, face down on the beach, the gentle lapping surf trying to claim him. Logan's head was turned and half buried and his broken limbs were twisted at strange angles, and around him the damp sand was beaten with, in addition to his own, four different sets of footprints.

Max Allan Collins is the first one to admit his writing is primarily in the "hard-boiled" tradition, so at first the idea behind this story may seem to be a departure from his usual work. However, once its true nature becomes apparent, this story has more in common with the great old pulp tales than one might think. More of his short fiction can be found in Murder Is My Business, Werewolves, *and* Vampire Detectives. *His current novel series features Nate Heller, a private eye in the 1940s.*

His Father's Ghost

by Max Allan Collins

The bus dropped him off at a truck stop two miles from Greenwood, and Jeff had milk and homemade cherry pie before walking the two miles to the little town. It was May, a sunny cool afternoon that couldn't make up its mind whether to be spring or summer, and the walk along the blacktop up and over rolling hills was pleasant enough.

On the last of these hills—overlooking where the undulating Grant Wood farmland flattened out to nestle the small collection of houses and buildings labeled "Greenwood" by the water tower—was the cemetery. The breeze riffled the leaves of trees that shaded the gravestones; it seemed to Jeff that someone was whispering to him, but he couldn't make out what they were saying.

Nobody rich was buried here—no fancy monuments, anyway. He stopped at the top and worked his way down. The boy—Jeff was barely twenty-one—in his faded jeans and new running shoes and Desert Storm sweatshirt, duffel bag slung over his arm, walked backward, eyes slowly scanning the names. When he reached the bottom, he began back up the hill, still scanning, and was threading his way down again when he saw the name.

Carl Henry Hastings—Beloved Husband, Loving Father. 1954–1992.

Jeff Carson studied the gravestone; put his hand on it. Ran his hand over the chiseled inscription. He thought about dropping to his knees for a prayer. But he couldn't, somehow. He'd been raised religious—or anyway, Methodist—but he didn't have much faith in any of that, anymore.

And he couldn't feel what he wanted to feel; he felt as dead as those around him, as cold inside as the marble of the tombstone.

The wind whispered to him through the trees, but he still couldn't make out what it said to him, and so just walked on into the little town, stopping at a motel just beyond the billboard announcing NEW JERSEY'S CLEANEST LITTLE CITY and a sign marking the city limits and population, six thousand.

He tapped the bell on the counter to summon a woman he could see in a room back behind there, to the right of the wall of keys, in what seemed to be living quarters, watching a soap opera, the volume so loud it was distorting. Maybe she didn't want to hear the bell.

But she heard it anyway, a heavyset woman in a floral muumuu with black beehive hair and Cleopatra eye makeup, hauling herself out of a chair as overstuffed as she was; twenty years ago she probably looked like Elizabeth Taylor. Now she looked more like John Belushi *doing* Elizabeth Taylor.

"Twenty-six dollars," she informed him, pushing the register his way. "Cash, check, or credit card?"

"Cash."

She looked at him for the first time, and her heavily mascaraed eyes froze.

"Jesus Christ," she said.

"What's wrong, lady?"

"Nuh . . . nothing."

He signed the register, and she stood there gaping at him. She hadn't returned to her soap opera when he exited, standing there frozen, an obese Lot's wife.

In his room he tossed his duffel bag on the bureau, turned on the TV to CNN just for the noise, and sat on the bed by the nightstand. He found the slim Greenwood phone book in the top drawer, next to the Gideon Bible, and he thumbed through it, looking for an address. He wrote it down on the notepad by the phone.

It was getting close enough to supper time that he couldn't go calling on people. But small-town people ate early, so by seven or maybe even six-thirty he could risk it. He'd been raised in a small town himself, back in Indiana—not this small, but small enough.

He showered, shaved, and after he'd splashed cold water on his face, he studied it in the bathroom mirror as if looking for clues:

gray-blue eyes, high cheekbones, narrow nose, dimpled chin. Then he shrugged at himself and ran a hand through his long, shaggy, wheat-colored hair; that was all the attention he ever paid to it.

Slipping back into his jeans and pulling on a light blue polo shirt, he hoped he looked presentable enough not to get chased away when he showed up on a certain doorstep. He breathed deep—half sigh, half determination.

He'd not be turned away.

Greenwood wasn't big enough to rate a McDonald's, apparently, but there was a Dairy Freez and a Mr. Quik-Burger, whatever that was. He passed up both, walking along a shady, idyllic residential street, with homes dating mostly to the 1920s or before he'd guess, and well-kept up. Finally, he came to the downtown, which seemed relatively prosperous: a corner supermarket, video store, numerous bars, and a café called Mom's.

Somebody somewhere had told him that one of the three rules of life was not eating at any restaurant called Mom's; one of the others was not playing cards with anybody named Doc. He'd forgotten the third and proved the first wrong by having the chicken-fried steak, American fries with gravy, corn, and slaw, and finding them delicious.

The only thing wrong with Mom's was that it was fairly busy—farm families, blue-collar folks—all of whom kept looking at him. It was as if he were wearing a KICK ME sign, only they weren't smirking; they had wide, hollow eyes and whispered. Husbands and wives would put their heads together; mothers would place lips near a child's ear for a hushed explanation.

Jeff's dad, back in Indiana, was not much of a man's man; Dad was a drama teacher at a small college, and if it hadn't been for Uncle Fred, Jeff would never have learned to hunt and fish and shoot. But Jeff's dad's guilty pleasure (Dad's term) was John Wayne movies and other westerns. Jeff loved them, too. *The Searchers* he had seen maybe a million times—wore out the video tape.

But right now he felt like Randolph Scott or maybe Audie Murphy in one of those fifties westerns where a stranger came to town and everybody looked at him funny.

Or maybe it was just his imagination. He was sitting in the corner of the café, and to his left, up on the wall, after all, was a little chalkboard with the specials of the day.

His waitress wasn't looking at him funny; she was a blonde of perhaps fifteen, pretty and plump, about to burst the buttons of her waitress uniform. She wanted to flirt, but Jeff wasn't in the mood.

When she brought the bill, however, he asked her directions to the address he'd written on the note paper.

"That's just up the street to Main and two blocks left and one more right," she said. "I could show you . . . I get off at eight."

"That's okay. How old are you?"

"Eighteen. That little pin you're wearing . . . were you really in Desert Storm?"

He had forgotten it was on there. "Uh, yeah."

"See any action?"

He nodded, digging some paper money out of his pocket. "Yeah, a little."

Her round pretty face beamed. "Greenwood's gonna seem awful dull, after that. My name's Tabitha, but my friends call me Tabby."

"Hi, Tabby."

"My folks just moved here, six months ago. Dad works at Chemco?"

"Mmmm," Jeff said, as if that meant something to him. He was leaving a five dollar bill and an extra buck, which covered the food and a tip.

"Jenkins!" somebody called.

It was the manager, or at least the guy in shirt and tie behind the register up front; he was about fifty with dark hair, a pot belly, and an irritated expression.

"You got orders up!" he said, scowling over at the girl.

Then he saw Jeff and his red face whitened.

"What's with him?" Tabby asked under her breath. "Looks like he saw a ghost. . . ."

The pleasantly plump waitress swished away quickly, and Jeff, face burning from all the eyes on him, got the hell out of there.

At dusk in the cool breeze, Greenwood seemed unreal, like something Hollywood dreamed up; as he walked back into the residential neighborhood—earlier he must have walked by within a block of the address he was seeking—he was thinking how perfect it seemed, when a red pickup rolled by with speakers blasting a Metallica song.

He hated that shit. Heavy metal was not his style, or drugs, either. His folks liked to joke about being "old hippies," and indeed he'd grown up used to the smell of incense and the sweet sickening aroma of pot. They weren't potheads or anything, but now and then, on a weekend night at home, they'd go in the den and put on Hendrix and Cream (music Jeff didn't care for in the least) and talk about the good old days.

Jeff loved his parents, but that Woodstock crap made him sick. He liked country western music—Garth Brooks, Travis Tritt—and found his folks' liberal politics naive. Some of his views came from Uncle Fred, no question; and maybe, like most kids, Jeff was just inclined to be contrary to his parents.

But a part of him had always felt apart from them. A stranger.

If it hadn't been for Dad liking western movies—Mom hated them and never had a kind word for "that fascist, John Wayne"—they might not have bonded at all. But when his father was a kid, *Gunsmoke* and *Have Gun Will Travel* were on TV, and that bug had bit his dad before the Beatles came along to screw up Jeff's parents' entire generation.

The streetlamp out front was burned out, but a light was on over the door of the one-and-a-half story 1950s era brick bungalow, with its four steps up to a stoop and its lighted doorbell. It was as if he were expected.

But he wasn't.

And he stood on the stoop the longest time before he finally had the nerve to push the bell.

The door opened all the way—not just a protective crack; this was still a small enough, safe enough town to warrant such confidence, or naivete. The cheerful-looking woman standing there in a yellow halter top and red shorts and yellow-and-red open-toed sandals was slender and redheaded with pale freckled-all-over skin; she was green-eyed, pug-nosed, with full lips—attractive but not beautiful, and probably about thirty.

"Danny," she began, obviously expecting somebody else, a bottle of Coors in a red-nailed hand, "I—"

Then her wide smile dissolved, and her eyes widened and saying "Jesus Christ!," she dropped the Coors; it exploded on the porch, and Jeff jumped back.

Breathing hard, she looked at him, ignoring the foaming beer and the broken glass between them.

"What . . . what is . . . who . . ."

Her eyes tightened and shifted, as if she were trying to get him in focus.

"Mrs. Hastings, I'm sorry to jump drop in on you like this."

Her voice was breathless, disbelieving: "Carl?"

"My name is Jeff Carson, Mrs. Hastings. We spoke on the phone?"

"Step into the light. Mind the glass."

He did.

Her eyes widened again and her mouth was open, her full lips quivering. "It's not possible."

"I called inquiring about your husband. And you told me he had died recently."

"Six months ago. I don't understand . . ."

"Is there somewhere we could talk? You seem to be expecting somebody. . . ."

She nodded; then swallowed. "Mr. Carson . . . Jeff?"

"Please."

"There's a deck in back; I was just relaxing there. Would you mind walking around and meeting me there? I don't . . . don't want you walking through the house just yet. My son is playing Nintendo and I . . . don't want to disturb him."

That made as little sense as anything else, but Jeff merely nodded.

In back, up some steps onto the wooden sun deck, Jeff sat in a white metal patio chair by a white metal table under a colorful umbrella; dusk was darkening into evening, and the backyard stretched endlessly to a break of trees. A bug light snapped and popped, eating mosquitoes; but a few managed to nibble Jeff, just the same.

In a minute or so she appeared through a glass door. She had two beers this time; she handed him one and took a manlike gulp from the other.

"So you're the one who called," she said.

"That's right."

"I almost forgot about that. All you did was ask for Carl, and when I said he'd died, you just said 'oh,' and asked when, and I said not long ago, and you said you were very sorry and hung up. Right? Wasn't that the conversation?"

"That was the conversation."

"Are you his son?"

That surprised Jeff, but he nodded and said, "How did you know? Is there . . . a resemblance?"

She had a mouthful of beer and almost spit it out. "Wait here."

She went inside the house and came back with a framed color photograph of a man in sheriff's uniform and hat—gray-blue eyes, high cheekbones, narrow nose, dimpled chin. Jeff might have been looking into a mirror of the future, showing him what he would look like in twenty-one years.

"No wonder everybody's been looking at me weird," he said. He couldn't stop staring at the picture; his hand shook.

"You never met him?"

"No. Except for this afternoon."

"This afternoon?"

"At the cemetery."

And then Jeff began to cry.

Mrs. Hastings rose and came over and put her arm around him; she patted his shoulder, as if to say, "There, there." "Listen . . . what's your name?"

"Jeff."

She moved away as Jeff dried his eyes with his fingertips. "Jeff, I never knew about you. Carl never told me. We were married a long time, but he never said anything about you."

"He was the local sheriff?"

"Yes. City, not county. For twelve years. You don't know much about your dad, do you?"

"My dad . . . my dad is a man named Stephen Carson."

"I don't understand."

"I was adopted." He said the obvious. "Carl Hastings was my natural father."

She was sitting again. She said, "Oh," drawing it out into a very long word. Then she pointed at him. "And the mother was Margie Holdaway!"

"That's right. How did you know?"

"Carl and Margie were an item in high school. Oh, I was just in grade school at the time, myself, but I've heard all about it. Not from Carl . . . from the gossips in this town that wanted to make sure I knew all about the Boy Most Likely and his hot affair with the Homecoming Queen. I just never knew anything had . . . come of it."

"Tell me about him."

"You . . . you don't know anything about him, do you, Jeff?"

"No. I always wanted to know who my real parents were. My *folks* knew . . . they didn't get me from an agency. There was some connection between Dad, that is, Stephen Carson, and a lawyer who went to school with Margie Holdaway's father. Anyway, that's how the adoption was arranged. My parents told me that when I turned twenty-one, if I still wanted to know who my natural parents were, they'd tell me. And they did."

"And you came looking for your dad."

"Six months too late, it looks like. Tell me about him."

She told him Carl Hastings was an only child, a farm boy from around Greenwood who was one of the little town's favorite sons—a high-school football star (All-State), he had gone on a scholarship and a successful run of college ball that led to pro offers. But in his senior year Carl had broken his leg in the final game of the season. He had returned to Greenwood where he went to work for a car dealership.

"My *daddy's* business," Mrs. Hastings said, and she sipped her Coors. "I was ten years younger than Carl . . . your daddy. I was working in the Greenwood Pontiac sales office, just out of high school, and things just sort of developed." She smiled and gazed upward and inward, then shook her head. "Carl was just about the handsomest man I ever saw. Least, till you came to my door."

"When did he become sheriff?"

She smirked a little, shook her head. "After we got married, Carl felt funny about working for his wife's daddy. Shouldn't have, but he did. When he got promoted to manager, he just . . . brooded. He was a funny sort of guy, your daddy—very moral. Lots of integrity. Too much, maybe."

"Why do you say that?"

"Oh, I don't know. It was his only fault, really . . . he could be kind of a stuffed shirt. Couldn't roll with the flow, or cut people much slack."

"Did that make him a good sheriff or a bad one?"

"He was re-elected five times, if that answers your question. He was the most dedicated lawman you can imagine."

"Is that what got him killed?"

The words hit her like a physical blow. She swallowed; her eyes began to go moist. She nodded. "I . . . I guess it was."

"I know it must be painful, ma'am. But what were the circumstances?"

Her expression froze, and then she smiled. "The way you said that . . . you said it, *phrased* it, just like Carl would have. Right down to the 'ma'am.' "

"How did my father die?"

"It *is* painful for me to talk about. If you wait a few minutes, Danny Simmons is stopping by—"

As if on cue, a man in the uniform of the local sheriff came out through the house via the glass doors. He was not Carl Hastings, of course: he was a tall, dark-haired man with angular features, wearing his sunglasses even though darkness had fallen.

"I let myself in, babe—I think Tim's gone numb from Nintendo . . . Judas Priest!"

The man in the sheriff's uniform whipped off his sunglasses to get a better look; his exclamation of surprise was at seeing Jeff.

"Danny, this is Carl's son." She had stood and was gesturing to Jeff, who slowly rose himself.

"Jesus, Annie." Simmons looked like he'd been pole-axed. "I didn't know Carl had a son, except for Tim."

"Neither did I," she said.

"He was my natural father," Jeff said, extending his hand, and the two men shook in the midst of the explanation.

"Adopted, huh? I'll bet I know who the mother was," Simmons said tactlessly, finding a metal patio chair to deposit his lanky frame in. "Margie Sterling."

"I thought her name was Holdaway," Jeff said.

"Maiden name," Mrs. Hastings explained. "Margie married Al Sterling right after college."

"Al Sterling?"

"His Honor Alfred Sterling," Simmons said, with a faint edge of nasty sarcasm. "Circuit judge. Of course, he wasn't a judge when Margie married him; he was just the golden boy who was supposed to take the legal profession by storm."

"And didn't?" Jeff asked.

Sheriff Simmons leaned forward, and Jeff could smell liquor on the man's breath, perhaps explaining the obnoxious behavior. "Fell on his ass in New York City with some major firm. Came crawling back to Greenwood to work in his daddy's law office. Now he's the biggest tight-ass judge around. You got a beer for me, babe?"

A little disgusted, a little irritated, Mrs. Hastings said, "Sure you need it, Danny?"

"I'd have to go some, to match that lush Sterling." He turned to Jeff and shrugged and smiled. "Have to forgive me, kid. I had a long day."

"No problem. Did you work with my father?"

"Proud to say I did. I was his deputy for five, no, six years. Stepping into his shoes was the hardest, biggest thing I ever had to try to do."

"Mrs. Hastings suggested I ask you about how he died."

Simmons lost his confident, smirky expression; he seemed genuinely sorrowful when he said, "Sorry, kid—I thought you knew."

"No. That's why I'm here. I'm trying to find out about him."

Simmons seemed to be tasting something foul. "Punks . . . goddamn gang scum."

"Gangs? In a little town like this?"

"Oh, they're not local. They come in from the big cities, looking for farmhouses to rent and set up as crack houses—quiet rural areas where they can do their drug trafficking out of and don't have big-city law enforcement to bother 'em."

"You've got that kind of thing going on here?"

Mrs. Hastings smiled proudly as she said, "Not now—Carl chased 'em out. He and Danny shot it out with a bad-ass bunch and chased 'em out of the county."

"No kidding," Jeff said. He felt a surge of pride. Had his real dad *been* John Wayne?

"This was about two weeks before it happened," Simmons said softly.

"Before what happened?"

Mrs. Hastings stood abruptly and said, "I'm getting myself another beer. Anybody else?"

"No thanks," Jeff said.

"I already asked for one and didn't get it," Simmons reminded her. She nodded and went inside.

Simmons leaned forward, hands folded, elbows on his knees. "It wasn't pretty. Classic urban-style drive-by shooting—as he come out of the office, some nameless faceless asshole let loose of a twelve-gauge shotgun and . . . sorry. Practically blew his head off."

Jeff winced. "Anybody see it?"

"Not a soul. It was three in the morning; we'd had a big accident out on the highway and he worked late. Office is downtown, and about then, it's deserted as hell. Practically tumbleweed blowin' through."

"Then how do you know it was that gang retaliating?"

Simmons shrugged. "Just the M.O., really. And we did have a report that a van of those Spic bastards was spotted rolling through town that afternoon."

"It was an Hispanic gang?"

"That's what I said."

"Nobody else had a motive?"

"You mean, to kill your dad? Kid, they would have elected that man president around here if they could. Everybody loved him."

"Not quite everybody," Jeff said.

Mrs. Hastings came back out and sat down with her Coors in hand. She still hadn't brought Simmons one.

"Sorry," she said. "I just didn't want to have to hear that again."

"I don't blame you," Jeff said. "I need to ask you something, and I don't mean for it to be embarrassing or anything."

"Go ahead," she said guardedly.

"Were my father and Margie Sterling still . . . friends?"

Her expression froze; then she sighed. She looked at the bottle of beer as her thumb traced a line in the moisture there. "You'll have to ask her that."

"You think she'd be around?"

"Probably. I can give you the address."

"I'd appreciate that."

Then she smiled one-sidedly, and it was kind of nasty. "Like to see the expression on her face when she gets a load of *you*. Excuse me a second—I'll go write that address down for you."

She got up and went inside again.

Simmons lounged his scarecrowlike body back in the patio chair and smiled affably. "So how long you going to be in town?"

"As long as it takes."

"To do what?"

"Find out why my father was killed."

The smile disappeared. "Look . . . kid. We investigated ourselves; plus, we had state investigators in. It was a gang shooting."

"Really? What gang exactly?"

"We didn't take their pedigree when Carl and me ran 'em off that farm!"

"You must have had a warrant."

"We did. It was a John Doe. Hey, hell with you, kid. You don't know me, and you don't know our town, and you didn't even know your damn father."

"Why do you call my father's wife, 'babe'?"

"What?"

"You heard me."

Mrs. Hastings came back out with the address on a slip of paper. She handed it to Jeff.

"Good luck," she said, and then, suddenly, she touched his face. Her hand was cold and moist from the beer bottle she'd been holding, but the gesture was overwhelmingly warm. He looked deep into the moist green eyes and found only love for his late father.

"You can answer my question later," he said to the sheriff, and walked down the steps and away from the deck.

The Sterling house was as close to a mansion as Greenwood had. On the outskirts of town in a housing development of split-level homes that looked as expensive as they did similar, dominating a circular cul-de-sac, it was a much larger structure, plantationlike, white, with pillars; through a large multipaned octagonal window high above the entry, a chandelier glimmered.

He rang the bell, and an endlessly bing-bonging theme played behind the massive mahogany door; a tall narrow row of windows on either side of the door provided a glimpse of a marble-floored entryway beyond.

He half expected a butler to answer, but instead it was a woman in a sweatshirt and slacks; at first he thought she was the housekeeper, but she wasn't.

She was his mother.

She was small and attractive. She had been cute, no doubt, when his father had dated her a lifetime ago; now she was a pixie-woman with short brown hair and wideset eyes and a thin, pretty mouth. The only sign of wealth was a massive glittering diamond on the hand she brought up to her mouth as she gasped at the sight of him.

". . . Carl?" Her voice was high-pitched, breathy, like a little girl's.

"No," Jeff said.

"You're not Carl. Who . . ."

Then she knew.

She didn't say so, but her eyes told him *she knew*, and she stepped back and slammed the door in his face.

He stood staring at it for a while, and was just starting to get angry, finger poised to press the bell again, and again, for an hour, for forever if he had to, when the door opened, slowly, and she looked at him. She had gray-blue eyes, too. Maybe his eyes had come from her, not his father.

Then the little woman threw herself around him. Held him. She was weeping. Pretty soon he was weeping, too. They stood outside the mansionlike home and held one another, comforting one another, until a male voice said, "What *is* this?"

They moved apart, then turned to see a man who could have been forty or fifty, but his dark eyes seemed dead already—a thin, gray-haired individual whose once-handsome features were tightened into a clenched fist of a face. He wore a cardigan sweater over a pale blue shirt with a tie. He had a pipe in one hand and a large cocktail glass in the other.

"What the hell is this about?" he demanded, but his voice was thin and whiny.

She pulled Jeff into the light. "Al, this is my son." Then she turned to Jeff and asked, "What's your name?"

Soon Jeff and Mrs. Sterling were seated on high chrome stools at the ceramic-tile island in the center of a large kitchen with endless dark-wood cabinets, appliance-loaded countertops, and stained glass windows. She had served him chocolate chip cookies and tea; the pot was still simmering on one of the burners opposite them on the ceramic island.

Judge Sterling had, almost immediately, gotten out of their way, saying morosely, "You'll be wanting some privacy," and disappearing into a study.

"I told Al all about my youthful pregnancy," she said. "We're both Catholic, and I like to think he respects my decision to have you."

"I'm certainly glad you did," Jeff said, and smiled. This should have felt awkward, but it didn't. He felt he'd always known this pretty little woman.

"I didn't show at all," she said. "When we graduated, I was six months along, and no one even guessed. I had you late that summer, and then started college a few weeks later . . . never missed a beat."

She had a perky way about her that endeared her to him immediately.

"I hope . . . I hope you can forgive me for never getting in touch with you. That's just the way it was done in those days. I don't know how it is now, but when you gave up a baby back then, you gave him up. His new parents *were* his parents."

"I don't hold any grudge. Not at all. I had good parents. I had a fine childhood."

She touched his hand; stroked it, soothingly. "I hope so. And I want to hear all about it. I hope we can be . . . friends, at least."

"I hope so, too."

He told her about his parents' pledge to reveal his true parentage to him at his twenty-first birthday.

"My only regret . . . my only resentment toward my folks . . . is that, by making me wait, they cost me knowing . . . or even meeting . . . my real father."

She nodded, and her eyes were damp. "I know. That's a terrible thing. I know everyone's already told you, but you're a dead ringer for your dad. Poor choice of words. I'm sorry."

"That's why I'm here, actually. The main reason."

"What do you mean?"

"To find out why and how my father died."

"Who have you spoken to?"

He filled her in.

"Terrible thing," she said, "what those gang kids did."

"You believe he died that way?"

"Oh, yes. We were proud of him, locally"—she lowered her voice—"although the board of inquiry into the farmhouse shooting, which my husband oversaw, was pretty hard on Carl and Dan."

"Really?"

"They were both suspended without pay for a month. Excessive use of force. Overstepping certain bounds of legal procedure. I don't know what, exactly. I'm afraid . . . nothing."

"What?"

She leaned close. "I'm afraid Alfred may have used the situation to get back at Carl."

"Your . . . romance with my father—it was strictly a high-school affair, wasn't it?"

She scooted off the chrome stool to get the tea kettle and pour herself another cup. Her back was to him when she said, "It wasn't entirely a . . . high-school affair."

He nibbled at a chocolate chip cookie; it was sweet and good. He wondered if it was homemade, and if so, if a cook had made it, or if his mother had.

She was seated again, stirring sugar into her tea. "For a lot of years, we didn't even speak, your father and I. Both our parents had made sure we were kept apart. We went to different colleges. The pregnancy—please don't take this wrong—but it was tragedy in our lives, not the joy it should have been. The baby . . . you . . . broke us apart instead of bringing us together, like it should." She shook her head. "Times were different."

"You don't have to apologize. I don't need explanations. I just want to know the basic facts. The . . . truth."

"The truth is, your dad and I would see each other, around town—I moved back here, oh, ten years ago, when Al's New York law practice didn't work out—and when we passed at the grocery store or on the street, Carl and me, we'd smile kind of nervously, nod from a distance, never even speak, really."

"I understand. Kind of embarrassed about it."

"Right! Well, last year . . . no, it was a year and a half ago . . . Al and I were separated for a time. We have two children, both college age, boy and a girl—they're your half brother and sister, you know. You *do* have some catching up to do."

That was an understatement.

"Anyway, when the kids moved out, I moved out. It's . . . the details aren't important. Anyway, we were separated, and as fate would have it, Carl and Annie were having some problems, too. Carl and I, we ran into each other at one of the local bars one night, kind of started crying into each other's beer . . . and it just happened."

"You got romantic again."

She nodded; studied her tea, as if the leaves might tell her something about the future—or the past. "It was brief. Like I said, I'm Catholic and have certain beliefs, and Al and I decided to go to marriage counseling, and Carl and Annie got back together, and . . . that was the end of it."

"I see."

She touched his hand again; clutched it. "But it was a sweet two weeks, Jeff. It was a reminder of what could have been. Maybe, what should have been."

"I see. The trouble my father and his wife were having, did it have anything to do with his deputy?"

"That weasel Danny Simmons? How did *you* know?"

"He was over at her house tonight. Calling her 'babe.' "

She laughed humorlessly. "She and Danny did have an affair. Cheap fling is more like it. Danny *was* the problem between her and Carl. Your father . . . he was too straight an arrow to have ever run around on her—anyway, before she had run around on him."

"But they got back together?"

"They did. And just because Annie and Danny have drifted back together, don't take it wrong. I truly believe she loved your father, and that they'd found their way back to each other."

"Well, she's found her way back to Simmons, now."

"You shouldn't blame her. People make wrong choices some-times . . . particularly when they're at a low ebb, emotionally."

"Well . . . I suppose she can use a man in her life, with a son to raise. Was there any sort of pension from my father being sheriff, or some kind of insurance? I mean, he was shot in the line of duty."

"I'm sure there is. But don't worry about Annie Hastings, finan-cially. Her father's car dealership is one of the most successful busi-nesses in the county, and she's an only child."

He slid off the stool. "Well, thank you, Mrs. Sterling. You've been very gracious."

"Must you go?"

"I think I should." He grinned at her. "The cookies were great. Did you make them?"

"I sure did." She climbed off her stool and came up and hugged him. "Any time you want some more, you just holler. We're going to get to know each other, Jeff. And Jeff?"

"Yes?"

"Would you work on something for me?"

"What's that?"

"See if you can work yourself up to calling me 'mom'—instead of Mrs. Sterling."

"Okay," he said.

She saw him to the door. Before he left, she tugged on his arm, pulling him sideways, and pecked his cheek. "You be good."

He started to say something, but then noticed her face was streaked with tears, and suddenly he couldn't talk. He nodded and walked away.

It was approaching ten o'clock now, and he walked back down-town; he wanted to see where his father worked, and around the corner from Mom's café—now closed—he found the County Sher-iff's office, a one-story tan brick building. He stood staring at the sidewalk out front, heavily bathed in light from a nearby streetlamp. He knelt, touched the cement, wondering where his father's blood had been. Heavy bushes stood to the right and left of the sidewalk and Jeff squinted at them. Then he looked up at the streetlamp and squinted again.

★   ★   ★

The sheriff's brown-and-white vehicle was still parked in front of the Hastings home. Jeff leaned against the car, waiting, hoping Simmons wouldn't be spending the night.

At a little after eleven, the tall sheriff came loping around from behind the house—apparently, they'd stayed out on the deck this whole time.

"Who is that?"

"Can't you see me?"

He chuckled, hung his thumbs in his leather gun belt. "The Hastings kid. No, I couldn't see you—streetlight's out."

"Actually, my name is Carson. The streetlight wasn't out in front of my father's office, was it?"

Simmons frowned; his angular face was a shadowy mask in the night. "What are you talking about?"

"Annie Hastings stands to come into her share of money, one of these days, doesn't she? Her father owns that car dealership and all."

"Yeah. So?"

"So I figure she wasn't in on it."

"On what?"

"Murdering my father."

Silence hung like a curtain. Crickets called; somewhere tires squealed.

"Your father was killed by street gang trash."

"He was killed by trash, all right. But it wasn't a street gang. Out in front of the sheriff's office, my father couldn't have been cut down in a drive-by shooting; he'd have dived for the bushes, or back inside. He'd have got a shot off in his own defense, at least."

"That's just nonsense."

"I think it was somebody who knew him—somebody who called to him, who he turned to, who shot his head off. I think it was you. You wanted his job, and you wanted his wife."

"You're just talking."

"All I want to know is, was she in on it?"

Simmons didn't answer; he went around the car to the driver's side door.

Jeff followed, grabbed the man's wrist as he reached for the car-door handle. "Was his wife in on it? Tell me!"

Simmons shoved him away. "Go away. Go home! Go back to Iowa or wherever the hell."

"Indiana."

"Wherever the hell! Go home!"

"No. I'm staying right here in Greenwood. Asking questions. Poking my nose in. Looking at the files, the autopsy, the crime-scene report, talking to the state cops, putting it all together until you're inside a cell where you belong."

Simmons smiled. It seemed friendly. "This is just a misunderstanding," he said and slipped his arm around Jeff's shoulder, all chummy, when the gun was out of its holster in Jeff's midsection *now*.

"Let's take a walk," Simmons said, softly; the arm around Jeff's shoulder had slipped around his neck and turned into a near choke hold. "There's some trees behind the house. We'll—"

Jeff flipped the man and the sheriff landed hard on the pavement on his back, but dazed or not, Simmons brought the gun up, his face a thin satanic grimace, and fired, exploding the night.

The car window on the driver's side spiderwebbed as Jeff ducked out of the way, and with a swift martial-art kick he sent the gun flying out of Simmons's hand, and it fell, nearby, with a *thunk*. The sheriff was getting to his feet but another almost invisible kick put him back down again, unconscious.

The night was quiet. Crickets. An automobile somewhere. Despite the shot, no porch lights were popping on.

Jeff walked over to where the gun had landed. He picked it up, enjoying the cool steel feel of the revolver in his hand, walked back to the unconscious Simmons, cocked it, pointed it down, and studied the skinny son of a bitch who had killed his father.

"It's not what your father would have done," she said.

Jeff turned, and Annie Hastings was standing there. At first he thought she had a gun in her hand, but it was only another Coors.

He said, "Did you hear any of that?"

She nodded. "Enough."

"He killed your husband."

"I believe he did."

"You didn't know?"

"I didn't know."

"You weren't part of it?"

"No, I wasn't."

"Can I trust you?"

"You'll know as much," she said, swigging the beer, then smiling bitterly, "when I back you up in court."

★   ★   ★

He stood at the gravestone in the cemetery on the hillside. He studied the words: *Carl Henry Hastings—Beloved Husband, Loving Father. 1954–1992.* He touched the carved letters: *Father.* He said a silent prayer.

The wind whispered a response through the trees.

"What was he like?" he asked. "What was he *really* like?"

His mother smiled; her pretty pixie face made him happy.

"He was like you," she said. "He was just like you."

The Theft of the White Queen's Menu

Edward D. Hoch

Nick Velvet first heard the White Queen mentioned as he was dining at one of the flashy Boardwalk casinos in Atlantic City. Across the table from him sat Rooster Vitale, a minor organized-crime figure who'd employed Nick's special talents more than once in the past.

"Have your assignments been falling off lately?" he asked Nick through a mouthful of duck.

"Not especially. I have all the work I want."

Vitale grunted. "I thought maybe the White Queen was cutting in on your territory."

"Who?"

"Sandra Paris. She calls herself the White Queen." Rooster fished into his vest pocket and produced a business card he passed over to Nick. It read simply:

THE WHITE QUEEN
Impossible Things Before Breakfast

There was a New York telephone number printed in the lower left corner.

"This is the first I've heard of her," Nick admitted. "What does she do?"

Rooster Vitale shrugged. "The same sort of impossible things you do, only she doesn't have your scruples about what she steals."

"I'll have to meet her sometime," Nick murmured, finishing his dinner and signaling the waiter for coffee. "Now let's get down to business. What can I do for you this time, Rooster?"

The stout man reached for his wine glass. "I want you to steal a roomful of furniture."

"Stop right there, Rooster. You know I don't steal anything of value."

"Hell, Nick, it's not like it was diamonds or bonds or a shipment of cocaine! This is just furniture! It's in the study of a guy's house down in Maryland. You could—"

"Sorry, Rooster, you know my rule. No money, jewelry, paintings, nothing of value. I've made a reputation, and a good living, stealing only worthless items. I don't intend to change now. A roomful of furniture is out of my line."

"You won't reconsider?"

"I can't."

"All right then," Rooster said sadly. "I'll have to look elsewhere."

"Who will you get?" Nick asked curiously.

"The White Queen, I suppose."

Douglas Shelton was a Baltimore attorney who knew how to live the good life. At fifty-five he was a senior partner in a firm that did a good deal of business with the local and state governments. He lived with his wife Angela in a fine old house near the shore of Chesapeake Bay. Their two children were doing well in college, and with time to themselves Doug and Angela had begun to travel more. She was ten years younger than Doug, a still beautiful woman who took pride in their home and the circle of influential friends in which they moved.

Shelton often worked at home, especially when the winter winds off the Bay brought snow or a chill temperature that made the long drive to his law firm in downtown Baltimore a less than pleasant experience. He'd converted an enclosed back porch into a private study with a desk, bookshelves, and filing cabinets, and made it so handsome that even the woman who'd come through to photograph the house recently for a national magazine and had seen some exquisite rooms had been especially impressed by it.

This morning in April, awakening from a deep sleep, Douglas Shelton's first thought was that he was alone in the wide king-sized bed. That was unusual and it took him a moment to clear his mind of sleep and remember that Angela had gone off to a parents' weekend at their daughter's college. A court appearance had kept Shelton from accompanying her. He opened one eye and could tell from the dim light that it was somewhere just after six. He thought he heard a noise downstairs, but decided it must be his imagination.

He slid out from beneath the covers and stretched, thinking he should fix himself some breakfast before driving into the city for his eleven o'clock court appearance. He went into the bathroom, brushed his teeth, and trod downstairs in his pajamas. Passing the open door of his study, he glanced in at the dim outlines of his furniture in the weak morning light, then continued on to the kitchen. He took some oranges from the refrigerator and started squeezing them.

After a few minutes the telephone rang.

Who would be calling him at 6:15 in the morning? Angela, perhaps? He picked up the wall phone in the kitchen. "Hello?"

"Douglas Shelton?" a woman's soft voice asked.

"Speaking."

"Take a look at your study, Mr. Shelton."

"What?"

The line went dead.

He grunted and replaced the phone, then retraced his steps through the dining and living rooms to the door of the study. Though he'd seen it only a few minutes earlier, it looked different now.

It looked empty!

He snapped on the overhead light and stared with unbelieving eyes. His desk, chair, bookcases, filing cabinet, sofa, and lamps, even the rug on the floor, were gone. The room was completely bare.

In the few minutes while he'd been preparing breakfast, someone had stolen all the furniture from his study.

The robbery at Douglas Shelton's home took place just three weeks after Nick Velvet's luncheon with Rooster Vitale, and when Nick spotted the item in the back pages of the New York newspaper he knew that Rooster had found someone to pull off his theft. Probably it had been the White Queen, and that bothered Nick the way successful competition always bothered a businessman.

"What's the matter, Nicky?" Gloria asked him over breakfast.

"Business. It's been a bit slow this month."

"It'll pick up."

He nodded, finishing his coffee. "Maybe I'll make a few phone calls."

The first person he called was Rooster Vitale in Atlantic City. "What happened with that furniture job you had?"

"It's taken care of, Nick. Sorry."

"I didn't want to do it. I'm just curious."

"The White Queen handled it. She did a neat job too. Maybe you saw it in the papers."

"I think I did."

"She's good, Nick. You better watch yourself or you'll be out of business."

"Thanks, Rooster."

Nick hung up and tried to forget about it. But the nagging memory remained with him. Now he had competition where there had been none before. He spent the following day learning what he could about Sandra Paris. She was a woman in her mid-thirties who'd turned to crime following a brief and unsuccessful career as an actress. Nick hunted out her picture in *The Times* and some show-business publications and was struck by the innocent beauty of her pale face, framed in platinum-blonde hair. Staring hard at the picture, he determined to meet her.

"Where can I find the White Queen?" He asked Rooster Vitale on the telephone.

"Hell, Nick, don't involve me in any feud."

"No feud, Rooster. I just want to meet the lady."

"The only time I ever see her is at breakfast. When she has an assignment she likes to finish it early and eat a big breakfast around ten o'clock."

"Impossible things before breakfast."

"What?"

"I was just quoting her motto. Where's her base—that New York phone number?"

"She moves around. That's just an answering service. I happen to know she's back in Atlantic City right now, on another assignment."

"For you?"

He hesitated. "Well, yeah."

"What?"

"You know I can't tell you, Nick. But chances are you'll find her having breakfast at the King's Fountain either tomorrow morning or the day after. Don't say I sent you."

"Thanks, Rooster."

She didn't show on the following morning. Nick managed to drink three cups of coffee while waiting, but by eleven-thirty he gave up and left. He spent the rest of the day gambling away small sums at the blackjack tables and wondering if he was wasting his time by staying over in Atlantic City for another night. A fierce April rainstorm was pelting the city from the ocean, confining his gaming to the mirrored luxury of the King's Fountain casino. He began to speculate about a scheme to cover over the Boardwalk and allow patrons access to other casinos in bad weather. It was a problem Las Vegas never had to face.

A voice he vaguely knew said, "Hello, Nick," and interrupted his thoughts. He turned to see Charlie Weston glaring down at him.

"Hello, Charlie. Long time no see."

Weston was an ex-cop who'd crossed Nick's path two or three times during the past fifteen years. He knew what Nick did for a living, and he was an honest man. The two taken together made him dangerous. He'd sworn on more than one occasion to put Nick behind bars. "What are you after in Atlantic City?" the big man asked, his meaty hand descending on Nick's shoulder.

"Just down for a little gambling. What about you?"

"I'm chief of security at the King's Fountain. My job is to protect the place from people like you, Nick."

"I never turned a crooked card in my life, Charlie. You know that." Nick was seated at a cocktail table for two and motioned toward the empty chair. "Sit down. I'll buy you a drink."

Weston sat down but waved away the offer. "I'm on duty. I suppose you are too."

"I'm not here to steal anything, Charlie. You have my word on that."

"I saw you here last month having dinner with Rooster Vitale. A few weeks later some evidence linking him to a bribery attempt in Maryland was stolen from a man named Shelton. All the furniture in Shelton's study was taken because Vitale wasn't sure where the incriminating papers were hidden. That sounds like your sort of caper, Nick."

"You know I never steal anything of value. Furniture has value."

"There's always a first time. Maybe the recession has forced you to be less fussy."

"It hasn't," Nick replied grimly. "I know nothing about the theft of Douglas Shelton's furniture."

"But you know his first name, don't you? And I hadn't mentioned it."

Nick silently cursed his slip-up. There was something about Charlie Weston that had always unnerved him. "I know nothing about it," he repeated. "I probably saw the name in the newspaper."

"Well, I'll tell you something about it. Rooster Vitale has always operated on the fringes of the organized-crime families. We know he was involved in bribing some Congressmen and state officials both here and in Maryland. Douglas Shelton, an attorney involved in some of the payoffs, had a number of papers that would incriminate Vitale hidden in his study. Since Rooster didn't know exactly where they were hidden, he had every stick of furniture stolen—even the rug on the floor. Shelton claims it was done in about five minutes, while he was squeezing oranges for breakfast."

"*I* didn't do it," Nick insisted. "It's not my sort of job."

Charlie Weston stood up. "We don't want trouble in our casino, Nick. We don't want Rooster Vitale or Nick Velvet hanging around. Understand?"

"I plan to leave tomorrow," Nick replied. Weston nodded and walked away.

Nick had barely reached the lobby the following morning when he heard the reports of The White Queen's latest escapade. Shortly before four, someone had stolen a roulette wheel from an unused gaming table at the Golden Fleece casino down the Boardwalk. Since the casino was open at the time, no one could imagine how the thieves had struck without being seen. The wheel had simply disappeared from the top of the table, leaving it bare.

She was already eating breakfast when he entered the dining room.

He walked over to her table and asked, "May I join you for coffee?"

She looked up, smiling the same enticing smile as in the newspaper photograph. An innocent beauty, caught between her toast and coffee. "I don't believe we've been introduced."

"My name is Nick Velvet."

"I know your name. I said I don't believe we've been introduced, Mr. Velvet."

"It's time we were," he said, pulling out the chair opposite her to sit down. "I hear you've had an active morning."

She arched an eyebrow at him but did not take the bait. Instead she said simply, "I slept late. Are you in the habit of asking personal questions, Mr. Velvet?"

For just an instant he wondered if Rooster could have steered him wrong. Perhaps she really was as innocent as she acted. Then he decided to plunge on. "You're cutting into my business, Miss Paris. I thought it was time we talked."

The waiter interrupted to take his order for coffee, and when he faced her again she said, "I understood that you were in a slightly different line of work. I don't bother myself with items of no value, like postcards and teabags."

"You're more familiar with me than I'd supposed. Who paid you to take the wheel this morning? Vitale?"

"Do you really expect me to answer that? You could be wearing a wire and recording every word."

"I don't work for the police."

"You were at a table with Weston, the casino security chief, yesterday."

"My, my—you have been keeping tabs on me. I'm sorry I didn't notice you."

"People rarely do, unless I smile. They think I'm in town for the librarians' convention."

"Tell me about Douglas Shelton's furniture."

"That," she said softly, "is a very sore subject."

"Oh? How well do you know Rooster Vitale?"

"Well enough. I've done some jobs for him." She lowered her voice still further and leaned across the table. "He hasn't paid me yet."

"It's usually cash on delivery," Nick said.

"Yes. Well—" She seemed about to say more, but changed her mind.

"Do you always eat a big breakfast after a job?"

"I suppose it's become my trademark." She passed him one of the cards he'd already seen. *Impossible Things Before Breakfast.* "Remember the White Queen in *Through the Looking Glass?* 'Sometimes I've believed as many as six impossible things before breakfast.' Well, I don't believe them, but I do them."

"Including the wheel this morning?"

She shrugged. "A simple little job."

"I hear it vanished with the casino full of people. You don't walk out the door with a roulette wheel under your arm and not attract attention."

The smile was back. "Someday I'll let you in on the secret, Mr. Velvet, but for now you needn't worry. I hope to be out of here in another day or so, heading for the West Coast. We won't be competitors then."

"I'm glad to hear it. But I admit a fondness for postcards and teabags. Furniture and roulette wheels are a bit out of my line, though I'll venture to say I could duplicate any one of your feats if I had to."

"Is that a challenge?"

"No, no. Let's part friends. I've enjoyed it, Miss Paris."

He rose to leave, but suddenly Sandra Paris seemed to make a decision. "Come stroll on the Boardwalk with me, where we can't be overheard."

"Gladly."

He let her pay for his coffee and then followed her across the hotel lobby to the Boardwalk entrance. The doors slid open automatically as they approached and then they were out in the morning air, breathing in the April warmth. "At least the rain has stopped," she commented. "We might have a decent day for a change."

"Looks like it."

She turned to him suddenly and said, "I need your help."

"Oh?"

"Rooster Vitale won't pay my fee until I deliver some papers he wants."

"That's between you and Rooster."

"But I know they're hidden in that furniture from Shelton's study. All I have to do is find them."

"That shouldn't be hard."

"But it is! I've taken the stuff apart piece by piece!"

"Maybe you've been double-crossed. You must have people working for you. One of them could have found the papers without letting you know."

She shook her head. "No, they've never been alone with the furniture."

"I don't find things," he said. "I steal them."

"What's your fee—twenty-five thousand?"

"That's right."

"I'll pay you that to steal the papers from their hiding place in the furniture and give them to me. It's easy money—no risk involved."

"Do I get to learn how you stole it all while Shelton was squeezing his orange juice?"

"Oh, no. That's not part of the agreement."

"I take a fee only for stealing valueless items. Those papers sound pretty valuable to me."

"Then do it as a professional favor. I'll owe you one, Mr. Velvet."

It was very hard resisting her smile. "You can call me Nick," he said.

They drove in her white Cadillac to a small warehouse west of the city. "I rented space here," Sandra explained. "Two men I've used before helped with the actual theft, but I trust them completely."

They entered the storage area and Nick was startled by the sight. Desk, sofa, chairs, filing cabinets—all but the rug had been reduced to rubble in a futile attempt to find the papers. "What do you think? Where haven't I looked?"

"Behind the pictures on the walls?"

"There were no pictures. The study was on an enclosed porch with big windows on three sides covered with roll-down blinds."

"The papers were rolled up in one of the blinds," he suggested.

"No, we've got them here someplace. And they're not in the filing cabinets. I've looked at every sheet of paper in every drawer."

"Maybe they were never in the study."

She shook her head. "He's frantic to get this stuff back."

"He won't be so frantic when he sees the condition it's in."

"He's not going to see—" She paused and stared at him. "Nick, are we thinking the same thing?"

"Could be," he answered with a grin. He was starting to like Sandra Paris. "If we can't find those papers, maybe Shelton can find them for us."

An hour later, after they'd talked it through, Nick phoned Shelton at his Baltimore law office. "Mr. Shelton, you don't know me but I have some information about your missing furniture."

"What? Where is it?"

"How much is it worth to get it back?"

There was silence for a moment. Then Shelton answered, "Five hundred dollars might be a reasonable reward."

"Double that and we'll talk business."

"Very well," he replied without hesitation. "Where is the furniture?"

"At a warehouse near Atlantic City. Can you drive up here this afternoon?"

"I suppose so. Give me the address."

"No," Nick said. "I'll meet you nearby." He gave the location of a fast-food restaurant in a shopping center on Route 322. "Meet me there at two o'clock with the money."

"How will I know you?"

"Don't worry. I'll know you."

Shelton arrived ten minutes early for the meeting. He was a stout, balding man who looked exactly like his newspaper photos. When Nick was reasonably certain he hadn't been tailed, he stepped up and made the contact. "Mr. Shelton? I'm the man who called you."

Shelton stared at him as if trying to memorize his face. "You're Mr.—?"

"The name's not important. Did you bring the money?"

"You'll get it when I see the furniture."

"All right," Nick agreed. "Let's go."

As they drove to the warehouse, the lawyer said, "But why? Why steal it in the first place? I never heard of anyone holding a roomful of furniture for ransom."

"I wasn't in on the robbery," Nick admitted. "That was my partner. I just want to get rid of the stuff." He turned into the warehouse parking lot.

"Is this the place?"

"Yeah."

Nick led him through the side door and unlocked the room Sandra had rented. He let the lawyer enter first. "My God!" Shelton gasped as Nick turned on the overhead light.

"Things got a little messed up on the trip."

Shelton hurried to the rug and Nick could see him testing the thick binding at the edge of it with his shoe. Then he looked at Nick seemingly satisfied. "This is all junk. You can't expect me to pay you for this."

"I thought you'd be happy to get your papers back," Nick said.

"Let me gather up a few things and you can take me back to my car. I'll take the rug and some of my files. You can keep the rest and I'll collect on the insurance."

Nick helped him carry the rug out to the car and then waited while the attorney went through his scattered files and pulled out more than a score of fat folders. "You can't expect me to pay for the rest of this," Shelton said again.

"Let's make it five hundred," Nick offered, shifting uneasily.

"Look, I've got your license number. You could be in big trouble," Shelton told him, responding to Nick's tone.

They drove back to the restaurant in silence and Nick helped Shelton move the rolled-up rug and file folders into his own car. As he was about to depart, the lawyer handed him a fifty-dollar bill. "Take this and be glad you're not in jail." Then he slid behind the wheel and drove off without another glance at Nick.

As his car disappeared from view, Sandra came out of the restaurant. "You look pleased with yourself, Nick. How'd it go?"

"Perfect. The papers were on microfilm, hidden in the binding of the rug. I removed it while he was sorting through his files. Here you are." He handed over the small strip of film.

She grinned and kissed him lightly on the cheek. "You know something? We'd make a pretty terrific pair."

They dined together that evening in the plush Guard Room at the King's Fountain. Over coffee she announced, "When I collect my money from Rooster Vitale I'm cutting you in for a share."

"That isn't necessary. I did it as a favor." He returned her smile. "After all, I'm anxious to get the competition out of town."

"You're not interested in teaming up?"

He thought of Gloria, waiting back home. "Not really. I've always worked best alone."

"I'm getting fifty thousand from Vitale," she told him.

"My regular fee is only half that."

"I know." She lit a cigarette. "Maybe I can subcontract some work to you. Do you have any suggestions?"

He shrugged. "I could steal your menu at breakfast some morning. Rob you of your celebration."

"I'll remember that and keep a tight grip on it. You steal it out of my hands and I'll pay you twenty-five thousand."

"It's a deal," he agreed, joining her laughter. They were both being silly, and he enjoyed it immensely. "Have you talked to Rooster yet?"

She nodded. "I'm meeting him after dinner. I told him on the phone I had what he wanted."

"Then I guess you'll be headed west."

"I could be tempted to stay."

"Don't tempt me to tempt you."

As they were leaving she said, "You know my room number, if you want to stop by after I see Vitale."

He spent the next hour randomly playing the casino slot machines. It was a crowded, noisy night, with busloads of evening gamblers down from New York and Philadelphia. After a while he strolled along the Boardwalk to the casino where the roulette wheel had been stolen. The bare table was no longer there. A guard told him it had been removed during the day by a storage company.

Nick had learned a great deal about Sandra Paris in the day he'd known her, but he felt he'd learned very little about her alter ego, The White Queen. He still didn't know how she'd stolen the furniture from Shelton's home or the roulette wheel from a busy casino. Maybe it would be worth teaming up with her just to learn how.

Maybe it would be worth a visit to her room, at least.

Nick strolled back along the Boardwalk to the King's Fountain, knowing he was being drawn to the woman like a fly to a honeyed web.

As he entered the lobby of the hotel, he was intercepted by Rooster Vitale. "Nick, I gotta talk to you."

"Right now?"

"Right now. Let's go have a drink."

Nick ordered a glass of wine and joined Rooster in the lounge. "What's the trouble? You look upset."

"That damned White Queen messed me up on the furniture deal."

"How could that be? I thought she found what you wanted today."

"You know about it, huh? She was supposed to find some papers for me. Instead she comes up with microfilm copies of them."

"Why isn't that good enough?"

"Hell, Nick—the papers are incriminating! I need the originals!"

"I see. Then you haven't paid Sandra her money?"

"Damn right I haven't paid her! She brings me the microfilm and tells me she gave the rest of everything back to Shelton."

"*I* gave it back, Rooster. I was helping Sandra. Whatever happened is my fault."

"Hell, Nick, I asked you to help me with this and you refused. Now you tell me you're the one that botched the job."

"You'd better explain what's involved. Just what are these papers?"

Rooster Vitale sighed and looked around as if seeking a way out. Finally he lowered his voice and said, "There were several letters and a typed contract. About ten years ago, before gambling was legal in Atlantic City, I was involved in a string of private clubs in Jersey and Maryland. You know what I mean—we had a few games in the back room for high rollers who didn't want to go all the way to Vegas for action. Shelton set up a dummy corporation for us, and those letters and the contract are my only link to it. Now I'm trying to go legit, to get into one of the casino corporations here. But Shelton's been blackmailing me, threatening to tell the State Gaming Commission about my past involvements. The White Queen stole all his study furniture to be sure of getting all the papers, but all she delivered was the microfilm."

"Maybe that's all there was."

Rooster shook his head. "Shelton phoned me an hour ago from home and boasted about getting the papers back."

"That's impossible! All he took back was the rug and a couple of dozen file folders. Sandra had been through every paper in them without finding what you wanted."

"All I know is what he told me, Nick. The problem is, what do I do now?"

"Tell me something, Rooster—did you also hire Sandra to steal the roulette wheel from the Golden Fleece?"

"She told you about that too, huh?"

"No, she didn't. But you told me she was doing another job for you."

"It was a wheel I sold to the Fleece when they first opened up," Rooster mumbled. "They needed equipment in a hurry. I decided I wanted it back. They weren't using it much any more."

"Was it rigged?"

"No. I've never run a crooked wheel, Nick."

"But you needed it stolen. Somehow it tied in with those papers, didn't it?"

"I can't go into all that."

"But you want my help."

"Can you get those letters and the contract?"

"You mean rob Douglas Shelton a second time?"

"Sure. Why not? I'll pay double your usual fee."

"Those papers have value now, Rooster. They're blackmail material. You know I can't take money for that."

"Hell, Nick, come down to earth! Either you're a thief or you're
not!"

"Let me think about it, Rooster."

"I got only one alternative, Nick. If you won't do it, I'll send a
couple of guys to his house with a firebomb. That'll finish the papers
and Shelton both at once."

For some reason the words shocked Nick. He'd known Rooster a
long time, and knew what he was, but the idea of murder had never
crossed his mind in connection with Rooster. Maybe Shelton didn't
deserve saving, but he didn't deserve killing either.

"All right," he said. "But if I do it it's as a favor to you—I'll take
no money for it."

"You gotta be paid, Nick."

"Give Sandra her money. I'll settle with her."

"Then I can count on you?"

Nick, who never thought he'd end up robbing a man to save the
man's life, replied, "You can count on me."

Douglas Shelton awakened suddenly, wondering if he heard
something downstairs. It was still early and his wife Angela was fast
asleep at his side. The first faint glow of dawn was just beginning to
outline the windows behind their draperies.

Remembering the morning he'd been robbed, he slipped silently
out of bed, taking with him the .38-caliber revolver he kept handy
now. All was dim and silent downstairs and as he passed the study
door he looked in at the shadowed shapes of the new furniture already
in place.

"Stand still, please," a voice from the study said. "And hand me
that gun."

"What—?"

"Please. I don't want to shoot you."

A hand reached out of the darkness to grab the gun and Shelton
saw the familiar face from the Atlantic City warehouse. "What do you
want? How'd you get in here?"

"Getting in was easy. Those study windows are simple to open.
And I think you know what I want. The files you took yesterday."

"Those are my private papers."

"Let's not waste time. You may not believe this, but I'm trying to save your life."

"With that gun?"

"Yes."

Shelton hesitated. The man's eyes were hard and businesslike, yet somehow Shelton believed him. "Very well," he said. "Ever since that girl photographed my house for the magazine I've had nothing but robberies. And the pictures haven't even appeared yet."

"Maybe I can do something to have them cancelled if you take me to those folders right now."

Shelton sighed and led the way to one of the new filing cabinets. "What makes you think you'll find anything this time when you didn't find anything before?"

"Because this time I know what I'm looking for," Nick Velvet said.

It was nearly ten-thirty when Sandra Paris settled down to breakfast at the King's Fountain. She was still studying the big gray menu when Nick walked in and took the chair opposite her. "Another celebration?" he asked.

She smiled, happy to see him again. "I was expecting you last night."

"I made no promises. And after I saw Rooster I figured you might not be in the mood for visitors."

"That's all settled. He paid me this morning. That's why I'm celebrating. Did you have anything to do with it, Nick?"

"A bit," he admitted.

"*Were* those papers in the batch I stole?"

"Yes."

"But how could they have been? I looked over every one!"

"I'll tell you that after you let me in on some of *your* secrets—how you stole the furniture and the roulette wheel, for instance."

"Are we partners, then?" She put down the menu and rested her folded hands on it.

"I'm no good at partners," Nick told her honestly. "And I think I know how you stole the furniture. I happened to see Douglas Shelton again this morning, and he mentioned a woman photographer who took pictures of his house for a national publication. He said the pictures hadn't appeared yet. They haven't appeared because *you* were the photographer, Sandra. You not only got the layout of the house while posing as a photographer, you also took a wide-angle photo of his study from the doorway. You blew up a print to life size and mounted it, probably on a large window shade, and placed it in the doorway of the study, blocking a view of the room and giving the impression, in dim light, that the furniture was still in place.

"You and some helpers worked quietly through the night, removing the furniture through those big porch windows. When Shelton finally heard something toward morning and came down for breakfast, you'd just about finished. He glanced at the study doorway but noticed nothing wrong. You rolled up the photo and left through the window while he was squeezing his orange juice, then you phoned him from down the road."

"You figured that out all by yourself?" she said, the irony of her tone not quite hiding a hint of admiration.

"Want me to tell you about the roulette wheel next?"

"Don't tell me you've solved that one too!"

"In a way it was one of the cleverest robberies I've come across. You simply walked up to the unused wheel in a casino full of people, waited until no one was looking your way, and pressed a hidden button that made the wheel drop inside the specially constructed table. It remained there until your men picked it up yesterday and took it to the warehouse."

"You're guessing now," she said, but her eyes had turned uncertain.

"It's a guess, but a knowledgeable one. Rooster told me he ran a string of illegal gambling houses in New Jersey some years back and that the roulette wheel at the Golden Fleece came from one of those houses. He needed it stolen so his past wouldn't accidentally come to light now that he's trying to get a legitimate gaming license. If the table came from an illegal house, I have a hunch it was gimmicked to look like an ordinary table when not in use. Of course, anyone could have pressed the hidden button to *hide* the wheel, but he needed your skill in removing the supposedly bare table from the casino later. That's when the real theft took place. Luckily for both of you, the people on duty at the casino never knew it was a gimmicked table. When a couple of workmen showed up with a truck, they let it go."

"All right," she admitted. "Suppose that's all true. It just proves you're a better detective than a thief, Nick."

"I'm still a pretty good thief. I got those papers back from Shelton," he reminded her.

"Are you going to tell me where they were?"

"Sure. You checked through all those papers, looking for the letters and contract Rooster described to you, but naturally you looked only at the *front* of the sheets. Shelton simply typed other, innocuous memos on the backs of the incriminating letters and contract and put them in his file with the back side up."

"But what did you get out of all this?" she asked, obviously miffed. "Did Rooster pay you?"

Nick shook his head. "The papers had value as blackmail. I don't steal anything of value. I took them to save a life, not for gain. Rooster's not paying me, you are."

"What?"

"Twenty-five thousand for stealing your menu—remember?"

"But my menu is right—" She picked it up and stared at it, then turned it over in her hands. The menu itself was gone. What she held was a blank piece of gray cardboard.

She sighed. "Damn it, Nick, you're always a jump ahead of me. I wish we could be partners." Then she reached for her checkbook.

"Cash would be better," he said quietly. "From the fifty Rooster gave you this morning."

By noon Nick had his suitcase packed and was ready to leave the hotel. When the knock came at his door he thought it might be the bellman. But it was Charlie Weston.

"You're leaving, are you, Nick?" he asked.

"I told you I would be."

"I thought you might want to know the police just arrested a couple of friends of yours—Rooster Vitale and Sandra Paris."

"I know the names," Nick admitted, trying not to show his surprise. "But I wouldn't exactly call them friends."

"We got them for stealing the roulette wheel out of the Golden Fleece. What do you think of that?"

"A crazy sort of a crime."

"Yeah. For a while I thought it was so crazy we might hang it on you, Nick. But no such luck. Turns out the wheel was hidden inside the table all along. A couple of guys picked it up yesterday at the casino and we traced the truck they were driving to a warehouse out on 322. I worked with the Fleece security men on it. The warehouse room had been rented by a woman we identified as Sandra Paris, and this morning we got films of Rooster Vitale paying her off. That's when we called in the local police."

"How does this concern me?"

Weston chewed nervously at his lower lip. "I don't exactly know. If I did, you'd be in a cell with them. We know you were out of town somewhere overnight, and when you came back early this morning you had a printer run off a copy of our breakfast menu done in disappearing ink that would fade after an hour or so. You slipped the hostess downstairs twenty bucks to give Sandra Paris that menu when she came in. Why'd you do that?"

Nick Velvet shrugged. "A practical joke. Last week was April Fools' Day."

The security man grunted. "Sandra Paris had only twenty-five thousand on her, but Rooster says he paid her fifty. You wouldn't happen to have the balance?"

"If you've got a search warrant you can find out."

They eyed each other until Weston finally looked away. "Go on, get out of here, Nick. Next time you won't be so lucky."

Nick thought about The White Queen all the way home, and he wondered what the penalty was for stealing a roulette wheel in New Jersey.

Carolyn Wheat brings a fresh, breezy style to any story she puts on paper. Her short stories are often instant classics, featuring engaging characters and inventive new takes on standard situations. "Ghost Station" is a bit of a departure for her into the dark world of the New York City transit system, and the lives that are lost—and found—there.

Ghost Station

Carolyn Wheat

If there's one thing I can't stand, it's a woman drunk. The words burned my memory the way Irish whiskey used to burn my throat, only there was no pleasant haze of alcohol to follow. Just bitter heartburn pain.

It was my first night back on the job, back to being Sergeant Maureen Gallagher instead of "the patient." Wasn't it hard enough being a transit cop, hurtling beneath the streets of Manhattan on a subway train that should have been in the Transit Museum? Wasn't it enough that after four weeks of detox I felt empty instead of clean and sober? Did I *have* to have some rookie's casually cruel words ricocheting in my brain like a wild-card bullet?

Why couldn't I remember the good stuff? Why couldn't I think about O'Hara's beefy handshake, Greenspan's "Glad to see ya, Mo," Ianuzzo's smiling welcome? Why did I have to run the tape in my head of Manny Delgado asking Captain Lomax for a different partner?

"Hey, I got nothing against a lady sarge, Cap," he'd said. "Don't get me wrong. It's just that if there's one thing I can't stand . . ." Et cetera.

Lomax had done what any standup captain would—kicked Delgado's ass and told him the assignment stood. What he hadn't known was that I'd heard the words and couldn't erase them from my mind.

Even without Delgado, the night hadn't gotten off to a great start. Swinging in at midnight for a twelve-to-eight, I'd been greeted with the news that I was on Graffiti Patrol, the dirtiest, most mind-numbing assignment in the whole transit police duty roster. I was a sergeant, damn it, on my way to a gold shield, and I wasn't going to earn it dodging rats in tunnels or going after twelve-year-olds armed with spray paint.

Especially when the rest of the cop world, both under- and aboveground, was working overtime on the torch murders of homeless people. There'd been four human bonfires in the past six weeks, and the cops were determined there wouldn't be a fifth.

Was Lomax punishing me, or was this assignment his subtle way of easing my entry back into the world? Either way, I resented it. I wanted to be a real cop again, back with Sal Minucci, my old partner. He was assigned to the big one, in the thick of the action, where both of us belonged. I should have been with him. I was Anti-Crime, for God's sake, I should have been assigned—

Or should I? Did I really want to spend my work nights prowling New York's underground skid row, trying to get information from men and women too zonked out to take care of legs gone gangrenous, whose lives stretched from one bottle of Cool Breeze to another?

Hell, yes. If it would bring me one step closer to that gold shield, I'd interview all the devils in hell. On my day off.

If there's one thing I can't stand, it's a woman drunk.

What did Lomax think—that mingling with winos would topple me off the wagon? That I'd ask for a hit from some guy's short dog and pass out in the Bleecker Street station? Was that why he'd kept me off the big one and had me walking a rookie through routine Graffiti Patrol?

Was I getting paranoid, or was lack of alcohol rotting my brain?

Manny and I had gone to our respective locker rooms to suit up. Plain clothes—and I do mean plain. Long johns first; damp winter had a way of seeping down into the tunnels and into your very blood. Then a pair of denims the Goodwill would have turned down. Thick wool socks, fisherman's duck boots, a black turtleneck, and a photographer's vest with lots of pockets. A black knit hat pulled tight over my red hair.

Then the gear: flashlight, more important than a gun on this assignment, handcuffs, ticket book, radio, gun, knife. A slapper, an oversize blackjack, hidden in the rear pouch of the vest. They were against regulations; I'd get at least a command discipline if caught with it, but experience told me I'd rather have it than a gun going against a pack of kids.

I'd forgotten how heavy the stuff was; I felt like a telephone lineman.

I looked like a cat burglar.

Delgado and I met at the door. It was obvious he'd never done vandal duty before. His tan chinos were immaculate, and his hiking boots didn't look waterproof. His red plaid flannel shirt was neither warm enough nor the right dark color. With his Latin good looks, he would have been stunning in an L. L. Bean catalog, but after ten minutes in a subway tunnel, he'd pass for a chimney sweep.

"Where are we going?" he asked, his tone a shade short of sullen. And there was no respectful "Sergeant" at the end of the question, either. This boy needed a lesson in manners.

I took a malicious delight in describing our destination. "The Black Hole of Calcutta," I replied cheerfully, explaining that I meant the unused lower platform of the City Hall station downtown. The oldest, darkest, dankest spot in all Manhattan. If there were any subway alligators, they definitely lurked in the Black Hole.

The expression on Probationary Transit Police Officer Manuel Delgado's face was all I could have hoped for. I almost—but not quite—took pity on the kid when I added, "And after that, we'll try one or two of the ghost stations."

"Ghost stations?" Now he looked really worried. "What are those?"

This kid wasn't just a rookie; he was a suburbanite. Every New Yorker knew about ghost stations, abandoned platforms where trains no longer stopped. They were still lit, though, and showed up in the windows of passing trains like ghost towns on the prairie. They were ideal canvases for the aspiring artists of the underground city.

I explained on the subway, heading downtown. The car, which rattled under the city streets like a tin lizzie, was nearly riderless at 1:00 A.M. A typical Monday late hour.

The passengers were one Orthodox Jewish man falling asleep over his Hebrew Bible, two black women, both reading thick paperback romances, the obligatory pair of teenagers making out in the last seat, and an old Chinese woman.

I didn't want to look at Delgado. More than once I'd seen a fleeting smirk on his face when I glanced his way. It wasn't enough for insubordination; the best policy was to ignore it.

I let the rhythm of the subway car lull me into a litany of the AA slogans I was trying to work into my life: EASY DOES IT. KEEP IT SIMPLE, SWEETHEART. ONE DAY AT A TIME. I saw them in my mind the way they appeared on the walls at meetings, illuminated, like old Celtic manuscripts.

This night I had to take one hour at a time. Maybe even one minute at a time. My legs felt wobbly. I was a sailor too long from the sea. I'd lost my subway legs. I felt white and thin, as though I'd had several major organs removed.

Then the drunk got on. One of the black women got off, the other one looked up at the station sign and went back to her book, and the drunk got on.

If there's one thing I can't stand, it's a woman drunk.

ONE DAY AT A TIME. EASY DOES IT.

I stiffened. The last thing I wanted was to react in front of Delgado, but I couldn't help it. The sight of an obviously intoxicated man stumbling into our subway car brought the knowing smirk back to his face.

There was one at every AA meeting. No matter how nice the neighborhood, how well dressed most people attending the meeting were, there was always a drunk. A real drunk, still reeling, still reeking of cheap booze. My sponsor, Margie, said they were there for a reason, to let us middle-class, recovery-oriented types remember that "there but for the grace of God . . ."

I cringed whenever I saw them, especially if the object lesson for the day was a woman.

"Hey, kid," the drunk called out to Delgado, in a voice as inappropriately loud as a deaf man's, "how old are you?" The doors closed and the car lurched forward; the drunk all but fell into his seat.

"Old enough," Manny replied, flashing the polite smile a well-brought-up kid saves for his maiden aunt.

The undertone wasn't so pretty. Little sidelong glances at me that said, *See how nice I am to this old fart. See what a good boy I am. I like drunks, Sergeant Gallagher.*

To avoid my partner's face, I concentrated on the subway ads as though they contained all the wisdom of the Big Book. "Here's to birth defects," proclaimed a pregnant woman about to down a glass of beer. Two monks looked to heaven, thanking God in Spanish for the fine quality of their brandy.

Weren't there any signs on this damn train that didn't involve booze? Finally an ad I could smile at: the moon in black space; on it, someone had scrawled, "Alice Kramden was here, 1959."

My smile faded as I remembered Sal Minucci's raised fist, his Jackie Gleason growl. "One of these days, Gallagher, you're goin' to the moon. To the *moon!*"

It wasn't just the murder case I missed. It was Sal. The easy part-
nership of the man who'd put up with my hangovers, my depressions,
my wild nights out with the boys.

"Y'know how old I am?" the drunk shouted, almost falling over
in his seat. He righted himself. "Fifty-four in September," he
announced, an expectant look on his face.

After a quick smirk in my direction, Manny gave the guy what he
wanted. "You don't look it," he said. No trace of irony appeared on his
Spanish altar boy's face. It was as though he'd never said the words that
were eating into me like battery-acid AA coffee.

The sudden jab of anger that stabbed through me took me by
surprise, especially since it wasn't directed at Delgado. *No, you don't
look it,* I thought. *You look more like seventy.* White wisps of hair over a
bright pink scalp. The face more than pink; a slab of raw calves' liver.
Road maps of broken blood vessels on his nose and cheeks. Thin
white arms and matchstick legs under too-big trousers. When he
lifted his hand, ropy with bulging blue veins, it fluttered like a pen-
nant in the breeze.

Like Uncle Paul's hands.

I turned away sharply. I couldn't look at the old guy anymore.
The constant visual digs Delgado kept throwing in my direction were
nothing compared to the pain of looking at a man dying before my
eyes. I didn't want to see blue eyes in that near-dead face. *As blue as the
lakes of Killarney,* Uncle Paul used to say in his mock-Irish brogue.

I focused on the teenagers making out in the rear of the car. A
couple of Spanish kids, wearing identical pink T-shirts and black
leather jackets. If I stared at them long enough, would they stop groping and kissing, or would an audience spur their passion?

Uncle Paul. After Daddy left us, he was my special friend, and I
was his best girl.

I squeezed my eyes shut, but the memories came anyway. The red
bike Uncle Paul gave me for my tenth birthday. The first really big new
thing, bought just for me, that I'd ever had. The best part was showing
it off to cousin Tommy. For once I didn't need his hand-me-downs, or
Aunt Bridget's clucking over me for being poor. *God bless the child who's
got her own.*

I opened my eyes just as the Lex passed through the ghost station
at Worth Street. Closed off to the public for maybe fifteen years, it
seemed a mirage, dimly seen through the dirty windows of the subway
car. Bright color on the white tile walls told me graffiti bombers had

been there. A good place to check, but not until after City Hall. I owed Manny Delgado a trip to the Black Hole.

"Uh, Sergeant?"

I turned; a patronizing smile played on Delgado's lips. He'd apparently been trying to get my attention. "Sorry," I said, feigning a yawn. "Just a little tired."

Yeah, sure, his look remarked. "We're coming to Brooklyn Bridge. Shouldn't we get off the train?"

"Right." *Leave Uncle Paul where he belongs.*

At the Brooklyn Bridge stop, we climbed up the steps to the upper platform, showed our ID to the woman token clerk, and told her we were going into the tunnel toward City Hall. Then we went back downstairs, heading for the south end of the downtown platform.

As we were about to go past the gate marked NO UNAUTHORIZED PERSONNEL BEYOND THIS POINT, I looked back at the lighted platform, which made a crescent-shaped curve behind us. Almost in a mirror image, the old drunk was about to pass the forbidden gate and descend into the tunnel heading uptown.

He stepped carefully, holding on to the white, bathroom-tile walls, edging himself around the waist-high gate. He lowered himself down the stone steps, the exact replica of the ones Manny and I were about to descend, then disappeared into the blackness.

I couldn't let him go. There were too many dangers in the subway, dangers beyond the torch killer everyone was on the hunt for. How many frozen bodies had I stumbled over on the catwalks between tunnels? How many huddled victims had been hit by trains as they lay in sodden sleep? And yet, I had to be careful. My friend Kathy Denzer had gone after a bum sleeping on the catwalk, only to have the man stab her in the arm for trying to save his life.

I couldn't let him go. Turning to Delgado, I said, "Let's save City Hall for later. I saw some graffiti at Worth Street on the way here. Let's check that out first."

He shrugged. At least he was being spared the Black Hole, his expression said.

Entering the tunnel's blackness, leaving behind the brightly lit world of sleepy riders, a tiny rush of adrenaline, like MSG after a Chinese dinner, coursed through my bloodstream. Part of it was pure reversion to childhood's fears. Hansel and Gretel. Snow White. Lost in dark woods, with enemies all around. In this case, rats. Their scuffling sent shivers up my spine as we balanced our way along the catwalk above the tracks.

The other part was elation. This was my job. I was good at it. I could put aside my fears and step boldly down into murky depths where few New Yorkers ever went.

Our flashlights shone dim as fireflies. I surveyed the gloomy underground world I'd spent my professional life in.

My imagination often took over in the tunnels. They became caves of doom. Or an evil wood, out of *Lord of the Rings*. The square columns holding up the tunnel roof were leafless trees, the constant trickle of foul water between the tracks a poisonous stream from which no one drank and lived.

Jones Beach. Uncle Paul's huge hand cradling my foot, then lifting me high in the air and flinging me backward, laughing with delight, into the cool water. Droplets clinging to his red beard, and Uncle Paul shaking them off into the sunlight like a wet Irish setter.

Me and Mo, we're the only true Gallaghers. The only redheads. I got straight A's in English; nobody's grammar was safe from me—except Uncle Paul's.

I thought all men smelled like him: whiskey and tobacco.

As Manny and I plodded along the four-block tunnel between the live station and the dead one, we exchanged no words. The acrid stench of an old track fire filled my nostrils the way memories flooded my mind. Trying to push Uncle Paul away, I bent all my concentration on stepping carefully around the foul-smelling water, the burned debris I didn't want to identify.

I suspected Delgado's silence was due to fear; he wouldn't want a shaking voice to betray his tension. I knew how he felt. The first nighttime tunnel trek was a landmark in a young transit cop's life.

When the downtown express thundered past, we ducked into the coffin-sized alcoves set aside for transit workers. My heart pounded as the wind wake of the train pulled at my clothes; the fear of falling forward, landing under those relentless steel wheels, never left me, no matter how many times I stood in the well. I always thought of Anna Karenina; once in a while, in my drinking days, I'd wondered how it would feel to edge forward, to let the train's undertow pull me toward death.

I could never do it. I'd seen too much blood on the tracks.

Light at the end of the tunnel. The Worth Street station sent rays of hope into the spidery blackness. My step quickened; Delgado's pace matched mine. Soon we were almost running toward the light, like cavemen coming from the hunt to sit by the fire of safety.

We were almost at the edge of the platform when I motioned Delgado to stop. My hunger to bathe in the light was as great as his, but our post was in the shadows, watching.

A moment of panic. I'd lost the drunk. Had he fallen on the tracks, the electrified third rail roasting him like a pig at a barbecue? Not possible; we'd have heard, and smelled.

I had to admit, the graffiti painting wasn't a mindless scrawl. It was a picture, full of color and life. Humanlike figures in bright primary shades, grass green, royal blue, orange, sun yellow, and carnation pink—colors unknown in the black-and-gray tunnels—stood in a line, waiting to go through a subway turnstile. Sexless, they were cookie-cutter replicas of one another, the only difference among them the color inside the black edges.

A rhythmic clicking sound made Delgado jump. "What the hell—?"

"Relax, Manny," I whispered. "It's the ball bearing in the spray-paint can. The vandals are here. As soon as the paint hits the tiles, we jump out and bust them."

Four rowdy teenagers, ranging in color from light brown to ebony, laughed raucously and punched one another with a theatrical style that said *We bad. We* real *bad.* They bounded up the steps from the other side of the platform and surveyed their artwork, playful as puppies, pointing out choice bits they had added to their mural.

It should have been simple. Two armed cops, with the advantage of surprise, against four kids armed with Day-Glo spray paint. Two things kept it from being simple: the drunk, wherever the hell he was, and the fact that one of the kids said, "Hey, bro, when Cool and Jo-Jo gettin' here?"

A very black kid with a nylon stocking on his head answered, "Jo-Jo be comin' with Pinto. Cool say he might be bringin' Slasher and T. P."

Great. Instead of two against four, it sounded like all the graffiti artists in New York City were planning a convention in the Worth Street ghost station.

"Sarge?" Delgado's voice was urgent. "We've gotta—"

"I know," I whispered back. "Get on the radio and call for backup."

Then I remembered. Worth Street was a dead spot. Lead in the ceiling above our heads turned our radios into worthless toys.

"Stop," I said wearily as Manny pulled the antenna up on his handheld radio. "It won't work. You'll have to go back to Brooklyn Bridge. Alert Booth Robert two-twenty-one. Have them call Operations. Just ask for backup, don't make it a ten thirteen." A 10-13 meant "officer in trouble," and I didn't want to be the sergeant who cried wolf.

"Try the radio along the way," I went on. "You never know when it will come to life. I'm not sure where the lead ends."

Watching Delgado trudge back along the catwalk, I felt lonely, helpless, and stupid. No one knew we'd gone to Worth Street instead of the Black Hole, and that was my fault.

"Hey," one of the kids called, pointing to a pile of old clothes in the corner of the platform, "what this dude be doin' in our crib?"

Dude? What dude? Then the old clothes began to rise; it was the drunk from the train. He was huddled into a fetal ball, hoping not to be noticed by the graffiti gang.

Nylon Stocking boogied over to the old drunk, sticking a finger in his ribs. "What you be doin' here, ol' man? Huh? Answer me."

A fat kid with a flat top walked over, sat down next to the drunk, reached into the old man's jacket pocket, and pulled out a half-empty pint bottle.

A lighter-skinned, thinner boy slapped the drunk around, first lifting him by the scruff of the neck, then laughing as he flopped back to the floor. The old guy tried to rise, only to be kicked in the ribs by Nylon Stocking.

The old guy was bleeding at the mouth. Fat Boy held the pint of booze aloft, teasing the drunk the way you tease a dog with a bone. The worst part was that the drunk was reaching for it, hands flapping wildly, begging. He'd have barked if they'd asked him to.

I was shaking, my stomach starting to heave. God, where was Manny? Where was my backup? I had to stop the kids before their friends got there, but I felt too sick to move. *If there's one thing I can't stand, it's a woman drunk.* It was as though every taunt, every kick, was aimed at me, not just at the old man.

I reached into my belt for my gun, then opened my vest's back pouch and pulled out the slapper. Ready to charge, I stopped cold when Nylon Stocking said, "Yo, y'all want to do him like we done the others?"

Fat Boy's face lit up. "Yeah," he agreed. "Feel like a cold night. We needs a little fire."

"You right, bro," the light-skinned kid chimed in. "I got the kerosene. Done took it from my momma heater."

"What he deserve, man," the fourth member of the gang said, his voice a low growl. "Comin' into our crib, pissin' on the art, smellin' up the place. This here *our* turf, dig?" He prodded the old man in the chest.

"I—I didn't mean nothing," the old man whimpered. "I just wanted a place to sleep."

Uncle Paul, sleeping on our couch when he was too drunk for Aunt Rose to put up with him. He was never too drunk for Mom to take him in. Never too drunk to give me one of his sweet Irish smiles and call me his best girl.

The light-skinned kid opened the bottle—ironically, it looked as if it once contained whiskey—and sprinkled the old man the way my mother sprinkled clothes before ironing them. Nylon Stocking pulled out a book of matches.

By the time Delgado came back, with or without backup, there'd be one more bonfire if I didn't do something. Fast.

Surprise was my only hope. Four of them, young and strong. One of me, out of shape and shaky.

I shot out a light. I cracked the bulb on the first shot. Target shooting was my best asset as a cop, and I used it to give the kids the impression they were surrounded.

The kids jumped away from the drunk, moving in all directions. "Shit," one said, "who shootin'?"

I shot out the second and last bulb. In the dark, I had the advantage. They wouldn't know, at least at first, that only one cop was coming after them.

"Let's book," another cried. "Ain't worth stayin' here to get shot."

I ran up the steps, onto the platform lit only by the moonlike rays from the other side of the tracks. Yelling "Stop, police," I waded into the kids, swinging my illegal slapper.

Thump into the ribs of the kid holding the kerosene bottle. He dropped it, clutching his chest and howling. I felt the breath whoosh out of him, heard the snap of rib cracking. I wheeled and slapped Nylon Stocking across the knee, earning another satisfying howl.

My breath came in gasps, curses pouring out of me. Blood pounded in my temples, a thumping noise that sounded louder than the express train.

The advantage of surprise was over. The other two kids jumped me, one riding my back, the other going for my stomach with hard little fists. All I could see was a maddened teenage tornado circling me with blows. My arm felt light as I thrust my gun deep into the kid's stomach. He doubled, groaning.

It was like chugging beer at a cop racket. Every hit, every satisfying *whack* of blackjack against flesh made me hungry for the next. I whirled and socked. The kids kept coming, and I kept knocking them down like bowling pins.

The adrenaline rush was stupendous, filling me with elation. I was a real cop again. There was life after detox.

At last they stopped. Panting, I stood among the fallen, exhausted. My hair had escaped from my knit hat and hung in matted tangles over a face red-hot as a griddle.

I pulled out my cuffs and chained the kids together, wrist to wrist, wishing I had enough sets to do each individually. Together, even cuffed, they could overpower me. Especially since they were beginning to realize I was alone.

I felt weak, spent. As though I'd just made love.

I sat down on the platform, panting, my gun pointed at Nylon Stocking. "You have the right to remain silent," I began.

As I finished the last Miranda warning on the last kid, I heard the cavalry coming over the hill. Manny Delgado, with four reinforcements.

As the new officers took the collars, I motioned Manny aside, taking him to where the drunk lay sprawled in the corner, still shaking and whimpering.

"Do you smell anything?" I asked.

Manny wrinkled his nose. I looked down at the drunk.

A trickle of water seeped from underneath him; his crotch was soaked.

Uncle Paul, weaving his way home, singing off-key, stopping to take a piss under the lamppost. Nothing unusual in that, except that this time Julie Ann Mackinnon, my eighth-grade rival, watched from across the street. My cheeks burned as I recalled how she'd told the other kids what she'd seen, her hand cupped over her giggling mouth.

"Not that," I said, my tone sharp, my face reddening. "The kerosene. These kids are the torch killers. They were going to roast this guy. That's why I had to take them on alone."

Delgado's face registered the skepticism I'd seen lurking in his eyes all night. Could he trust me? He'd been suitably impressed at my chain gang of prisoners, but now I was talking about solving the crime that had every cop in the city on overtime.

"Look, just go back to Brooklyn Bridge and radio"—I was going to say Captain Lomax, when I thought better—"Sal Minucci in Anti-Crime. He'll want to have the guy's coat analyzed. And make sure somebody takes good care of that bottle." I pointed to the now-empty whiskey bottle the light-skinned boy had poured kerosene from.

"Isn't that his?" Manny indicated the drunk.

"No, his is a short dog," I said, then turned away as I realized the term was not widely known in nondrunk circles.

Just go, kid, I prayed. *Get the hell out of here before*—

He turned, following the backup officers with their chain gang. "And send for Emergency Medical for this guy," I added. "I'll stay here till they come."

I looked down at the drunk. His eyes were blue, a watery, no-color blue with all the life washed out of them. Uncle Paul's eyes.

Uncle Paul, blurry-faced and maudlin, too blitzed to care that I'd come home from school with a medal for the best English composition. I'd put my masterpiece by his chair, so he could read it after dinner. He spilled whiskey on it; the blue-black ink ran like tears and blotted out my carefully chosen words.

Uncle Paul, old, sick, and dying, just like this one. Living by that time more on the street than at home, though there were people who would take him in. His eyes more red than blue, his big frame wasted. I felt a sob rising, like death squeezing my lungs. I heaved, grabbing for air. My face was wet with tears I didn't recall shedding.

I hate you, Uncle Paul. I'll never be like you. Never.

I walked over to the drunk, still sprawled on the platform. I was a sleepwalker; my arm lifted itself. I jabbed the butt of my gun into old, thin ribs, feeling it bump against bone. It would be a baseball-size bruise. First a raw red-purple, then blue-violet, finally a sickly yellow-gray.

I lifted my foot, just high enough to land with a thud near the kidneys. The old drunk grunted, his mouth falling open. A drizzle of saliva fell to the ground. He put shaking hands to his face and squeezed his eyes shut. I lifted my foot again. I wanted to kick and kick and kick.

Uncle Paul, a frozen lump of meat found by some transit cop on the aboveground platform at 161st Street. The Yankee Stadium stop, where he took me when the Yanks played home games. We'd eat at the Yankee Tavern, me wolfing down a corned beef on rye and cream soda, Uncle Paul putting away draft beer after draft beer.

Before he died, Uncle Paul had taken all the coins out of his pocket, stacking them in neat little piles beside him. Quarters, dimes, nickles, pennies. An inventory of his worldly goods.

I took a deep, shuddering breath, looked down at the sad old man I'd brutalized. A hot rush of shame washed over me.

I knelt down, gently moving the frail, blue-white hands away from the near-transparent face. The fear I saw in the liquid blue eyes sent a piercing ray of self-hatred through me.

If there's anything I can't stand, it's a woman drunk. Me too, Manny, I can't stand women drunks either.

The old man's lips trembled; tears filled his eyes and rolled down his thin cheeks. He shook his head from side to side, as though trying to wake himself from a bad dream.

"Why?" he asked, his voice a raven's croak.

"Because I loved you so much." The words weren't in my head anymore, they were slipping out into the silent, empty world of the ghost station. As though Uncle Paul weren't buried in Calvary Cemetery but could hear me with the ears of this old man who looked too damn much like him. "Because I wanted to be just like you. And I am." My voice broke. "I'm just like you, Uncle Paul. I'm a drunk." I put my head on my knee and sobbed like a child. All the shame of my drinking days welled up in my chest. The stupid things I'd said and done, the times I'd had to be taken home and put to bed, the times I'd thrown up in the street outside the bar. *If there's one thing I can't stand . . .*

"Oh, God, I wish I were dead."

The bony hand on mine felt like a talon. I started, then looked into the old man's watery eyes. I sat in the ghost station and saw in this stranger the ghost that had been my dying uncle.

"Why should you wish a thing like that?" the old man asked. His voice was clear, no booze-blurred slurring, no groping for words burned out of the brain by alcohol. "You're a young girl. You've got your whole life ahead of you."

My whole life. To be continued . . .

One day at a time. One night at a time.

When I got back to the District, changed out of my work clothes, showered, would there be a meeting waiting for me? Damn right; in the city that never sleeps, AA never sleeps either.

I reached out to the old man. My fingers brushed his silver stubble.

"I'm sorry, Uncle Paul," I said. "I'm sorry."

Charles Ardai's fiction has appeared in many anthologies, notably Alfred
Hitchcock's Mystery Magazine *and* Isaac Asimov's Science Fiction
Magazine. *Able to cut right to the heart of a character or situation with equal ease,*
he has a voice as unforgettable as his stories. In "Nobody Wins," he takes a look at
love and the Mob, and finds them an uneasy match.

Nobody Wins

Charles Ardai

Leon Culhane was one of those men you look at twice when they
pass you on the street, the sort who looks as though he stepped off a
poster for a horror movie once and couldn't figure out how to step
back on again. He had the kind of face that would scare small children,
and more than a few adults.

When he came into my office, he had to duck, and even so, the
top of his head brushed the lintel of the door. I offered him a seat
across from me, but we could both see he wouldn't fit in the chair. I
only wished I had seen it before I had offered. He didn't take offense;
he just leaned one elbow on top of my filing cabinet, put his chin in
his hand and started telling his story.

I tried to listen without looking. I tried to—I couldn't. His face
was flat, as though someone had smashed it with an iron, and when he
talked, the words came out of a pair of lips that looked drawn on—
they never moved. His eye sockets could have held golf balls with
room to spare, and if there was an inch of skin on his face that wasn't
pocked with acne scars, I couldn't see it. It wasn't a face you wanted to
look at, but it wasn't a face you could do anything but look at, either.

When he came to a pause, I shook my head and asked him to start
again. I hadn't heard one word.

"Carmine Stampada gave me your name," he said slowly, and this
time I just looked down at my notepad and listened. "He said you
know your way around a missing persons case, that you found his wife
when she took off for the Keys."

"Yeah," I said. "I found her facedown in a swimming pool."

"You found her," he said. "Now I want you to find somebody for me. Her name is Lila, and she's my fiancée. I have a picture that I'll show you if you look up."

I looked. He held out a four-by-five still of a lovely girl with auburn hair. I couldn't imagine her marrying him in a million years. But imagining isn't my job. I handed the photo back. "Attractive," I said.

He nodded. "Three days ago she told me she was going to her brother's for the weekend. She was supposed to be home this morning. She never showed up."

I looked at my watch. It was only twelve thirty. "Maybe she's stuck in traffic."

"Maybe she is," he said, "but the traffic's not on the way home. I called her brother, and he never saw her. He didn't know anything about her coming for the weekend."

I thought I knew what he was implying. "You think she—" how to put this delicately? "—headed for the Keys?"

He shook his head. "Not Lila."

"So what do you think happened?" I asked.

He squeezed his hands together, cracking some knuckles. "I think someone took her."

"And why do you think that?"

"I think that, Mr. Mickity, because when I woke up I found this on my doorstep." He reached into a jacket pocket, pulled out a velvet-covered jewelry box, and placed it on my desk. I had a feeling there was more in it than jewelry.

There was. A woman's little finger, severed between the first and second knuckles.

I closed the box before the bile that was crawling up my throat could reach my mouth.

"Lila's?" I asked.

"How the hell should I know?" Culhane walked up to my desk and leaned on it with both hands. "I hope the answer is no. But I'm supposed to think it's yes. I want to know why. I want to know who sent it, I want to know where my fiancée is, and I want you to bring her back."

"You realize," I said, "that it may very well be her finger. That there's a good chance she's already dead and that if she's not, she may have disappeared of her own free will."

"Well, that's what you're going to find out," Culhane said.

"Both of us," I told him.

*   *   *

Culhane gave me all the information he wanted me to have and left out all that he didn't, simple things like what he did for a living. He could have told me. He wouldn't have been the first Family man I've done a turn for. But he didn't know that I didn't have a wire in my pants or a brother on the police force or a Good Citizen complex cluttering up my head, so I couldn't really blame him for keeping a lid on his more questionable activities.

Of course, I didn't know for certain that that's what he wasn't telling me. For all I knew he earned his keep in some legitimate way, like opening doors in a ritzy apartment house, or babysitting. The fact that a man has Mafia written all over him doesn't make him a wiseguy any more than my looking like a P.I. makes me a detective. It's my license that makes me a detective, that and the fact that people are willing to hire me to find their fiancées. It was the bodies dumped in the East River that made Culhane a mob boy, that or maybe the broken kneecaps in Canarsie, or Little Italy, or wherever. That his hands had held a baseball bat, and not in regulation play, I'd have been willing to bet the agency on.

What else didn't Leon Culhane tell me? Things like where I could reach him after hours, how well-laundered the hundreds were that he was paying me with, what cute names his mamma had had for him when he was just a little Culhane, things like that.

What he did tell me was where I could find Lila's brother Jerome and, while we were at it, her sister Rachel. Culhane had called Rachel, to no avail, but I wrote her number down anyway. He gave me the number of an answering service that could get a message to him at any hour of the day as long as the hour was between nine in the morning and five in the afternoon. He gave me five hundred-dollar bills, each with its own serial number—I checked. And he gave me a stiff neck from looking up at him leaning over me for so long.

When he left, I got out the bottle of Excedrin I kept in my desk drawer, poured a few pills into a cloth handkerchief, wrapped them up, and then smashed them six or seven times with the butt of my revolver. I took the handkerchief into the bathroom, poured its contents into my toothbrushing cup, and filled the cup with cold water from the tap. I stirred it all up with the handle of my toothbrush and watched as the fragments pretended to dissolve.

I drank the medicine quickly, refilled the cup, and drank again.

I felt sick. Seeing a woman's severed finger is not my idea of lunchtime entertainment. To top it off, Culhane had left the finger behind. He didn't want it.

Well, I didn't want it, either. But I couldn't throw it away, I couldn't do anything with it, and I certainly didn't want to look at it. So I wrapped it in aluminum foil and stuck it in the freezer compartment of my office's miniature refrigerator. The velvet box, lined inside and out, was ruined by bloodstains. That, at least, I threw away.

I sat down to look over my notes. Lila Dubois, pronounced the un-French way, do-*boys*, soon to be Lila Culhane, had vanished. Maybe, I thought, she took a good look at the marriage bed she was climbing into and bailed out. If so, who could blame her? On the other hand, if so, where did the finger come from?

Could Culhane's rivals have kidnapped his fiancée? Sure. Kidnapping was their stock in trade. And the finger? Why not? If I could imagine Culhane cutting off a girl's finger, and I could, in a Bronx minute, it didn't take much to imagine his peers doing the same.

But "could have" is not the same as "did," and even if Culhane's rivals did send the grisly package, "why" was still a big question. Fingers usually come with notes of explanation. There had been no note with this finger.

No, it didn't add up—not yet. But Lila Dubois had to be somewhere. And someone had to know where.

Jerome Dubois answered the door in a Ralph Lauren bathrobe and slippers that must have cost a hundred dollars apiece. He had a tidily cropped beard and unhappy eyes that looked like they were looking at something they didn't want to see. Right now they were looking at me, but I didn't take it personally. Guys like this are unhappy looking at anything except their well-groomed faces in their gold-framed bathroom mirrors.

"Good afternoon," he said. "I am Dr. Dubois. Leon told me you were coming today." He lifted a cut-glass decanter from the minibar set up in one corner of the living room. "Port?" I shook my head. He poured himself a glass and carried it to the couch in the center of the room. He waited for me to join him before sitting down.

Then he waited for me to talk.

"When did you see Lila last?" I said.

He rolled his eyes back in his head for a second. "Oh, a week ago, two weeks. Something like that."

"Can't you be more specific?"

"Not really, I'm afraid. I have a terrible memory for dates."

"I'm not asking about the Civil War, doctor. I'm asking you did you see her last Tuesday or the Tuesday before that."

"I don't remember."

I waited while the doctor sipped his drink.

"She didn't ask to come visit you over the weekend?"

"No."

"She didn't come here Friday night?"

"No."

"She wasn't here at all over the weekend?"

"No."

"You didn't talk to her—"

"No."

"—over the weekend."

"No."

We sat.

"Listen," I said finally. "Leon Culhane has hired me to find out what happened to your sister. I'd think you'd be interested in knowing this, too, except maybe you don't give a damn or maybe you know and just aren't telling me. That's fine with me. It's stupid, but it's fine. What is not fine is wasting my time, which is what you are doing. So why don't you just tell me what you're going to tell me and then I'll go find out how much of it is a lie?"

"I imagine," Dubois said, "that you find this approach effective when you deal with men in Leon's circle. I find it vulgar, personally." We stared at each other for a while.

"What do you do, doctor?" I asked.

"If you mean what do I do professionally, I have a successful private practice, in addition to which I spend a good part of each year preparing and presenting papers for seminars. I also teach a graduate-level course at Columbia."

"In the field of psychology?"

"Abnormal psychology, yes."

"And in your successful private practice, doctor, if one of your patients is uncooperative, what do you do?"

"I work with him to identify the root cause underlying this behavior and then eliminate it. But if you are implying that I am being uncooperative, you are mistaken. There are better ways I could be spending my time than speaking with a friend of Leon Culhane's."

"Leon Culhane's not my friend."

"Neither am I—nevertheless, I am spending the time. I am answering your questions to the best of my ability. I do not know where Lila is. That question I cannot answer. But if you have others, by all means ask them. I may not satisfy you, but it will not be because I am unwilling to cooperate."

"What do you think happened to your sister?"

Jerome raised his shoulders and let them fall. "I don't know."

"I said what do you *think* happened. You don't know what you think?"

"I think she is fine."

"Why?"

"Because she is always fine."

"But she's missing."

"She has been missing before."

"When?"

Jerome shrugged again. "Now and again."

"*When?* "

"When she was a teenager, Lila would disappear for days at a time. She would go off without telling anyone where she was going. Then, a week later, she would return and tell us all about it: I went to the Hague! I went to Bourbon Street for Mardi Gras! Vanishing is nothing new for Lila."

"When was the last time she took off like that?"

"I don't remember."

"Would Rachel?"

"She might."

I stood up, put my hat back on, and walked myself to the door. Dubois followed me with his eyes only. "I am sorry that I can be of no more help," he said.

"No, you're not," I said. "Don't lie. You don't do it well."

"You have a great deal of hostility, Mr. Mickity. Why is that?"

I opened the door and walked out. The door didn't swing shut on its own—it wasn't that kind of door—and I didn't pull it closed behind me. I looked back and saw Dubois still sitting on the couch, his arms stretched wide along the top, his glass dangling from one hand.

I walked. He could close the door himself, or he could let the flies in, I didn't care.

★   ★   ★

Rachel Dubois looked a lot like her sister, or at least like the photo of her sister Culhane had shown me. The same color hair, though Rachel's was cut short, and the same long, old-money face. Pretty, but offputting to a guy like me, and I'd have thought to a guy like Culhane as well. I couldn't imagine Culhane planting a kiss on lips like those with lips like his.

Rachel was a little friendlier than her brother had been. She took my hat and hung it on a brass peg, and then she took my coat and passed it to a tall man in a suit that hung on him like a shroud. She didn't introduce us, and he didn't make eye contact. I asked about him when we sat down.

"Oh, that's Maren," Rachel said, taking a second to dredge the man's name out of memory. "He's our valet. We couldn't function without him."

"We?"

"My husband and I."

I looked around. The walls were covered with portraits, but the only man in any of them was Dr. Jerome. "Your husband live here with you?"

Rachel smiled. "Certainly. But he never paints himself."

"Your husband is a painter?"

Color rose to her cheeks. "No. My husband paints." By which she meant, *A painter is someone who paints for a living. My husband doesn't do anything for a living.*

"What does he do when he's not painting?" I asked.

"What does anyone do? What do you do when you're not . . ." The blush returned as she remembered that she was speaking with a member of the working class. "I suppose he reads. He chairs committees. He spends time with me."

"Does he spend any time with your sister?"

"Some."

"Does he spend time with Leon Culhane?"

"No."

"Will he, once they are married?"

A little shudder passed through Rachel's shoulders. "Lila will always be welcome here."

If she ever turns up, I thought. "Will Leon?"

"Excuse me?"

"Will Leon always be welcome here, too?"

"I will not bar my door to any member of my family, by blood or by marriage. But he will not be welcome. I'm sorry, Mr. Mickity. I imagine it sounds awful to you. I simply do not feel comfortable with that man."

It didn't sound awful to me at all. I'd have been surprised if she had felt comfortable with him.

"Lila is a headstrong child," she said, in an almost maternal tone. "She will have her way, whether the rest of us like it or not. She will marry that man—there is no way around it now—and she will suffer."

"Suffer? How?"

"Men like that make people suffer," she said. "That's their role in life. Don't think it doesn't extend to their families."

I thought of Dahlia Stampada, who ran away with a pugnosed sweet-talker whose sole redeeming feature was that he didn't beat her up the way Carmine did. When he found out that Carmine was on his trail, he had shot her in the head and left her in a swimming pool. But at least he hadn't beat her up.

I remembered Carmine's expression when I told him that Dahlia was dead: no regret, no anger, just a sort of facial shrug. Dead was better than missing, since missing you can do with another man but dead you do alone.

And Leon had gotten my name from Carmine Stampada.

"You're right," I said. Rachel's eyes opened a little wider at that, as though she felt a sudden need to reappraise me. "Leon Culhane is not the kind of man I'd want my sister marrying."

"That's very frank of you."

I shrugged. "I'm always honest. In my business, it doesn't pay to be a liar."

"If you feel that way about Culhane, why are you working for him?"

"I don't have a sister," I said. "I have nothing to worry about."

Rachel led me upstairs via a thickly carpeted staircase that made no sound at all when we climbed it. I think it was the first time in my life that I had climbed stairs that didn't creak.

The hallway was hung with more of Rachel's husband's paintings. The style was bland and conservative, the way you would have expected it to be. Horseriding foxhunters. Landscapes in the Everglades. Storm clouds over the Cape. At least the horses looked like horses and the clouds looked like clouds.

Rachel opened a door at the end of the hall and took me into a room furnished with a bed, a writing desk, a telephone, and a large dresser. The room was bigger than my office. "This is where Lila stays when she's here."

"When was she here last?"

"In June."

"How often did she normally come?"

"About once a month."

"Don't you think it's odd that you haven't seen her in three months?"

"Yes, I do. But a great deal has been odd since she started seeing Culhane. This is the least of it."

"Oh? What else?"

"Phone calls during which she sounded as though she was about to break into tears, but wouldn't admit that anything was wrong. Letters we would get from her that said things like, 'Darling, Leon and I are so wonderfully happy together!' She was trying to put on a good face, but she wasn't doing a very good job of it. I could tell she was unhappy."

"Why did she stay? Was she afraid of leaving him?"

"Wouldn't you be? She probably was. But really it didn't matter. You see, she's taken her stand with us, and she'd sooner go through all sorts of unhappiness with him than admit she was wrong. She'll go through with the marriage now no matter how wrong she knows it is, because she told us she would."

"Except that now she's missing," I said.

Rachel didn't say anything for a second. "Yes, except for that."

"Do you know where your sister is?"

"No." It sounded like the truth, unfortunately.

"Your brother said that Lila has disappeared before, when she was younger. She went to New Orleans, he said."

"Yes, and to Amsterdam, and to Paris, and once to Greenwich Village. I think that little adventure made our mother most unhappy of all. Lila liked to travel, and of course, we had the resources to do it. She would occasionally just pick up her travel bags and go."

"When was the last time this happened?"

"When she was about seventeen."

"So not for quite a long time."

"No."

"Do you think that's what happened this time? Your brother seems to think it is."

"I don't know, Mr. Mickity. Maybe Jerome is right. I just have a bad feeling about it. If she comes back a week from now smiling and carefree, I'll eat my words. But I don't think she will."

"Why not?"

"Because I think that man did something to her. I know it makes no sense, because then why did he hire you, but in my heart I feel it. Tell me something, how much is he paying you?"

I thought about it for a second and then I told her.

"While you're investigating, could you do me a favor and do a little investigating of him as well? I'll pay you the same amount, and no one need know."

I almost told her that she didn't have to do that, that I would be looking into Leon Culhane's life as a matter of course. But instead I just thanked her, said yes, I would, and took her money. There's honest and then there's stupid, after all.

"By the way," I asked her as she took me back to the front door, "what kind of doctor is your brother, exactly?"

"He's a Jungian psychiatrist. He specializes in devising therapy to repair what he calls 'antisocial disinhibitions.' That's as much of it as I understand, I'm afraid. Why?"

"I was just wondering." I thought of asking her whether his patients ever concealed important information from him, the way my clients do from me. Then I decided that the answer had to be yes, and if it wasn't she wouldn't know anyway.

"Thanks for being open with me," I said. "It's a nice change of pace."

"Just find my sister, Mr. Mickity. Please."

The 17th Precinct is not the busiest in the city, but it's busy enough. When I looked in on my way back to my office, Scott Tuttle, my ex-partner, was on two phones at once. He was a big guy with a head that had always looked too small for his body; now that he'd lost the last of his hair it looked even smaller. With a phone at either ear and a stack of reports up to his chin he looked like more of a prisoner than the guys in the cage at the back of the room.

I took a Post-it note off his desk, scribbled on it, and added it to the stack in front of him. It said, "Back in a minute. Help with fingerprint?" He glanced at the note and nodded.

My office was just two blocks away. I went over there, took the foil-wrapped package from my freezer, and carried it back to the precinct house. Scott was only on one phone now, and when I dropped the package on his desk, he looked at it and said, "I'll call you back" to the person on the other end of the line. He hung up slowly.

"Is that what I think it is?"

"I want to run a print from it."

I followed him into a back room where he got out a stamp pad, unwrapped the finger, and rolled it in the ink. Then he pressed it down firmly on a piece of white cardboard, his thumb pushing on the nail and rolling it slightly to either side. He lifted the finger carefully and used a paper towel to wipe it off.

"What the hell is this, Doug?"

"It's a case."

"A case." He held the finger out to me. I didn't really want to take it, but I took it. "This is what you work on now? Someone cuts off a woman's finger and you carry it around in your pocket? I thought you left the force to get away from stuff like this."

"I thought so, too."

"So what happened?"

"You can't get away from it," I said. "It's everywhere." I wrapped the finger in the aluminum foil again.

"Jesus," he said. "What a world."

The library at 50th Street and Lexington was a one room wonder. To get there, you had to descend a flight of stairs into a subway station and then take a sharp left turn through a pair of doors so heavy I had trouble moving them. Past the doors was a windowless chamber with only enough room for six or seven rows of stacks, a checkout desk, and two computers. Whose idea it had been to cram a library in there, I don't know.

But one had been crammed in, and because it was so close to my office, I was probably its best customer. Not for the books—for the computers. A computer can be kept in a broom closet; if it's connected to the right source of information, it's still the most powerful tool in the world.

I ran all the names I had through the machine. "Lila Dubois" came up blank. "Rachel Dubois" got me a few newspaper articles, including the notice in the *Times* from when she got married. I hadn't realized that the Dubois family was as well known or as well-to-do as the article led me to believe. They weren't Rockefellers, and Rachel had certainly married up when she wed the scion of the Hoeffler clan, but they weren't exactly hurting for cash, either. Papa Dubois, the *Times* was careful to note, had been a prime source of funds for the Reagan reelection campaign. Mamma Dubois had the maiden name of Kelter, as in the Kelter Inn chain of hotels.

"Jerome Dubois" produced a long list of publications, including contributions to scholarly journals and books with impenetrable, forty-word-long titles. I dug up a few reviews of his work, one of which started, "If Jerome Dubois would spend more time in the real world and less in his head, he would surely have a different outlook on human psychology." There was also an article in *New York* magazine on the city's psychiatric establishment. The author of that article described Dubois as a "consummate theoretician" and "a zealous proponent of his ideas," which ideas he called "reactionary and barbaric."

I went to the stacks to see if I could find any of these reactionary and barbaric books, but that was asking too much. This branch hardly had two books to rub together, and neither was by Jerome Dubois.

Before logging off the computer, I also had it do a search on "Leon Culhane." None of what it found surprised me. Fourteen arrests. Two convictions. References to him in articles in the *Village Voice,* the *News,* and the *Post.* No books with long titles. No contributions to scholarly journals.

I dialed the number Leon Culhane had given me and left a message for him saying that I wanted to talk to him. I didn't have anything to tell him that couldn't have waited, but I wanted him to know what I had done. He called back in about ten minutes.

"Have you found her?"

I hate that question. "Not yet, Mr. Culhane. The search is still young. You get any more fingers?"

"That isn't funny."

"It's not meant to be. I think there's a good chance you'll be hearing again from the people who sent you the finger, especially since they didn't send a note the first time. They didn't send a note, did they?"

"No, they didn't. I told you."

"You did. I just wanted to make sure you hadn't found one since then."

"No."

I waited. Nothing came.

"Okay, in that case, let me tell you where I've been." I opened my notebook and made sure he could hear the pages turning. "I've talked to Jerome and Rachel. They don't seem to like you very much."

"Don't fool yourself, Mickity—they don't like you either."

"I'm sure they don't. But they seem to have a particular dislike for you."

"What's your point?"

"My point is that they think that if something happened to Lila, you're probably the one behind it. Now, I don't believe that's the case. But I want you to know that that's what they're saying."

"I don't care what they're saying. All I care about is where Lila is."

I flipped some more pages. "A friend of mine in the police department took the print from the finger. He'll run it through the computer and see what comes up."

"That won't help," Culhane said. "Lila never had her fingerprints taken."

"No, I wouldn't have thought she had. But maybe the person who lost that finger has. Assuming that it's not Lila's."

"Oh."

"Right: oh. We should have results on that in a day or two."

"Fine. What else?"

He didn't need to know I'd looked up his rap sheet. "That's it," I said. "I'll let you know if anything happens. And you'll call me if you get any more packages?"

"Yeah, I'll call you." He hung up. I took an Excedrin. It stuck in my throat, the way they always do when I'm too lazy to break them up. It took three shots of whisky to get it down.

I went to visit Carmine Stampada down on Mott Street. When I'd found his wife, he'd paid me handsomely and told me his door was always open. Since then, I'd never had a reason to see if that was true. This seemed like as good an occasion as any.

His face didn't exactly light up when he saw me, but my arrival didn't obviously make him unhappy, either. He disengaged from the conversation he was having with two slickhaired men who were about as tall and broad-shouldered as Leon Culhane and came over to pump my hand. I looked at the two men and suddenly realized how Leon must fit into this world. It was babysitting, all right—after a fashion.

The two bodyguards followed Carmine as he led me down the block to a trattoria called Intimo. They took a table near the front; we took one in the back.

"Sorry to bother you—"

"No bother. I needed to take lunch anyway. What can I do for you?"

"Leon Culhane," I said.

Stampada nodded. "So he did go to you. That's what I figured. When I saw you coming, I said to Jimmy, this is a good man, but I'll bet he is not just coming to pass the time with us."

"No, Mr. Stampada, I wouldn't waste your time like that."

"No waste, but go on."

"Who is Leon?" I asked.

"Who is Leon? Leon and me, we grew up together. Just a couple of blocks away from here, in fact. Leon's a good man."

"What does he do for you?"

Stampada gave me a tight little smile. "I know you're a trustworthy man, Douglas. But what a person does, you don't discuss."

"Does he do what Jimmy does, for instance?"

Stampada looked over at his bodyguards. I didn't know which one was Jimmy, but it hardly mattered. "Leon's older. He's been through a lot more than Jimmy has. But yeah, more or less."

"Do you have any idea how he met Lila Dubois?"

"Of course I do."

A waiter arrived with two cups of espresso on his tray. He placed them on the table along with a glass of anisette for Stampada. Stampada took a sip from each.

"It was about—what?—five, six years ago? Six, I think. Leon was on his way home, it's maybe one o'clock in the morning, and he passes this guy and this girl making out in a doorway. Nothing so unusual about that, right? So he walks on. But one thing Leon's got is good hearing, and maybe five steps later he hears this girl making sounds and she does not sound like she is enjoying herself, you know what I mean? Now he could have kept walking. It's a big city; lots of people in it and you can't mind everyone's business. But he didn't keep walking. He turned around and went back."

He took another sip of espresso. "The guy had a knife to her throat. When Leon pulled him off her, her neck was all bloody from little cuts. The guy hadn't meant to cut her, but he was so excited he couldn't help himself. He slashed Leon across the forearm, and let me tell you, I saw it afterwards, that cut was down to the bone. But Leon picked the guy up—this is with blood pouring down his arm, remember—and he smashed that little bastard against the wall so hard that if I took you there right now you could still see the marks."

"God."

"That's how they met. A regular Harlequin love story, right? Leon took her home—his home—and they bandaged each other up. I didn't see Leon for a week. Then she disappeared back to her Cadillacs and her Riverdale mansion and Leon came back to work. I thought that was the end of it. But they stayed in touch. Just this year they started seeing each other again. Now they're supposed to be married." He finished the anisette in one swallow. "And that's the whole story."

"Except now she's missing and her family thinks Leon's done something to her."

"You tell them different. You tell them that's impossible." Stampada leaned forward. "Listen, I know this man, thirty-six years now I know this man, and this is a man who, I'm not telling you anything you don't know, has made more than one person wish he were dead. This goes no farther than this table, Douglas, but between you, me, and the lamppost, Leon Culhane has done some things to some people that even make me uncomfortable. And I am not an easy man to make uncomfortable. But I'm telling you Leon Culhane would kill himself before he'd hurt that girl. And if anyone else did anything to hurt her . . . let's just say I wouldn't want to be in that man's shoes for any amount of money."

"So what do you think happened to her?"

"I have no idea."

"Could it have been another woman, someone who was jealous of her? Someone who wanted Leon for herself?"

Stampada pointed to his bodyguards. "Look at Jimmy. There's a boy who never has to go to bed alone. And Aldo, maybe he's not so handsome, but he's big, and ugly he ain't. Those boys dress well, they comb their hair every day, they get looked at on the street. They carry big guns and they work for me. Now Leon carries a big gun and he works for me, but the only woman I ever saw look at him is Lila Dubois. Most people, when they see him, they just pray to God he's not looking at them. Leon's not a pretty sight, Douglas. He's a damn good man, loyal, but he's also ugly as sin. Until he met Lila, there's never been any woman in Leon's life—and if you don't find her, I have a feeling there's never going to be another."

"Then could it be someone who's trying to get at you?"

"What, through Leon?" Stampada shook his head. "Or did you mean someone who wants his job? No, then they'd just kill him. Or try to. Why take the girl?"

"Then who would have done it?"

"You're the detective," Stampada said. "If I could answer that, we should trade jobs."

I got two things from Stampada before I left. The first was Leon Culhane's address in Hoboken. The second was a promise that he wouldn't tell Leon he'd given it to me. I didn't want Leon to know I was poking around in his life.

On the bus over to Jersey I thought about what Stampada had told me. The man was not known for his honesty in general, but everything he'd said to me had the ring of truth. He'd had no reason to lie.

Culhane was as violent and unregenerate a sociopath as any I had met. That's what Stampada had been telling me in his careful, delicate way. Here was a man who had no friends and no lovers, who'd spent his life feared and hated, and who had been good enough at what he did to earn the respect of one of the most violent capos in the Mob. Leon Culhane was probably a killer many times over, and worse things, too.

He was also in love.

Was this possible? Could it be that this monster was tame in the presence of Lila Dubois? Could Rachel have been wrong? Maybe. Maybe.

The bus let me off next to a video arcade. I crossed to the other side of the avenue, away from the beeps and lasers and the sound of quarters being gobbled up, and turned down a side street. All the houses here looked the same. This was the border between the good and the bad parts of Hoboken: good enough not to be slums, but not good enough to keep from being crammed with identical prefabs. Some of the houses had building numbers; others had lost theirs. I consulted the slip of paper on which I had written Leon's address and made my way slowly down the block.

It was only by counting doorways that I figured out which one was 1317. It was a two story rectangular box with a cinder block foundation and pale blue siding. The roof was gabled, and the drainpipes were rusty. There were no curtains in the windows. The lawn was patchy, but well-kept.

There was a row of cars parked in the street, and I kept them between me and the house the first time I passed. I chanced a glance in one of the windows. I didn't see anyone.

I went back, this time walking on the sidewalk, going slowly, looking in each window. The rooms looked comfortable, though they didn't have much in the way of furniture. The kitchen was well stocked with sixpacks, and I saw a shotgun leaning against the refrigerator.

I rounded the corner, hoping to get a look at the rest of the house and maybe even find a way inside. Instead, I got a look at another shotgun, the twin of the one I had seen in the kitchen. This one was pointed directly at me. It was in the unsteady hands of a man who, though both tall and ugly, was not Leon Culhane.

"Step back, put your hands up, and don't even think of trying to run," he said.

I stepped back until my back was against the wall of the house. I put my hands up. I thought about trying to run but tried not to let it show. "My name is Douglas Mickity," I said. "I'm a private investigator. I was hired by the owner of this house to—"

"Like hell you were," the man said, jamming the barrel of the shotgun under my chin. "I'm the owner of this house, and you're sure as hell not the P.I. I hired. Now you start talking or I'll blow your head off."

I felt the metal at my throat, pressing against my Adam's apple. "I was looking for Leon Culhane's house. Thirteen seventeen." I opened my left hand and let him see the slip of paper in it. The shotgun wavered at my throat, brushing my chin. "Leon Culhane hired me to find his fiancée. That's the truth."

"So why do you want to go snooping around his house?"

"I don't know." My mind was racing for an acceptable answer. "To be thorough. To make sure he didn't miss anything."

"What agency do you work for?"

"I work for myself."

"Take your I.D. out and show it to me," he said. "Slowly."

I did what he said. He looked at my driver's license and my investigator's license. Then he lowered his gun. I started to breathe again.

"Sorry," he said. He turned away and started walking toward the back porch of his house.

"Hold on," I called after him. "What did you mean 'You're not the P.I. I hired'?"

"Just what it sounds like," the man said. "I hired Arthur Chase. You're not him. When you said you're a detective, I thought maybe you work for him. But you don't, so that's that." He opened the door and waited for me to leave.

"Can you at least tell me which house is Culhane's?"

He nodded toward the house behind me.

"And your name?"

"None of your business."

The door banged shut behind him.

I rubbed my throat. I could still feel where he had held the gun on me. I had accidentally miscounted houses, and for that simple mistake I had almost gotten killed. Scott's words came back to me: *Jesus, what a world.* Two houses picked at random in Hoboken, New Jersey, and both of the owners had hired detectives, both had guns, both were willing to use them. . . . No, it didn't matter whether you were on the force or not. You couldn't get away from it.

I went down the block to Culhane's house. It was a little better furnished than the other house, his lot a little worse maintained. There was a small stack of mail at the front door. I looked through it. Most of the mail was addressed to Leon R. Culhane, but two envelopes were addressed to Howard Gross at 1319 and a supermarket circular was addressed to Sheila Hanover at 1315. So I had been speaking to Mr. Gross—or Mr. Hanover, if there was a Mr. Hanover.

There was more I could have done if I hadn't been so jumpy, but I couldn't shake the feeling that Mr. Shotgun, whatever his name was, was peeking out at me from between his Venetian blinds.

I took one last look at the doorstep where Culhane had found the finger and then I headed back to the bus stop.

My first stop in the city was at 41st Street and Fifth Avenue: the Mid-Manhattan Library. I used one of their computers for a few more database searches, and I found something under "Hanover" that caught my eye. It was a newspaper article from a few weeks back. I printed it out and took it with me.

But the main reason I was there was not for the computer. I went through the stacks until I came to the D's. Of five books listed in the card catalogue, only one was on the shelf. I took it.

I also went back to the 17th Precinct. Scott dug through his files while I read the PBA announcements tacked above the Quick-Cool Ice Cream Bar Machine. Eventually he turned up the print match he'd run for me.

I promised Scott dinner at the restaurant of his choice. In return, he told me whose finger I had stashed in my office icebox.

It wasn't Lila's.

The book was fascinating. I tore through it the way some people read potboiler mysteries and others the sports pages.

Its title was *Strategies for Mental Retrogression*. The title was followed on the book's cover by a subtitle of three or four lines, the gist of which was that psychology had taken a wrong turn some time around the middle of the century, and that we would all be better off if we stopped coddling the mentally ill and went back to reliable methods of treatment such as straitjackets, wet-ties, electric shocks, and lobotomies. It was a book calculated to shock and titillate its audience of white-coated academicians, whom I pictured reading it under the covers with a flashlight.

I didn't understand half the words, which I'm sure was the point of his using them. The half I did understand kept adding up to such hogwash that I wanted to throw the book down the incinerator chute and start fresh with a good Robert Ludlum or Lawrence Block. But I didn't. I made it all the way from the first chapter, about making the insane aware that they are insane, to the last, which said that if all methods of treatment were unsuccessful, one should incarcerate the mad person until, inevitably, new methods are developed.

The text was peppered with cheery anecdotes, most about well-intentioned but naive psychiatrists who started out by asking their patients for input into their therapy and ended up roasted on a spit, strangled with their stethoscopes, or chopped up into little bits. On the other side were case studies that showed how electroshock helped Clara S. lead a normal life and how being restrained for a solid year turned Allan G. into a productive citizen.

I took the book along with me on the train up to Riverdale.

When Jerome came to the door, I asked him to autograph it. He almost smiled, then saw that it was a library book and frowned. He stared into my eyes, as though trying to pry open my odd, aberrant psyche. "Is this a joke?"

"No joke. I read the book. It's very impressive."

"*You* read the book?" He said this in a tone that suggested that what he really wanted to say was, You can *read?*

"I did. Cover to cover. Didn't get all the fine points, I admit, but the generalities sank in very nicely, thank you. Do you think I could come in?"

He stepped back from the door. "Suit yourself."

I suited myself and shut the door behind me. Jerome retreated to the couch. He did not offer me a drink this time. Maybe something in my eyes told him not to.

"Has Lila come back?" he said.

"I think I've found her."

"Really?" Jerome drummed his fingers on the back of the couch. "Delightful. I'm very glad to hear it. Please ask her to telephone sometime and tell me all about where she has been."

I shook my head. "Why bother? I told you you're a terrible liar."

"What am I lying about?"

"What are you lying about? Mister, if you told me your name, I'd want to see a birth certificate to confirm it."

Jerome extended a finger toward the door. "On second thought, no, you can't come in. Get out of my house."

"What, and skip my lecture?"

"What are you talking about?"

"Case study: Jerome D.," I said. "Here we have a respected doctor from a more than respectable family. He didn't marry into money the way one sister did, but he went to a prestigious medical school and he has plenty to keep himself fed and clothed."

"Get out of my house."

"Jerome and his two sisters received the best of everything and, what's more, they had identical upbringings. So how could it have happened that while two of the siblings turned out as might have been predicted one went so horribly wrong?"

"If you don't get out this second, I'm calling the police." He grabbed the phone.

"Put the phone down," I said. His face went pale. I raised my gun to chest level. "I have six bullets in here, and I only need one. I'd go to jail, but so what? I've been there before."

Jerome's hand, suddenly a bloodless white, was still clenched around the receiver. We could both hear the dial tone's purr.

"Put the phone down. Or do you want to bet on whether I could miss six times at this range?"

He put the phone down.

"Now sit down."

He sat down.

"Case study: Lila D.," I continued. "A thankless little renegade from adolescence on. Ran away on pappa's charge card while Jerome and Rachel were behaving the way proper young adults should. Ran away to New York City and almost got herself raped. Took up with a Mafia thug. Lost her blueblood virginity to a man almost twice her age whose profession is making people beg for him to stop. Had the temerity to fall in love with this man and to be suckered by his sly impersonation of a normal human being. Wouldn't be talked out of it for love or money—and you probably tried both. What could account for this? How could one third of the same seed that bred you turn out so . . . so . . . dare I say, crazy?"

Sweat was pooling around the collar to Jerome's robe. His hands were at his sides. His eyes were riveted on my gun.

"I know what happened, Jerome. It isn't that hard to figure out.

"You tried to reason with her. You suggested she seek help. You tried to make her aware of the obvious insanity of her plan. How could a sane woman dream of marrying Leon Culhane? But she wouldn't budge. She insisted that she loved him.

"So you invited her down here for the weekend, and when she arrived, you did what any good psychiatrist would do, if only—how did you put it?" I opened the book and found the page I was looking for. " 'If only proven therapeutic methods had never to answer to the sobbing, pitiful wail we call conscience, then psychiatry would no longer be a hobbled science. It is as though we asked a surgeon, prior to his making the initial incision, to pause to consider whether he would want himself similarly cut open. Steps must be taken; the ill must be cured; nothing should stand in the way.' "

I closed the book.

"Where is she? Where have you locked up your sister, doctor?"

"You are wrong." He spoke in a whisper.

"Don't make me search this place, or you won't recognize it when I'm—"

"She is not here," he whispered. "Search if you like."

"Then where? Did you stick her in one of the hospitals you consult with?" I aimed the gun at his legs. "I'm no Leon Culhane, but I think I can figure out how he gets people to tell him things before they die. I might make a mistake, and hurt you more than I'd like to, but what can I say? I'm not an expert. Talk. You've got three seconds."

He didn't even wait for me to count to two. His head dropped, and I thought I saw tears well up in his eyes. I know I heard them in his voice.

"Your analysis was admirable," he said. "You would make a good psychiatrist. But I am afraid your conclusion is incorrect. Yes, it was quite clear that Lila was afflicted. Unfortunately, in this case her madness threatened not only herself, but her sister and myself as well. It threatened the good name of my family. It threatened my professional reputation. Can you imagine what effect it would have on my standing in the community to have it known that my younger sister is insane? Even if I were treating her for it?" His voice was a ragged wail. "Never mind insanity—can you imagine what it would have meant for a Dubois to marry a gangster?"

Jerome rose slowly from the couch and extended his arms toward me, as though he expected me to slap a pair of handcuffs on him. "I didn't abduct her. She came of her own free will. But she wouldn't listen to reason. There was no other choice. I couldn't risk incarcerating her. So I killed her."

"Oh, please don't say that." Now I was the one whispering.

"I did," Jerome said. "I forced myself to overcome my internalized inhibitions. I had to."

"You poor man," I whispered.

I closed the door behind me this time.

Leon Culhane arrived at my office a little after eleven. I had my radio on. When he came in, I turned it down low. I didn't turn it off. Somehow I didn't want mine to be the only voice in the room.

I hauled out the foil-wrapped finger and showed him the printout Scott had given me. The finger belonged to Liana Hanover, daughter of Anthony and Sheila. According to police records, the Hanovers had reported their daughter missing two weeks earlier. According to the newspaper articles I'd found in the library, the parents had had no contact from the kidnappers.

Except that they had—the kidnappers had just left their grisly package on the wrong doorstep by mistake. And had they left a note with it, one that blew away in the morning wind? Who knows?

I told Leon that I would be sending the finger to Arthur Chase and that I would leave his name out of it.

Leon listened to this impassively. It was not Lila's finger; this was good. But maybe in my voice he could hear that this was the last of the good news, because he showed no relief.

I told him.

I told him the whole story, I showed him Jerome's book, I explained what had been going through Jerome's head. Culhane stared me in the eyes through every word of it, showing no sign of anger, grief, or pain.

After a while I ran out of things to say.

"Job well done, Mr. Mickity," he said. "You earned your money." He turned to leave.

I stopped him at the door with a hand at the small of his back. I felt him recoil at my touch. "Please," I said, looking up into his enormous eyes, "don't hurt him too much."

"I couldn't possibly hurt him too much," he said.

Winner of the Grand Master Award from the Mystery Writers of America, Lawrence Block has been turning out some of the finest mystery fiction for the past twenty years. Although he is best known for his series characters Matt Scudder, a melancholy private eye, and Keller, a philosophical hit man, his stand-alone short fiction packs just as powerful a punch. "Someday I'll Plant More Walnut Trees," a dark tale of domestic abuse, is no exception.

Someday I'll Plant More Walnut Trees

Lawrence Block

There is a silence that is just stillness, just the absence of sound, and there is a deeper silence that is more than that. It is the antithesis, the aggressive opposite, of sound. It is to sound as antimatter is to matter, an auditory black hole that reaches out to swallow up and nullify the sounds of others.

My mother can give off such a silence. She is a master at it. That morning at breakfast she was thus silent, silent as she cooked eggs and made coffee, silent while I spooned baby oatmeal into Livia's little mouth, silent while Dan fed himself and while he smoked the day's first cigarette along with his coffee. He had his own silence, sitting there behind his newspaper, but all it did was insulate him. It couldn't reach out beyond that paper shield to snatch other sound out of the air.

He finished and put out his cigarette, folded his paper. He said it was supposed to be hot today, with rain forecast for late afternoon. He patted Livia's head, and with his forefinger drew aside a strand of hair that had fallen across her forehead.

I can see that now, his hand so gentle, and her beaming up at him, wide-eyed, gurgling.

Then he turned to me, and with the same finger and the same softness he reached to touch the side of my face. I did not draw away. His finger touched me, ever so lightly, and then he reached to draw me into the circle of his arms. I smelled his shirt, freshly washed and sun-dried, and under it the clean male scent of him.

We looked at each other, both of us silent, the whole room silent. And then Livia cooed and he smiled quickly and chucked me under the chin and left. I heard the screen door slam, and then the sounds of the car as he drove to town. When I could not hear it anymore I went over to the radio and switched it on. They were playing a Tammy Wynette song. "Stand by your man," Tammy urged, and my mother's silence swallowed up the words.

While the radio played unheard I changed Livia and put her in for her nap. I came back to the kitchen and cleared the table. My mother waved a hand at the air in front of her face.

"He smokes," I said.

"I didn't say anything," she said.

We did the dishes together. There is a dishwasher but we never use it for the breakfast dishes. She prefers to run it only once a day, after the evening meal. It could hold all the day's dishes, they would not amount to more than one load in the machine, but she does not like to let the breakfast and lunch dishes stand. It seems wasteful to me, of time and effort, and even of water, although our well furnishes more than we ever need. But it is her house, after all, and her dishwasher, and hers the decision as to when it is to be used.

Silently she washed the dishes, silently I wiped them. As I reached to stack plates in a cupboard I caught her looking at me. Her eyes were on my cheek, and I could feel her gaze right where I had felt Dan's finger. His touch had been light. Hers was firmer.

I said, "It's nothing."

"All right."

"Dammit, Mama!"

"I didn't say anything, Tildie."

I was named Matilda for my father's mother. I never knew her, she died before I was born, before my parents met. I was never called Matilda. It was the name on my college diploma, on my driver's license, on Livia's birth certificate, but no one ever used it.

"He can't help it," I said. "It's not his fault."

Her silence devoured my words. On the radio Tammy Wynette sang a song about divorce, spelling out the word. Why were they play-ing all her records this morning? Was it her birthday? Or an anniver-sary of some failed romance?

"It's not," I said. I moved to her right so that I could talk to her good ear. "It's a pattern. His father was abusive to his mother. Dan grew up around that. His father drank and was free with his hands. Dan swore he would never be like that, but patterns like that are almost impossible to throw off. It's what he knows, can you understand that? On a deep level, deeper than intellect, bone deep, that's how he knows to behave as a man, as a husband."

"He marked your face. He hasn't done that before, Tildie."

My hand flew to the spot. "You knew that—"

"Sounds travel. Even with my door closed, even with my good ear on the pillow. I've heard things."

"You never said anything."

"I didn't say anything today," she reminded me.

"He can't help it," I said. "You have to understand that. Didn't you see him this morning?"

"I saw him."

"It hurts him more than it hurts me. And it's my fault as much as it's his."

"For allowing it?"

"For provoking him."

She looked at me. Her eyes are a pale blue, like mine, and at times there is accusation in them. My gaze must have the same quality. I have been told that it is penetrating. "Don't look at me like that," my husband has said, raising a hand as much to ward off my gaze as to threaten me. "Damn you, don't you look at me like that!"

Like what? I'd wondered. How was I looking at him? What was I doing wrong?

"I do provoke him," I told her. "I make him hit me."

"How?"

"By saying the wrong thing."

"What sort of thing?"

"Things that upset him."

"And then he has to hit you, Tildie? Because of what you say?"

"It's a *pattern*," I said. "It's the way he grew up. Men who drink have sons who drink. Men who beat their wives have sons who beat their wives. It's passed on over the generations like a genetic illness. Mama, Dan's a good man. You see how he is with Livia, how he loves her, how she loves him."

"Yes."

"And he loves me, Mama. Don't you think it tears him up when something like this happens? Don't you think it eats at him?"

"It must."

"It does!" I thought how he'd cried last night, how he'd held me and touched the mark on my cheek and cried. "And we're going to try to do something about it," I said. "To break the pattern. There's a clinic in Fulton City where you can go for counseling. It's not expensive, either."

"And you're going?"

"We've talked about it. We're considering it."

She looked at me and I made myself meet her eyes. After a moment she looked away. "Well, you would know more about this sort of thing than I do," she said. "You went to college, you studied, you learned things."

I studied art history. I can tell you about the Italian Renaissance, although I have already forgotten much of what I learned. I took one psychology course in my freshman year and we observed the behavior of white rats in mazes.

"Mama," I said, "I know you disapprove."

"Oh, no," she said. "Tildie, that's not so."

"It's not?"

She shook her head. "I just hurt for you," she said. "That's all."

We live on 220 acres, only a third of them level. The farm has been in our family since the land was cleared early in the last century. It has been years since we farmed it. The MacNaughtons run sheep in our north pastures, and Mr. Parkhill leases forty acres, planting alfalfa one year and field corn the next. Mama has some bank stock and some utilities, and the dividends plus what she's paid for the land rent are enough to keep her. There's no mortgage on the land and the taxes have stayed low. And she has a big kitchen garden. We eat out of it all summer long and put up enough in the fall to carry us through the winter.

Dan studied comparative lit while I studied art history. He got a master's and did half the course work for a doctorate and then knew he couldn't do it anymore. He got a job driving a taxi and I worked waiting tables at Paddy Mac's, where we used to come for beer and hamburgers when we were students. When I got pregnant with Livia he didn't want me on my feet all day but we couldn't make ends meet on his earnings as a cabdriver. Rents were high in that city, and everything cost a fortune.

And we both loved country living, and knew the city was no place to bring up Livia. So we moved here, and Dan got work right away with a construction company in Caldwell. That's the nearest town, just six miles from us on country roads, and Fulton City is only twenty-two miles.

After that conversation with Mama I went outside and walked back beyond the garden and the pear and apple orchard. There's a stream runs diagonally across our land, and just beyond it is the spot I always liked the best, where the walnut trees are. We have a whole grove of black walnuts, twenty-six trees in all. I know because Dan counted them. He was trying to estimate what they'd bring.

Walnut is valuable. People will pay thousands of dollars for a mature tree. They make veneer from it, because it's too costly to use as solid wood.

"We ought to sell these off," Dan said. "Your mama's got an untapped resource here. Somebody could come in, cut 'em down, and steal 'em. Like poachers in Kenya, killing the elephants for their ivory."

"No one's going to come onto our land."

"You never know. Anyway, it's a waste. You can't even see this spot from the house. And nobody does anything with the nuts."

When I was a girl my mama and I used to gather the walnuts after they fell in early autumn. Thousands fell from the trees. We would just gather a basketful and crack them with a hammer and pick the meat out. My hands always got black from the husks and stayed that way for weeks.

We only did this a few times. It was after Daddy left, but while Grandma Yount was still alive. I don't remember Grandma bothering with the walnuts, but she did lots of other things. When the cherries came in we would all pick them and she would bake pies and put up jars of the rest, and she'd boil the pits to clean them and sew scraps of cloth to make beanbags. There are still beanbags in the attic that Grandma Yount made. I'd brought one down for Livia and fancied I could still smell cherries through the cloth.

"We could harvest the walnuts," I told Dan. "If you want."

"What for? You can't get anything for them. Too much trouble to open and hardly any meat in them. I'd sooner harvest the trees."

"Mama likes having them here."

"They're worth a fortune. And they're a renewable resource. You could cut them and plant more and someday they'd put your grandchildren through college."

"You don't need to cut them to plant more. There's other land we could use."

"No point planting more if you're not going to cut these, is there? What do we need them for?"

"What do our grandchildren need college for?"

"What's that supposed to mean?"

"Nothing," I'd said, backing away.

And hours later he'd taken it up again. "You meant I wasted my education," he said. "That's what you meant by that crack, isn't it?"

"No."

"Then what did you mean? What do I need a master's for to hammer a nail? That's what you meant."

"It's not, but evidently that's how you'd rather hear it."

He hit me for that. I guess I had it coming. I don't know if I deserved it, I don't know if a woman deserves to get hit, but I guess I provoked it. Something makes me say things I shouldn't, things he'll take amiss. I don't know why.

Except I do know why, and I'd walked out of the kitchen and across to the walnut grove to keep from talking about it to Mama. Because he had his pattern and I had mine.

His was what he'd learned from his daddy, which was to abuse a woman, to slap her, to strike her with his fists. And mine was a pattern I'd learned from my mama, which was to make a man leave you, to taunt him with your mouth until one day he put his clothes in a suitcase and walked out the door.

In the mornings it tore at me to hear the screen door slam. Because I thought, Tildie, one day you'll hear that sound and it'll be for the last time. One day you'll do what your mother managed to do, and he'll do like your father did and you'll never see him again. And Livia will grow up as you did, in a house with her mother and her grandmother, and she'll have cherry-pit beanbags to play with and she'll pick the meat out of black walnuts, but what will she do for a daddy? And what will you do for a man?

All the rest of that week he never raised his hand to me. One night Mama stayed with Livia while Dan and I went to a movie in Fulton City. Afterward we went to a place that reminded us both of

Paddy Mac's, and we drank beer and got silly. Driving home, we rolled down the car windows and sang songs at the top of our lungs. By the time we got home the beer had worn off but we were still happy and we hurried upstairs to our room.

Mama didn't say anything the next morning but I caught her looking at me and knew she'd heard the old iron bedstead. I thought, *You hear a lot, even with your good ear pressed against the pillow.* Well, if she had to hear the fighting, let her hear the loving, too.

She could have heard the bed that night, too, although it was a quieter and gentler lovemaking than the night before. There were no knowing glances the next day, but after the screen door closed behind Dan and after Livia was in for her nap, there was a nice easiness between us as we stood side by side doing the breakfast dishes.

Afterward she said, "I'm so glad you're back home, Tildie."

"So you don't have to do the dishes all by yourself."

She smiled. "I knew you'd be back," she said.

"Did you? I wonder if I knew. I don't think so. I thought I wanted to live in a city, or in a college town. I thought I wanted to be a professor's wife and have earnest conversations about literature and politics and art. I guess I was just a country girl all along."

"You always loved it here," she said. "Of course it will be yours when I'm gone, and I had it in mind that you'd come back to it then. But I hoped you wouldn't wait that long."

She had never left. She and her mother lived here, and when she married my father he just moved in. It's a big old house, with different wings added over the years. He moved in, and then he left, and she just stayed on.

I remembered something. "I don't know if I thought I'd live here again," I said, "but I always thought I would die here." She looked at me, and I said, "Not so much die here as be buried here. When we buried Grandma I thought, *Well, this is where they'll bury me someday.* And I always thought that."

Grandma Yount's grave is on our land, just to the east of the pear and apple orchard. There are graves there dating back to when our people first lived here. The two children Mama lost are laid to rest there, and Grandma Yount's mother, and a great many children. It wasn't long ago that people would have four or five children to raise one. You can't read what's cut into most of the stones, it's worn away with time, and it wears faster now that we have the acid rain, but the stones are there, the graves are there, and I always knew I'd be there, too.

"Well, I'll be there, too," Mama said. "But not too soon, I hope."

"No, not soon at all," I said. "Let's live a long time. Let's be old ladies together."

I thought it was a sweet conversation, a beautiful conversation. But when I told Dan about it we wound up fighting.

"When she goes," he said, "that's when those walnuts go to market."

"That's all you can think about," I said. "Turning a beautiful grove into dollars."

"That timber's money in the bank," he said, "except it's not in the bank because anybody could come in and haul it out of there behind our backs."

"Nobody's going to do that."

"And other things could happen. It's no good for a tree to let it grow beyond its prime. Insects can get it, or disease. There's one tree already that was struck by lightning."

"It didn't hurt it much."

"When they're my trees," he said, "they're coming down."

"They won't be your trees."

"What's that supposed to mean?"

"Mama's not leaving the place to you, Dan."

"I thought what's mine is yours and what's yours is mine."

"I love those trees," I said. "I'm not going to see them cut." His face darkened, and a muscle worked in his jaw. This was a warning sign, and I knew it as such, but I was stuck in a pattern, God help me, and I couldn't leave it alone. "First you'd sell off the timber," I said, "and then you'd sell off the acreage."

"I wouldn't do that."

"Why? Your daddy did."

Dan grew up on a farm that came down through his father's father. Unable to make a living farming, first his grandfather and then his father had sold off parcels of land little by little, whittling away at their holdings and each time reducing the potential income of what remained. After Dan's mother died his father had stopped farming altogether and drank full time, and the farm was auctioned for back taxes while Dan was still in high school.

I knew what it would do to him and yet I threw that in his face all the same. I couldn't seem to help it, any more than he could help what followed.

*   *   *

At breakfast the next day the silence made me want to scream. Dan read the paper while he ate, then hurried out the door without a word. I couldn't hear the screen door when it banged shut or the car engine when it started up. Mama's silence—and his, and mine—drowned out everything else.

I thought I'd burst when we were doing the dishes. She didn't say a word and neither did I. Afterward she turned to me and said, "I didn't go to college so I don't know about patterns, or what you do and what it makes him do."

The *quattrocento* and rats in a maze, that's all I learned in college. What I know about patterns and family violence I learned watching Oprah and Phil Donahue, and she watched the same programs I did. ("He blacked your eye and broke your nose. He kicked you in the stomach while you were pregnant. How can you stay with a brute like this?" "But I love him, Geraldo. And I know he loves me.")

"I just know one thing," she said. "It won't get better. And it will get worse."

"No."

"Yes. And you know it, Tildie."

"No."

He hadn't blacked my eye or broken my nose, but he had hammered my face with his fists and it was swollen and discolored. He hadn't kicked me in the stomach but he had shoved me from him. I had been clinging to his arm. That was stupid, I knew better than to do that, it drove him crazy to have me hang on him like that. He had shoved me and I'd gone sprawling, wrenching my leg when I fell on it. My knee ached now, and the muscles in the front of that thigh were sore. And my rib cage was sore where he'd punched me.

But I love him, Geraldo, Oprah, Phil. And I know he loves me.

That night he didn't come home.

I couldn't sit still, couldn't catch my breath. Livia caught my anxiety and wouldn't sleep, couldn't sleep. I held her in my arms and paced the floor in front of the television set. Back and forth, back and forth.

At midnight finally I put her in her crib and she slept. Mama was playing solitaire at the pine table. Only the top is pine, the base is maple. An antique, Dan pronounced it when he first saw it, and better than the ones in the shops. I suppose he had it priced in his mind, along with the walnut trees.

I pointed out a move. Mama said, "I know about that. I just haven't decided whether I want to do it, that's all." But she always says that. I don't believe she saw it.

At one I heard our car turn off the road and onto the gravel. She heard it, too, and gathered up the cards and said she was tired now, she'd just turn in. She was out of the room and up the stairs before he came in the door.

He was drunk. He lurched into the room, his shirt open halfway to his waist, his eyes unfocused. He said, "Oh, Jesus, Tildie, what's happening to us?"

"Shhh," I said. "You'll wake the baby."

"I'm sorry, Tildie," he said. "I'm sorry, I'm so goddam sorry."

Going up the stairs, he spun away from me and staggered into the railing. It held. I got him upstairs and into our room, but he passed out the minute he lay down on our bed. I got his shoes off, and his shirt and pants, and let him sleep in his socks and underwear.

In the morning he was still sleeping when I got up to take care of Livia. Mama had his breakfast on the table, his coffee poured, the newspaper at his place. He rushed through the kitchen without a word to anybody, tore out the door and was gone. I moved toward the door but Mama was in my path.

I cried, "Mama, he's leaving! He'll never be back!"

She glanced meaningfully at Livia. I stepped back, lowered my voice. "He's leaving," I said, helpless. He had started the car, he was driving away. "I'll never see him again."

"He'll be back."

"Just like my daddy," I said. "Livvy, your father's gone, we'll never see him again."

"Stop that," Mama said. "You don't know how much sticks in their minds. You mind what you say in front of her."

"But it's true."

"It's not," she said. "You won't lose him that easy. He'll be back."

In the afternoon I took Livia with me while I picked pole beans and summer squash. Then we went back to the pear and apple orchard and played in the shade. After a while I took her over to Grandma Yount's grave. We'll all be here someday, I wanted to say, your grandma and your daddy and your mama, too. And you'll be here when your time comes. This is our land, this is where we all end up.

I might have said this, it wouldn't hurt for her to hear it, but for what Mama said. I guess it's true you don't know what sticks in their minds, or what they'll make of it.

She liked it out there, Livia did. She crawled right up to Grandma Yount's stone and ran her hand over it. You'd have thought she was trying to read it that way, like a blind person with Braille.

He didn't come home for dinner. It was going on ten when I heard the car on the gravel. Mama and I were watching television. I got up and went into the kitchen to be there when he came in.

He was sober. He stood in the doorway and looked at me. Every emotion a man could have was there on his face.

"Look at you," he said. "I did that to you."

My face was worse than the day before. Bruises and swellings are like that, taking their time to ripen.

"You missed dinner," I said, "but I saved some for you. I'll heat up a plate for you."

"I already ate. Tildie, I don't know what to say."

"You don't have to say anything."

"No," he said. "That's not right. We have to talk."

We slipped up to our room, leaving Mama to the television set. With our door closed we talked about the patterns we were caught in and how we seemed to have no control, like actors in a play with all their lines written for them by someone else. We could improvise, we could invent movements and gestures, we could read our lines in any of a number of ways, but the script was all written down and we couldn't get away from it.

I mentioned counseling. He said, "I called that place in Fulton City. I wouldn't tell them my name. Can you feature that? I called them for help but I was too ashamed to tell them my name."

"What did they say?"

"They would want to see us once a week as a couple, and each of us individually once a week. Total price for the three sessions would be eighty dollars."

"For how long?"

"I asked. They couldn't say. They said it's not the sort of change you can expect to make overnight."

I said, "Eighty dollars a week. We can't afford that."

"I had the feeling they might reduce it some."

"Did you make an appointment?"

"No. I thought I'd call tomorrow."

"I don't want to cut the trees," I said. He looked at me. "To pay for it. I don't want to cut Mama's walnut trees."

"Tildie, who brought up the damn trees?"

"We could sell the table," I said.

"What are you talking about?"

"In the kitchen. The pine-top table, didn't you say it was an antique? We could sell that."

"Why would I want to sell the table?"

"You want to sell those trees bad enough. You as much as said that as soon as my mama dies you'll be out back with a chain saw."

"Don't start with me," he said. "Don't you start with me, Tildie."

"Or what? Or you'll hit me? Oh, God, Dan, what are we doing? Fighting over how to pay for the counseling to keep from fighting. Dan, what's the matter with us?"

I went to embrace him but he backed away from me. "Honey," he said, "we better be real careful with this. They were telling me about escalating patterns of violence. I'm afraid of what could happen. I'm going to do what they said to do."

"What's that?"

"I want to pack some things," he said. "That's what I came home to do. There's that Welcome Inn Motel outside of Caldwell, they say it's not so bad and I believe they have weekly rates."

"No," I said. "No."

"They said it's best. Especially if we're going to start counseling, because that brings everything up and out into the open, and it threatens the part of us that wants to be in this pattern. Tildie, from what they said it'd be dangerous for us to be together right now."

"You can't leave," I said.

"I wouldn't be five miles away. I'd be coming for dinner some nights, we'd be going to a movie now and then. It's not like—"

"We can't afford it," I said. "Dan, how can we afford it? Eighty dollars a week for counseling and God knows how much for the motel, and you'd be having most of your meals out, and how can we afford it? You've got a decent job but you don't make that kind of money."

His eyes hardened but he breathed in and out, in and out, and said, "Tildie, just talking like this is a strain, don't you see that? We can afford it, we'll find a way to afford it. Tildie, don't grab on to my arm like that, you know what it does to me. Tildie, stop it, will you for God's sake stop it?"

I put my arms around my own self and hugged myself. I was shaking. My hands just wanted to take hold of his arm. What was so bad about holding on to your husband's arm? What was wrong with that?

"Don't go," I said.

"I have to."

"Not now. It's late, they won't have any rooms left anyhow. Wait until morning. Can't you wait until morning?"

"I was just going to get some of my things and go."

"Go in the morning. Don't you want to see Livvy before you go? She's your daughter, don't you want to say good-bye to her?"

"I'm not leaving, Tildie. I'm just staying a few miles from here so we'll have a chance to keep from destroying ourselves. My God, Tildie, I don't want to leave you. That's the whole point, don't you see that?"

"Stay until morning," I said. "Please?"

"And will we go through this again in the morning?"

"No," I said. "I promise."

We were both restless, but then we made love and that settled him, and soon he was sleeping. I couldn't sleep, though. I lay there for a time, and then I put a robe on and went down to the kitchen and sat there for a long time, thinking of patterns, thinking of ways to escape them. And then I went back up the stairs to the bedroom again.

I was in the kitchen the next morning before Livia woke up. I was there when Mama came down, and her eyes widened at the sight of me. She started to say something but then I guess she saw something in my eyes and she stayed silent.

I said, "Mama, we have to call the police. You'll mind the baby when they come for me. Will you do that?"

"Oh, Tildie," she said.

I led her up the stairs again and into our bedroom. Dan lay facedown, the way he always slept. I drew the sheet down and showed her where I'd stabbed him, slipping the kitchen knife between two ribs and into the heart. The knife lay on the table beside the bed. I had wiped the blood from it. There had not been very much blood to wipe.

"He was going to leave," I said, "and I couldn't bear it, Mama. And I thought, Now he won't leave, now he'll never leave me. I thought, This is a way to break the pattern. Isn't that crazy, Mama? It doesn't make any sense, does it?"

"My poor Tildie."

"Do you want to know something? I feel safe now, Mama. He won't hit me anymore and I never have to worry about him leaving me. He can't leave me, can he?" Something caught in my throat. "Oh, and he'll never hold me again, either. In the circle of his arms."

I broke then, and it was Mama who held me, stroking my forehead, soothing me. I was all right then, and I stood up straight and told her she had better call the police.

"Livia'll be up any minute now," she said. "I think she's awake, I think I heard her fussing a minute ago. Change her and bring her down and feed her her breakfast."

"And then?"

"And then put her in for her nap."

After I put Livia back in her crib for her nap Mama told me that we weren't going to call the police. "Now that you're back where you belong," she said, "I'm not about to see them take you away. Your baby needs her mama and I need you, too."

"But Dan—"

"Bring the big wheelbarrow around to the kitchen door. Between the two of us we can get him down the stairs. We'll dig his grave in the back, we'll bury him here on our land. People won't suspect anything. They'll just think he went off, the way men do."

"The way my daddy did," I said.

Somehow we got him down the stairs and out through the kitchen. The hardest part was getting him into the old wheelbarrow. I checked Livia and made sure she was sleeping soundly, and then we took turns with the barrow, wheeling it out beyond the kitchen garden.

"What I keep thinking," I said, "is at least I broke the pattern."

She didn't say anything, and what she didn't say became one of her famous silences, sucking up all the sound around us. The barrow's wheel squeaked, the birds sang in the trees, but now I couldn't hear any of that.

Suddenly she said, "Patterns." Then she didn't say anything more, and I tried to hear the squeak of the wheel.

Then she said, "He never would have left you. If he left he'd only come back again. And he never would have quit hitting you. And each time would be a little worse than the last."

"It's not always like it is on *Oprah,* Mama."

"There's things you don't know," she said.

"Like what?"

The squeaking of the wheel, the song of birds. She said, "You know how I lost the hearing in the one ear?"

"You had an infection."

"That's what I always told you. It's not true. Your daddy cupped his hands and boxed my ears. He deafened me on the one side. I was lucky, nothing happened to the other ear. I still hear as good as ever out of it."

"I don't believe it," I said.

"It's the truth, Tildie."

"Daddy never hit you."

"Your daddy hit me all the time," she said. "All the time. He used his hands, he used his feet. He used his belt."

I felt a tightening in my throat. "I don't remember," I said.

"You didn't know. You were little. What do you think Livia knows? What do you think she'll remember?"

We walked on a ways. I said, "I just remember the two of you hollering. I thought you hollered and finally he left. That's what I always thought."

"That's what I let you think. It's what I wanted you to think. I had a broken jaw, I had broken ribs, I had to keep telling the doctor I was clumsy. I kept falling down. He believed me, too. I guess he had lots of women told him the same thing." We switched, and I took over the wheelbarrow. She said, "Dan would have done the same to you, if you hadn't done what you did."

"He wanted to stop."

"They can't stop, Tildie. No, not that way. To your left."

"Aren't we going to bury him alongside Grandma Yount?"

"No," she said. "That's too near the house. We'll dig his grave across the stream, where the walnut grove is."

"It's beautiful there."

"You always liked it."

"So did Dan," I said. I felt so funny, so light-headed. My world was turned upside down and yet it felt safe, it felt solid. I thought how Dan had itched to cut down those walnut trees. Now he'd lie forever at their feet, and I could come back here whenever I wanted to feel close to him.

"But he'll be lonely here," I said. "Won't he? Mama, won't he?"

The walnut trees lose their leaves early in the fall, and they put on less of a color show than the other hardwoods. But I like to come to the grove even when the trees are bare. Sometimes I bring Livia. More often I come by myself.

I always liked it here. I love our whole 220 acres, every square foot of it, but this is my favorite place, among these trees. I like it even better than the graveyard over by the pear and apple orchard. Where the graves have stones, and where the women and children of our family are buried.

Joyce Harrington is a mainstay of mystery magazines such as Ellery Queen's Mystery Magazine *and* Alfred Hitchcock's Mystery Magazine. *Her mystery stories often examine the ups and downs of human relationships, both marital and otherwise. "August Is a Good Time for Killing" illustrates this perfectly.*

August Is a Good Time for Killing

Joyce Harrington

Augustis a good time for killing," the old woman said, peering solemnly over the honeysuckle. There must have been shock on my face, for she added quickly, "I mean weeds, of course."

"Of course," I agreed just as quickly. I knew she meant weeds. What else could she mean?

"There's not much else to do in the garden in August. Strawberries are finished. Peas are petering out. Tomatoes are still bearing but they're tired. Killing is the only thing."

"The peas were awfully good. Thank you again."

Was it true that she was a witch? Josh had refused to eat the peas; said they were poisoned and he didn't want to get turned into a frog or fall asleep for a zillion years. Fact of the matter was that Josh hated peas—canned, frozen, or fresh from Mrs. Abel's garden. Peter ate four and survived. I had eaten the rest, greedily enjoying every mouthful. I love fresh peas. Mrs. Abel couldn't have sent over a more welcome gift. And now I wished I could uneat them somehow. The ghost of those peas was rising in my throat and fuddling my brain, making it difficult to think or speak with any sense at all. Maybe they *were* bewitched.

"You should put those boys to work," she said. "And the honeysuckle is a good place to start. You have to cut it back quite severely. If you don't, it will take over."

"But it's so beautiful. I don't mind if it does take over. The boys thought you were offering them a job. To help you in *your* garden."

"Nonsense. I've gardened for years without a stitch of help, I'm certainly not going to start needing it now. But the honeysuckle is growing over onto *your* side. It's my honeysuckle, so I'm willing to take the responsibility for cutting it back. The least you could do is make your boys pull up the runners. They'll be all over the place if you don't. I assume you're too busy to do it yourself."

What could I tell her? Everything she said was a challenge. We seemed to be an affront to her sense of order—a young woman and her two sons living alone without benefit of a man around the house. Not unusual in New York City, but obviously not quite respectable in this quiet backwater town. Or was I being too sensitive? Was Mrs. Abel mean and spiteful to everybody? *Was* she, as Josh and Peter insisted, a witch?

"Well, I am pretty busy," I said. "I'm working on a book." And instantly felt queasy and self-conscious, as if I'd just mouthed some lame excuse for not having my homework done. I knew she had been a schoolteacher.

"So I heard." She dismissed my labors with those three words. "It's always been my experience with boys that if you keep them busy, they won't have time to get into mischief. I taught school for fifty years, you know."

"So I heard."

My sarcasm was wasted. She plowed on with her dreadful philosophy of how boys should be handled. It wasn't much different from her attitude toward honeysuckle. She must have warped a lot of young minds in her day.

"You must always keep the upper hand with boys. Now girls are much easier to control. Oh, once in a while you'll get a wild one—" she eyed me speculatively "—but for the most part you can handle girls with a system of rewards for good behavior."

Bribery, I thought. Just like the peas.

"I always made sure the boys in my classes had plenty of work to do. And I wasn't afraid to use the paddle."

"Were they afraid of you?" I asked.

"They respected me," she replied. "Lots of them come to visit me now that I've retired. They don't forget Mrs. Abel. They come to me for advice with their own children. And I tell them just what I told you—don't be afraid to enforce hard work and strong discipline."

I was dying to get away, but I didn't want to be rude. And a kind of horrid fascination glued me to my side of the honeysuckle hedge and kept me prompting her for more.

"Did you have any children of your own?" I asked.

"No. I've been a widow for a long time. I never thought once about remarrying after Mr. Abel died. He never came back from the Great War. They never even found his body. I have a flag. I raise it on Memorial Day." She sounded as if the flag gave her more pleasure and less trouble than the living man might have done.

"Now your husband," she went on. "He must have been a handsome man. The boys are quite good-looking. They don't resemble you at all."

I stared at the wart on Mrs. Abel's chin. Every witch worth her eye of newt has a wart on her chin; Mrs. Abel's had the requisite three long hairs growing out of it.

"He still is a handsome man. We're divorced."

"So much of that nowadays." She wagged her head and the corners of her mouth dripped sadness. "It's always the children who suffer."

"The boys aren't suffering. They're having the time of their lives." What a talent the woman had for raising hackles! She'd neatly put me on the defensive in the most vulnerable area of my already shaky emotional fortifications.

"It'll show up later," she assured me. "Mark my words, you'll have your hands full."

Mrs. Abel spoke in clichés, but she imbued them with such eager ill-will, such certainty of disaster, that I found myself glancing nervously over my shoulder to see if maybe Josh and Peter had emerged from the woods dripping blood or trailing broken limbs. The early afternoon continued blamelessly still and sun-filled. Bees and squirrels went about their business.

"Well," I said. "Back to work. It's been nice chatting with you." And what exactly did I mean by *that?* It was horrible chatting with her. Was I trying to be charming and disarming so she wouldn't cast an evil spell on me? I crossed the yard feeling her flat eyes boring malevolently into the small of my back. It made me walk funny, as if my legs had turned to stilts.

Our house is a dingy white clapboard affair, squatted at the edge of a little upstate town near a shallow creek and a pleasant wooded area. It is small, in need of paint, and its facilities are primitive, but the rent is cheap and as a sanctuary from the havoc of divorce and the hustle of the city it is perfect.

The screen door shrieked as I entered my sanctuary. The manuscript glared at me from a rickety card-table at one end of the screened porch. Blank yellow paper rolled onto the platen of my old Olivetti issued its challenge. The book, while not precisely the cause of the divorce, had played its part in the final breakup. It had been all right as long as I just diddled around writing an occasional clever little story for clever little magazines. Hal could afford to be proud and say, "This is my wife. She writes."

But as soon as the writing got serious, as soon as I got the grant from the Endowment and really started working on the book, as soon as the cooking fell off and the laundry got behind and dust accumulated on the hi-fi, Hal started obstructing me. In little ways at first—like calling me up from the office when he knew I was working and telling me his grey suit had to be taken to the cleaners immediately. Or inviting hordes of people over for dinner on the day *after* I'd done the weekly shopping so I'd have to dash out and do it all over again and spend the rest of the day cooking. And be hung over and worn out the next day, so there were two days lost from the book. It grew from an accumulation of petty annoyances to a monster bristling with lawyers, recriminations, hurt pride, and no return ticket.

I sighed and settled down in my swivel chair. I swiveled once, viewing my domain. Plants in pots helped hide the lack of paint. At one side of the porch, a lumpy daybed undulated beneath a bright Indian coverlet. I would make some pillows soon, turn the place into a regular den of Oriental luxury, maybe even put a priceless Persian rug on the splintery floor. I might even oil the hinges on the screen door. After I sold the book. I swiveled back to the Olivetti and groped for a thought.

"Ma! Ma! Josh found a dead body!" Peter came screeching across the yard.

"That's nice," I mumbled.

"Ma! Ma! No kidding!" Peter pounded up the stairs and through the screen door, letting it slam behind him. The whole porch shook and the Olivetti inched closer to the edge of the table. "There's an old dead guy in the woods! Josh is guarding him."

I shoved back from the typewriter and stared, disbelieving, at my younger son. Dead guys did not turn up in peaceful woods outside of lurid fiction. Or could this be some of Mrs. Abel's witchery in action?

"Oh, Ma! It's real weird. This old guy is in a cave and he has a long beard and he smells funny."

Peter was hopping up and down with fearful excitement. Stay calm, I told myself, and calmly said to him, "Maybe I'd better take a look."

I followed Peter across the yard and into the quiet aisles between the trees. How strange to be walking through August woods, trailing my capering child, played on by rays of tinkling sunlight, toward the possibility of a corpse. This couldn't be happening.

And it was not. When we reached the cave, a steepled indentation beneath two slabs of angled rock, the corpse was sitting up and talking to Josh.

"Sure we got bears. Ain't you heard 'em? They come in the night. Come for bacon, beans, and boys. Beans and bacon they like to eat. What d'you think they wants with boys?"

"Don't believe you," Josh challenged. "I ain't seen no bears."

"*Any* bears," I corrected automatically. "And don't say 'ain't.'"

Josh shrugged and kicked at a rock.

"Who are you?" I asked the revenant.

The bearded, funny-smelling, no longer dead old guy scrambled to his feet, knocking his head against the overhanging roof of his cave.

"Morning, ma'am. Afternoon. How dee do. Luther's who I am. You's livin' in my house."

"Your house?"

He was not old beneath his effluvium of cheap wine; I would guess around forty. His beard was patchy black and grey, his arms long, sinewy, and tanned. He wore a ribbed undershirt splotched with wine and sweat stains, grey pin-striped trousers that had come down in the world, and a pair of out-at-the-pinkie-toe sneakers.

"Yes, ma'am. I was livin' in that house. Miz Abel said I could. Then she said I had to leave, cuz you's was comin'."

"How long did you live there?"

The question seemed to puzzle him. He gazed off into the rustling top of the trees and scratched absently at the back of his head.

"Where do you live now?"

He shrugged and glanced over his shoulder at the tiny cave. In it there lay a grimy quilt, the batting poking through the ancient calico, an empty muscatel bottle, and a shabby zippered satchel.

"Can you paint a house, Luther?"

"I can paint," he said, nodding energetically. "I did paint for Miz Abel. She give me two dollars. Said I wa'n't worth no more'n that. I can wash windows. Set traps too."

"For bears?"

"Ain't no bears 'round here." His bloodshot eyes swiveled around at me, pityingly, as if I were loony. "Rabbits mostly. I gets twenty-five cents apiece." His tongue flicked out to lick dry lips, and he turned to gaze longingly at the empty bottle.

The boys had lingered until it was certain that Luther was neither corpse nor ghost, and then they'd scampered away toward the creek. I could hear them whooping and splashing. Luther hung before me, loose-limbed and expectant. What now? I thought of the small building at the back of the yard, no more than a shed really, designated by the rental agent as "the washhouse." I had done no more than poke my head into it and retained a hazy collection of a stone tub with a single faucet, a rusty gas ring, and a single light bulb hanging from a frayed black cord. Not much, but better surely than a cave in the woods. Was I about to hire a resident handyman? It would be nice to have the house painted. Painting was not included in the lease. It would be nice to get on with the book. I couldn't do both.

"Luther, would you like to paint my house?"

"Yes, ma'am."

"Would you like to live in the washhouse?"

"Yes, ma'am."

"I'll pay you." I hesitated over naming an amount. Best wait and see what kind of a painter Luther turned out to be, although anything would be an improvement.

As if he could read my mind, Luther stated proudly, "I paint real good."

"Fine," I said. "You can move into the washhouse this afternoon. It needs to be cleaned up and so do you. Then we'll go into town and buy some paint."

I walked away, leaving Luther to round up his belongings and say goodbye to his cave. It had always been a tenet of my city life that winos were harmless. Repugnant maybe, and a sad waste of good human material, but basically no threat at all. Luther had a quality of childlike simplicity. No. Not childlike. Children were far from simple.

I set a broom, a bucket, some soap, and a towel outside the washhouse, and for the third time that day confronted my typewriter. It must have been several hours later that I became aware of a tentative scratching at the screen door. The sun threw a long shadow across my yellow paper. Luther stood on the porch steps transformed. He wore white painter's overalls, clean but flecked with many-colored drips of paint. His face, bereft of beard, shone red above and white below, his chin oozing blood from tiny razor nicks. Good Lord! I hadn't asked him to shave!

"Time to get paint," he said.

"Right you are," I agreed. The book was alive again, running through the typewriter like a wild thing. I could be generous with my time. The boys trailed across the yard, obviously about to utter their eternal plaintive cry, "I'm hungry, Ma!"

"Hurry up!" I called to them. "We're going into town."

"Can we eat at McDonald's?"

"Why not?"

In the hardware store, the proprietor eyed me curiously as I shuffled through paint chips. The boys prowled, fascinated by nails in barrels and nuts and bolts in little wooden drawers with curved brass handles. It was an old-fashioned hardware store that carried the very latest in power tools and electrical appliances alongside stacks of Mason jars and rows of kerosene lamps. Luther clutched a bright red paint chip and stared at his sneakers as if already beyond hope that anything so beautiful could be his to work with.

"White," I said. "And some brushes and whatever else we need. A ladder, I guess."

"I can rent you an extension ladder, ma'am. No sense in buying one of those." The proprietor beamed at me with kindly fat-cheeked goodwill. "Luther doin' the job for you?"

"Yes." I looked around for the boys. They were hypnotized by a display of flashlights. What is it about boys and flashlights? I decided I would let them each choose one.

"Luther's a good enough painter." The proprietor's rich jolly voice called me back to the business at hand. "But he's slow." The man tapped the side of his head significantly. Luther continued to stare at his sneakers; the hand holding the red paint chip began to shake.

"And he has some funny ideas about color. Well, just look at him. I bet he's thinkin' it would be real nice to paint your whole house fire-engine red. Crazy!" The man spoke as if Luther were deaf or so deficient in understanding that he could say any cruel thing without penetrating to a nerve. "But if you want to get the job done, just make sure he stays off the bottle. Right, Luther?"

Luther's mouth twisted into a witless wet grin. He said, "Bub-bub-bub." His eyes filmed over into a semblance of idiocy.

"We'll paint the house white," I said, "but there's no reason why we can't have a red door. Let me have a can of this." I took the red paint chip from Luther's shaking hand and waved it at the hardware man's complacent smirk.

"Yes, ma'am," he said.

Later, with the painting gear stowed in the trunk and the ladder secured to the roof of the car, Luther's face returned to normal. Normal? The boys, in the back seat, shone their flashlights into each other's eyes and threatened mutual mayhem.

Luther said, "Time to eat?"

"McDonald's, here we come."

We carried our hamburgers and french fries home. I was not about to subject Luther to any more of the mindless bullying I had witnessed in the hardware store. It was for my own protection as much as for his. He had evolved his means of dealing with it; turning himself into a slack-jawed drooling caricature of a mental defective. But I couldn't bear to watch that awful transformation again.

We ate in the twilit backyard, Luther and the boys munching in companionable silence while I pondered how I had managed to appoint myself protector of the downtrodden. It was totally out of character; I was far from overprotective with the boys and not notable for coddling my husband. My ex-husband. What was there about this alcoholic reject that evoked my righteous indignation? Was that all it was, or was I, God forbid, infected with missionary zeal? Did I have some inane notion that I could reform him, educate him, bless his life with meaning? Maybe he had all the meaning he could handle.

The boys crammed the last of the french fries into their mouths and swooped off shrieking across the darkening lawn, drawn by the wildly flailing beams of their flashlights. Luther gathered up the greasy papers, methodically wadding them into the smallest possible bundle.

"Time to paint now?"

"No. It's too dark. You can start in the morning."

"Don't pay no mind to that Miz Abel. Luther never did no wrong thing."

"Mrs. Abel has never mentioned you, Luther. Now I want to get some more work done. Good night."

As I entered the screen porch, I heard Luther's disjointed mumble fading across the yard to the washhouse.

"Paint in the morning. Get up early. Miz Abel is ugly. This one is pretty. Paint the door *red*. Nice. Miz Abel better not tell."

Tell what? I wondered, and then forgot as my fingers flew over the keys.

In the morning, I awoke to the sound of scraping. It was barely light and a fuzzy mist floated about two feet off the ground. It made the ladder seem to rise from incalculable depths up the side of the house and, for all I could tell, extend all the way to heaven. The scraping came from somewhere above. My Little Ben windup alarm clock said 5:45 and my bed felt clammy from the tendrils of mist that had crept onto the porch and fingered my lumpy bedding. I scrambled into my robe and went outside.

Luther was on the ladder, a great white bird of pure light, elbows flapping as he scraped away old paint blisters from the flanks of the house.

"Time to paint now!" He beamed down at me.

"Time to paint, Luther." I went inside to plug in the coffeepot. Time for the book too, before the boys woke up. I left Cheerios and bananas on the kitchen table for them.

The scraping from above melted into a rhythmic slap-slap, which in turn blended into the tap-tap of words arranging themselves on paper. I vaguely heard the boys clanking spoons on bowls and then clumping past me to offer their services to Luther. Good, I thought. Let him teach them how to paint a house. Just a few more lines and then on to the next chapter. Then I leaped at an imperative rapping on the screen door and whirled to see who was barging into my morning. It was Mrs. Abel.

"May I come in? I have to talk to you." Her wart pulsed with secrets to unfold. I opened the door and she creaked through.

"Can we talk in the kitchen? I don't want *him* to hear." She rolled her eyes upward and I wondered if she meant Luther or God.

We went into the kitchen. The boys had left behind a crunching of spilled sugar and some flaccid "O's" in milky puddles. Mrs. Abel tiptoed around a shriveled banana peel.

"I thought I ought to warn you," she mouthed, making up in exaggerated lip movements what she lacked in volume. Her teeth were long and yellow.

"About what?" I mouthed back at her.

"Luther. I see he's painting for you."

"Right. He seems to know what he's doing."

"Oh, he's a good enough painter. A bit . . ."

". . . slow? I know. But I'm in no hurry."

"That isn't what I came to tell you. Frankly, I hoped I wouldn't have to tell you this. Luther was supposed to go stay with his brother. I told him to go. He's never disobeyed me before."

"First time for everything."

"What?" Her flat eyes suspected irreverence, but she carried on. "As far as I knew, he went. His brother lives on the other side of town. Luther always has a home there, whenever he chooses to appear."

She stopped for breath and to marshal her thoughts.

"Coffee?" I asked.

"What? Oh. Yes, please. Two sugars, no milk. Luther killed a boy."

Coffee slopped into the saucer and from there over my thumb and onto the gritty linoleum.

"I didn't mean to startle you." She smiled. "But truth is truth and must be told, now that you've got yourself mixed up with him."

"I'm not mixed up. He's only painting the house."

"*And* living in the washhouse. I saw him hanging his quilt out to air. But of course you couldn't know anything about what happened here thirty years ago. You couldn't know the *danger* you're in— or your boys." She sipped coffee primly and smacked her thin lips. Either my coffee was to her liking, or her story was making her mouth water.

One thing was certain. Her evil was infectious. I wanted to rush out of the house and snatch Josh and Peter away from the contaminated person of the house painter. But a small voice said, "Wait a minute. Find out what *really* happened."

"What happened?" I asked. "Thirty years ago."

"What happened was that a boy who lived in this house, about eight years old—isn't your younger boy about that age?—was drowned in the creek. He used to go fishing and trapping with Luther, and then one night he didn't come home for supper. Luther was about ten years old then, living at home with his mother and father just down the road. They've passed on since. He was a child of their old age; a mistake if you ask me, and he never was very bright. Well, the parents of the missing child were very upset and a search was organized.

"They found Luther first, in a little cave in the woods. Oh, he was a mess, crying and blubbering and making less sense than usual. He never did have any backbone. I remember him carrying on the same way over an arithmetic problem. Anyway, all they could get out of him was that he didn't do it and he didn't know who did it. Well, *that* made them search even harder, and eventually they found the boy—Bobby Albright was his name—face down in the creek. They say you can drown in a teacup, but it's always been my opinion that you would need a little help. I've always believed that Luther held Bobby's face in the water."

"What did the police say?"

"Accident," she snapped. "Accident! There was a lump on poor Bobby's head, so they guessed he fell on a rock and drowned while unconscious. But I knew better. Why do you suppose Luther took it so hard? Guilt, pure and simple."

"But why would Luther do such a thing?"

"You and I need reasons, my dear. But Luther is different. He was a willful, disobedient child. One of those who stubbornly refused to learn anything, and no amount of paddling could make him a good student. Well, I just wanted to let you know what kind of person you have painting your house. If I were you, I'd keep my doors and windows locked at night."

"Wait a minute," I said. "If he's so dangerous, why did you give him permission to camp out in this house while it was vacant?"

"Oh, he's no danger to me. I know how to handle him. The owners asked me to keep an eye on the house, and what better way to prevent vandalism than to let it be known that crazy Luther might be lurking about the premises?"

"Has he ever done . . . anything else?"

"No. But who knows what he might do when he's full of wine. Well, I suppose you're busy." She glanced pointedly around my untidy kitchen. "And Lord knows I have plenty of work to do."

I stood at the screen door and watched her wade laboriously across the yard. What's worse than a witch? I thought. I hoped I wouldn't have too many more visitations from Mrs. Abel now that she'd sown her vile seeds of ancient gossip. With half an ear I listened to the slapping at the side of the house, and the low murmur of Peter's voice telling one of his favorite stories.

"So Dorothy had to get the broomstick but she got caught by the flying monkeys . . ."

"You gotta hold the brush like this," came Luther's voice. "And go this way, back and forth."

"And they all came to save her and they ran all over the castle and then Dorothy spilled a bucket of water on the witch and she melted and that was the end of her."

And Josh, ever the realist and puncturer of his little brother's balloons, said, "The Wizard was a fake and it was all only a dream. But Mrs. Abel is a real witch and she'll getcha!"

If you only knew, I thought, and went to take a shower, hoping to dispel the heavy sense of oppression that my visitor had left behind.

Later that evening, I paid Luther for his day's work. The front and one side of the house were finished except for the trim, and the boys had spent a glorious day covering themselves with paint. As I handed him a ten-dollar bill, his eyes shifted to the little house beyond the honeysuckle hedge.

"Miz Abel came here this morning," he stated.

"Yes, she did."

"She told you things about Luther."

I wouldn't lie to him, but I wondered how much I could safely tell him. I suspected that he was only crazy "north by northwest," but I wasn't ready to bank on it. "She told me about something that happened a long time ago. An accident."

He nodded gravely and sloped off across the yard to the wash-house. I wanted to call after him, let him know I was on his side, but if he didn't know that already nothing I said would make any difference.

That night I was very conscious of not locking my doors and windows. For a long moment, my hand hovered over the hook and eyebolt on the screen door, but then I reminded myself that this was not paranoid New York City. This was the safe, clean, all-American, true-blue small town of everyone's nostalgic dreams. Anyway, the flimsy hook wouldn't stop anyone determined to get in. I went to bed.

For a long time I lay listening to the sleepy murmurs of the boys in their nook under the eaves. After they quieted down, I listened to the hooting of owls and the rustling of trees in the mild night air. Once I got up and stared through the screen into the blackness of the backyard. I thought I'd seen a flash of light from the direction of the washhouse, but decided it must have been a firefly. At last I slept, but dreamed strange, struggling, blood-tinged dreams that kept me on the edge of consciousness, fading as soon as I opened my eyes. Toward dawn, I finally fell into exhausted and dreamless oblivion . . .

I was awakened by the slap-slap-slap on the side of the house. It was mid-morning of a hot humid day, and I'd lost precious hours from the book. I dressed quickly and went outside to see what progress the painters were making.

I rounded the side of the house and stopped in shock. Luther, on the ladder, twisted around and waved to me, grinning and pleased with himself. The front of his white overalls was streaked and splashed with red. My knees went weak and my empty stomach lurched. The boys were nowhere in sight.

"Where . . . ?" My nightmares were coming true. Mrs. Abel was right. My mind leaped to horrid discoveries in the woods or behind the washhouse. I stared up at Luther, wondering what to do next.

"Painted the door already," he announced proudly.

Josh pounded around from the front of the house and took my hand in his sticky one.

"Come and see, Ma. It looks terrific."

Peter followed, gripping a reddened paintbrush. Both boys were generously splattered with red paint.

"Can we paint the stairs red too?"

"No, not the stairs. That would be too much red." It was already too much red for one morning, but I let them lead me around to the front of the house.

The door had, indeed, been painted. Bright red and still tacky, it gleamed on the front of the house like the half-remembered bloodstains of my dreams.

"It looks very nice," I said. And tottered back into the house to plug in the coffeepot. While the coffee perked and I scrambled eggs, I chastised my hyperactive imagination. Was I going to let that vicious old woman distort my mind with her ugly suspicions? No, I was not. It occurred to me that her tale might be just that, a fabrication designed to frighten me into leaving. I didn't know what she had against me, but I wasn't going to be frightened out of my sanctuary. I called everybody in to breakfast. Luther ate with good appetite.

The rest of the morning I spent organizing my notes and my own feelings. I didn't know what to make of Mrs. Abel's story, but if anybody ever needed a friend, it was Luther. If he'd really killed that boy, why hadn't the police found out about it? Mrs. Abel had seemed so certain that he'd done it. Surely she would have told the police. They must have been satisfied that he was innocent, or at least not responsible. Why had she continued to believe him guilty for thirty years? And why try to frighten me off when all I was doing was giving him an honest day's work and a semblance of dignity? I was still puzzling over Mrs. Abel's purpose when I heard voices outside. I ran out and around the house to see who was there.

Josh and Peter were huddled together at the corner of the house, being uncharacteristically quiet. When I appeared, they bolted for the porch, but I sensed their noses pressed to the screen from the inside.

"Good morning," I said to the tall dry man in the quasi-military uniform with the small American flag sewn onto the sleeve. Luther stood dumb and downcast before him. There was no mistaking the family resemblance. Mrs. Abel had neglected to tell me that Luther's brother was a policeman.

"Morning, ma'am," he said, politely and deliberately removing his Smokey Bear hat. "I came to find Luther. I hope he hasn't been bothering you."

I said what was obvious. "Luther's been painting my house."

"Yes. Well, there's more to it than that. I called Mrs. Abel earlier this morning. She always knows what he's been up to."

My blood began to boil. "Luther hasn't been 'up to' anything. Mrs. Abel is a vicious old busybody."

I glanced at Luther. He was wearing his village idiot face, and his lips began to move in the slobbering "bub-bub-bub" I'd heard in the hardware store.

"That may be," said his brother. "But she didn't answer her phone. I called three times. So I came on over to see for myself."

"Luther's doing a job for me, and doing it well. Are you satisfied?"

"Not exactly." He turned to peer intently up the road toward the center of town. "The ambulance should be getting here soon. I called from over to her place."

"Ambulance? What for? Is she sick?"

"Not exactly. She's dead." His eyes, when they swung back to me, were a chilly grey. "May I use your phone?"

"Sure. But wait a minute. What did she die of? Heart?"

He paused with his hand on the screen door. I heard the boys scuffing away upstairs.

"You might say that. Somebody stopped it for her. With a pair of hedge-clippers."

Now that he'd opened up, I wanted him to stop. But he droned on in his official monotone.

"Somebody threw a bucket of water on her. Maybe trying to clean up the mess. Just made it worse. She put up a fight though. Somebody likely got a broomstick busted over his head. I got to make that phone call now." He went inside.

Luther stood beside the ladder, the red-stained front of his overall glowing obscenely in the noonday sun.

"She's a witch," he muttered. He took his painter's cap off and tenderly massaged the top of his head.

"Luther, don't." Everybody was telling me things I didn't want to hear.

"I thrown water on her but she don't melt. She hit Luther with that broom. Luther hit her with that . . . that . . ."

I sat down on the porch steps. Luther came closer, earnestly explaining.

"She hit Bobby with that shovel. Bobby taken two tomatoes."

"What tomatoes? Who's Bobby?"

"Bobby fallen down. She tell Luther help carry. Put Bobby in the water. She say Luther never tell nobody or else go to jail forever. Luther didn't do no wrong thing. Bobby was Luther's friend. She a witch. She kill Bobby."

It came together then and I wanted to cry. But my tears wouldn't help Luther. The only thing I could do was respect his confidence and hope for the best. But what would be best for Luther? To continue playing his role of village idiot, a role he was comfortable with? Or to spend the rest of his life in some institution for the criminally insane? Not if I could help it by keeping his confession to myself. Mrs. Abel had got what was coming to her.

Heavy footsteps shook the porch and the screen door screamed on its rusty hinges. I got up to face Luther's brother with what I hoped was a look of puzzled ignorance.

"Ma'am," he said with exaggerated respect. "I just talked with the station. It seems they think they have a suspect."

I looked at Luther. He had retreated behind his moronic facade.

"It seems they picked up this stranger for speeding through town. It seems they put two and two together and came up with five." Doubt clouded his steely grey eyes as he glanced at his brother. "It seems they're holding him on suspicion."

"Do you believe he did it?"

"I don't know what to believe, ma'am, I truly don't. All I know for sure is that one old woman is dead, and I can't say I regret her passing. But it's my duty to find out who killed her."

"And this stranger, this speeder, what about him?" My voice came strangely from my throat, taut and stifled. If I didn't speak, if I didn't betray Luther's confidence, would another man live wasted years in the wake of Mrs. Abel's malevolence? I couldn't speak. Only Luther could do that. I whirled on him, clutching his red-smeared sleeve. "Luther! Tell him! Tell your brother what you told me."

"Bub-bub-bub." Wet lips and vacant eyes. He was gone. This was no role-playing. Luther had crossed the line to the only safety he knew.

A gentle hand took my arm and held it firmly.

"Ma'am," said the expressionless voice. "I know. Luther told me. I've been waiting thirty years for him to tell me. Now it's too late."

I looked at the dry creased face under the silvery brush cut. The grey eyes had lost their chill, and I saw there a sadness deeper than any I had ever known. I felt tears in my own eyes then, for Luther struggling dimly in his silent prison and for this man with the sad grey eyes who must finally crucify his brother.

"Ma'am?" The man's questioning voice reached through my sobs. "Would it be all right with you if Luther finishes painting the house before I take him in? It would make him feel better, and I'll stay and keep an eye on him."

"Yes, oh yes." I broke away and stumbled into the house. I had packing to do. All the clothes into all the duffel bags. All the toys, books, toothbrushes. The lid onto the typewriter. We would go back to the city. Back to a world I knew well and could cope with, where violence and evil were anonymous and did not reach into my life with red hands smearing me with indelible accountability.

Josh and Peter stood one above the other on the narrow stairway, watching, large-eyed and frightened, as I swept through the house indiscriminately tossing objects into boxes and bags, whatever was handy. "Get your things together, boys," I shouted at them. "We're leaving!"

"Aw, Ma," said Josh. "Can't we help Luther finish painting?"

I stopped in my tracks, one hand clutching a damp pair of swimming trunks. My children in their red-stained jeans, with streaks of red on their hands and arms and even in their hair, were telling me something. It was, after all, only paint. Luther had been their friend. He still was. There was nothing to run away from.

"I can't pack these. They're all wet. Sure, go and help Luther. We won't be leaving yet a while . . ."

On the outside of the house, the rhythmic slap of Luther's paintbrush is the most melancholy sound I have ever heard.

Bruce Holland Rogers is no stranger to anthologies, having appeared in Feline and Famous *and* Cat Crimes Takes a Vacation. *When he's not plotting feline felonies, he's writing excellent fantasy stories for such collections as* Enchanted Forests, The Fortune Teller, *and* Monster Brigade 3000. *Winner of the Nebula Award for best short science fiction story, he creates fiction that is at once evocative and unforgettable. In the following piece, he puts the screws to government inefficiency as only he can.*

Enduring as Dust

Bruce Holland Rogers

I drive past the Department of Agriculture every morning on my way to work, and every morning I slow to a crawl so that I can absorb the safe and solid feel of that building as I go by. The north side of Agriculture stretches for two uninterrupted city blocks. The massive walls look as thick as any castle's. Inside, the place is a warren of offices and suboffices, a cozy organizational hierarchy set in stone. I've often thought to myself that if an H–bomb went off right over the Mall, then the White House, the Capitol, the memorials and the reflecting pools would all be blown to ash and steam, but in the midst of the wreckage and the settling dust, there would stand the Department of Agriculture, and the work inside its walls would go securely on.

I don't have that kind of security. The building that houses the Coordinating Administration for Productivity is smaller than our agency's name. The roof leaks. The walls are thin and haven't been painted since the Great Depression.

That I am here is my own fault. Twenty years ago, when I worked for the Bureau of Reclamation, I realized that the glory days of public dam building were over. I imagined that a big RIF wave was coming to the bureau, and I was afraid that I'd be one of those drowned in the Reduction In Force. So I went looking for another agency.

When I found the Coordinating Administration for Productivity, I thought I had found the safest place in Washington to park my career. I'd ask CAP staffers what their agency did.

"We advise other agencies," they would say.

"We coordinate private and public concerns."

"We review productivity."

"We revise strategies."

"We provide oversight."

"But clearly, clearly, we could always do more."

In other words, nobody knew. From the top down, no one could tell me precisely what the administrative mission was. And I thought to myself, I want to be a part of this. No one will ever be able to suggest that we are no longer needed, that it's time for all of us to clear out our desks, that our job is done, because no one knows what our job *is*.

But I was wrong about the Bureau of Reclamation. It hasn't had a major project for two decades, doesn't have any planned, and yet endures, and will continue to endure, through fiscal year after fiscal year, time without end. It is too big to die.

The Coordinating Administration for Productivity, on the other hand, employs just thirty civil servants. We're always on the bubble. With a stroke of the pen, we could vanish from next year's budget. All it would take is for someone to notice us long enough to erase us. And so, as I soon learned, there was an administrative mission statement after all: Don't Get Noticed.

That's why we never complained to GSA about the condition of our building, why we turned the other cheek when FDA employees started parking in our lot and eventually took it over. That's also why no one ever confronted the secretaries about the cats named Dust. And above all, that is why I was so nervous on the morning that our chief administrator called an "urgent meeting."

I sat waiting outside of the administrator's office with Susana de Vega, the assistant administrator, and Tom Willis, Susana's deputy. "I don't like this," Tom said. "I don't like this one damn bit."

Susana hissed at him and looked at the administrator's secretary. But Roxie wasn't listening to us. She was talking, through an open window, to the cat on the fire escape. The cat was a gray tom with the tattered ears of a streetfighter. He backed up warily as Roxie put the food bowl down. "Relax, Dust," she said. "I'm not going to hurt you."

It was January, a few days before the presidential inauguration, and the air coming in through the window was cold, but nobody asked Roxie to close it.

"When has Cooper ever called an *urgent* meeting?" Tom continued in a lower voice. "Hell, how many times has he called a meeting of any damn kind? He's up to something. He's got to throw his goddam Schedule-C weight around while he still has it to throw."

Throwing his weight around didn't sound like Bill Cooper, but I didn't bother to say so. After all, Cooper was a political appointee on his way out, so whether he threw his weight around or not, Tom's underlying point was correct: Cooper was a loose cannon. He had nothing to lose. Intentionally or not, he might blow us up.

Roxie waited to see if the cat would consent to having his chin scratched, but Dust held his ground until the window was closed. Even then, he approached the food warily, as if checking for booby traps.

Susana told Tom to relax. "Two weeks," she reminded him. "Three at the outside."

"And then God only knows what we'll be getting," Tom said, pulling at his chin. "I hate politics."

Roxie's intercom buzzed, and without turning away from the cat she told us, "You can go in now."

I followed Susana and Tom in, and found Cooper nestled deeply in his executive chair, looking as friendly and harmless as he ever had. His slightly drooping eyelids made him seem, as always, half asleep. He waved us into our seats, and as I sat down, I realized how little he had done to personalize his office in the twelve years of his tenure. Everything in the room was government issue. There weren't any family pictures or the usual paperweights made by children or grandchildren. In fact, there wasn't anything on the surface of his desk at all. It was as if Cooper had been anticipating, from the day he moved in, the day when he would have to move out.

There was *some* decoration in the room, a pen and ink drawing on the wall behind Cooper, but that had been there for as long as I had been with the CAP. It showed an Oriental-looking wooden building next to a plot of empty ground, and I knew from having looked once, maybe fifteen years ago, that the drawing wasn't just hung on the wall. The frame had been nailed into the paneling, making it a permanent installation.

"People," Cooper said from deep inside his chair, "we have a problem." He let that last word hang in the air as he searched for what to say next.

Susana, Tom and I leaned forward in our chairs.

"An impropriety," he went on.

We leaned a little more.

"A mystery."

We watched expectantly as Cooper opened his desk drawer and took out a sheet of paper. He studied it for a long time, and then said, "You people know my management style. I've been hands-off. I've always let you people handle the details," by which he meant that he didn't know what we did all day and didn't care, so long as we told him that everything was running smoothly. He tapped the sheet of paper and said, "But here is something that demands my attention, and I want it cleared up while I'm still in charge."

And then he read from the letter in his hand. The writer represented something called the Five-State Cotton Consortium, and he had come to Washington to get advice on federal funding for his organization. He had taken an employee of the Coordinating Administration for Productivity to lunch, picking her brain about the special appropriations process as well as various grant sources. The woman had been very helpful, and the letter writer just wanted Cooper to know that at least one member of his staff was really on the ball. The helpful staffer's name was Kim Semper.

At the sound of that name, I felt ice form in the pit of my stomach. I stared straight ahead, keeping my expression as plain as I could manage. I knew some of what Cooper was going to say next, but I tried to look genuinely surprised when he told us what had happened after he received the letter.

"I wanted to touch base with Ms. Semper and make sure that the citizen hadn't actually paid for her lunch. You people know as well as I do that we don't want any conflict of interest cases."

"Of course not," said Susana. "But I don't see how there could be any such conflict. We don't actually make funding decisions."

"We don't?" Cooper said, and then recovered to say, "No, of course not. But you people will agree that we wouldn't want even the *appearance* of impropriety. And anyway, that doesn't matter. What matters is that in my search for Kim Semper, I came up empty. We don't have an employee by that name."

Trying to sound more convincing than I felt, I said, "Maybe it's a mistake, Bill. Maybe the letter writer had the name wrong, or sent the letter to the wrong agency."

"Hell, yes!" Tom said with too much enthusiasm. "It's just some damn case of mistaken identity!"

But Cooper wasn't going to be turned easily. "I called the citizen," he told us. "No mistake. Someone is posing as an officer of our agency, a criminal offense."

I said, "Doesn't there have to be intent to defraud for this to be a crime?"

Cooper frowned. "The citizen did buy lunch for this Kim Semper. She benefitted materially." He shook the letter at me. "This is a serious matter."

"And one we'll get to the bottom of," Susana promised.

"I want it done before my departure," Cooper said. "I don't want to saddle my successor with any difficulties," by which he meant that he didn't want to leave behind any dirty laundry that might embarrass him when he was no longer in a position to have it covered up.

Susana said again, "We'll get to the bottom of it."

Cooper nodded at Tom. "I want a single point of responsibility on this, so the personnel director will head up the investigation."

With Cooper still looking at him, Tom looked at me expectantly, and I felt compelled to speak up. "That would be me," I said. "Tom's your deputy assistant."

"Of course," Cooper said, covering. He turned to me. "And you'll report to him." Then he added, "You aren't too busy to take care of this matter, I assume."

"It'll be tight," I said, thinking of the Russian novel I'd been wading through for the last week, "but I'll squeeze it in."

Outside of Cooper's office, Susana patted Tom's shoulder, then mine, and said with complete ambiguity, "You know what to do." Then she disappeared down the hall, into her own office.

Roxie's cat was gone, but Roxie had something else to distract her now. She was reading a GPO publication called, *Small Business Administration Seed Projects: Program Announcement and Guidelines.* She didn't even look up when Tom hissed at me, "Sit on it!"

"What?"

"You know damn well what I mean," Tom said through his teeth. "I don't know what this Kim Semper thing is all about, and I don't want to know! This is just the kind of problem that could blow us out of the goddam water!"

I said, "Are you telling me to ignore an assignment from the chief administrator?"

I could see in Tom's eyes the recognition that he had already been too specific. "Not at all," he said in a normal voice, loud enough for Roxie to overhear if she were listening. "I'm telling you to handle this in the most appropriate fashion." Then he, too, bailed out, heading for his own office.

I found my secretary, Vera, trying to type with a calico cat in her lap. The cat was purring and affectionately digging its claws into Vera's knee.

"Damn it, Vera," I said, surprising myself, "the memo specifies feeding only. Everybody knows that. You are not supposed to have the cat inside the building!"

"You hear that, Dust?" Vera said as she rubbed behind the cat's ears. "It's back out into the cold with you." But she made no move to get up.

"Hold my calls," I growled. I went into my office and closed the door, wishing that I had a copy of the legendary memo so that I could read chapter and verse to Vera. It was bad enough that the secretaries had distorted the wording of the memo, issued well over twenty years ago, that had allowed them to feed a stray cat named Dust, "and only a cat named Dust." It seemed like every so often, they had to push beyond even the most liberal limits of that allowance, and no manager was willing to make an issue of it, lest it turn into a civil service griev-ance that would bring an OPM investigation crashing down around our ears.

I didn't stew about the cat for long. I still had Kim Semper on my mind. It took me a few minutes to find the key to my file cabi-net, but once I had the drawer open, there weren't many folders to search through before I found what I wanted. I untaped the file folder marked PRIVATE and pulled out the letter. It was addressed to me and sported an eleven-year-old date. "After failing to determine just who her supervisor is," the text began, "I have decided to write to you, the Director of Personnel, to commend one of your adminis-trators, Miss Kim Semper." The story from there was pretty much the same: a citizen had come to Washington looking for information, had stumbled across the Coordinating Administration for Productiv-ity, and had ended up buying Semper's lunch in exchange for her insights on the intricacies of doing business in the Beltway. Though he had been unable to contact her subsequently, her advice had been a big help to him.

After checking the personnel files, I had called the letter writer to tell him that he'd been mistaken, that there was no Kim Semper here at the CAP. Maybe, I suggested, he had gone to some other agency and confused the names? But he was sure that it was the CAP that he had consulted, and he described our building right down to the tiny, nearly unreadable gray lettering that announced the agency's name on the front door.

In a government agency, a mystery, any mystery, is a potential bomb. If you're not sure of what something is, then you assume that it's going to blow up in your face if you mess with it. At the CAP, where everything was uncertain and shaky to begin with, the unknown seemed even more dangerous. So I had buried the letter.

Now maybe it was coming back to haunt me. I wondered if I should cover my tail by Xeroxing my letter and bringing Cooper a copy right now. "Hey, Bill. I had to check my files on this, to make sure, but would you believe . . ." Maybe that would be good damage control.

But maybe not. After all, Cooper seemed to think this was an urgent matter. I had known about it for eleven years and done nothing. And my letter was so old that I probably didn't have to worry about it hurting me if I didn't bring up its existence. By now, the writer himself might not even remember sending it to me. Perhaps the man was even dead. If I kept my mouth shut, it was just possible that no one would ever know about my Kim Semper letter. And if that was what I wanted, then it would help my cause to do just what Tom had urged: To sit on the investigation, to ignore Kim Semper until the executive branch resignations worked their way down, layer by layer, from the new president's cabinet to our agency, and Cooper was on his way.

Either option, hiding the letter or revealing it, had its dangers. No matter how I played it out in my mind, I couldn't see the safe bet. I returned to what I'd been doing before the meeting with Cooper, and I should have been able to concentrate on it. Napoleon was watching this Polish general, who wanted to impress him, trying to swim some cavalry across a Russian river, but the horses were drowning and everything was a mess. It was exciting, but it didn't hold my attention. I read the same page over and over, distracted with worry.

At the end of the day, there was no cat in Vera's lap, but there was a skinny little tabby begging on the fire escape. At her desk, Vera was pouring some cat food into a bowl labeled, "Dust."

"Sorry I snapped earlier," I said.

"Bad day?" Vera said, opening the window.

"The worst," I told her, noticing the stack of outgoing mail on her desk. "Is that something I asked you to do?"

"Oh, I'm just getting some information for the staff library," she said.

I nodded, trying to think of something managerial to say. "You're self-directed, Vera. I like to see that."

"Oh, I've always been that way," she told me. "I can't stand to be idle." She opened the window to feed the cat and said, "Here you go, Dust."

Cooper called another meeting for Thursday of the next week. It was the day after the inauguration, and he must have felt the ticking clock. Before the meeting, Tom called me.

"How's your investigation coming?" he said.

"Slowly."

"Good. That's damn good. See you in the old man's office."

For once there wasn't a cat on Roxie's fire escape. Cooper's door was open, and I walked right in. Susana and Tom were already there, and Cooper motioned me to a seat. Cooper didn't waste any time.

"What have you got?"

I opened my notebook. "First, I double-checked the personnel files, not just the current ones, but going back twenty-five years." I looked at Cooper grimly. "No one by the name of Kim Semper has *ever* worked for the Coordinating Administration for Productivity."

"Yes, yes," Cooper said. "What else?"

"I called over to the Office of Personnel Management. There is not now, nor has there ever been, anywhere in the civil service system, an employee named Kim Semper." I closed the notebook and put on the face of a man who has done his job well.

Cooper stared at me. I pretended to look back at him earnestly, but my focus was actually on the framed pen and ink behind him. If I had to give it a title, I decided, it would be, "Japanese Shed With Empty Lot."

At last Cooper said, "Is that all?"

"Well, Bill, I haven't been able to give this my full attention."

"It's been a week, a *week* since I brought this up to you people."

"And a hellish week it's been," I said, looking to Tom for help.

"That's true," Tom jumped in. "The inauguration has stirred things up. We've had an unusually, ah, unusually heavy run of requests." Cooper frowned, and I could see Tom's hands tighten on the side of his chair. He was hoping, I knew, that Cooper wouldn't say, "Requests for what? From whom?"

Susana saved us both by saying, "I'm ashamed of the two of you! Don't you have any sense of priorities? And, Tom, you're supposed to be supervising this investigation. That means staying on top of it, making sure it's progressing." She turned to Cooper. "We'll have something substantial next week, Bill."

"I don't know, people," Cooper said. "Realistically, something like this is out of your purview. Maybe it calls for an outside investigator."

Cooper was almost certainly bluffing. Any dirt at the bottom of this would cling to him like tar if we brought in the consul general's office. He wanted to keep this internal as much as we did.

Even so, Susana paled. She played it cool, but it was a strain on her. "Why don't you see what we come up with in seven working days? Then you can decide."

Minutes later, in the hallway, Tom said, "So what now?"

"Don't look at me," Susana told him without breaking stride. "I pulled your bacon out of the fire, boys. Don't ask me to think for you, too." Then over her shoulder, she added, "You'd just better appear to be making progress by our next little get-together."

Before he left me standing alone in the hallway, Tom said, "You heard the lady, Ace. Let's see some goddam action."

In my office, with the door closed behind me, I finished another chapter of the Russian novel and then got right on the case. I cleared space on the floor and laid out the personnel files for the last eleven years. It made sense to assume that "Kim Semper" was an insider, or had an inside confederate who could arrange her lunchtime meetings. And I knew that Ms. Semper had been working this free-lunch scam since at least the date of my letter. I figured that I could at least narrow down my suspect pool by weeding out anyone who hadn't been with the CAP for that long.

Unfortunately, this didn't narrow things much. Even Cooper, by virtue of three straight presidential victories for his party, had been with the CAP for longer than that.

So what did I really have to go on? Just two letters of praise for Kim Semper, dated eleven years apart. The letter writers themselves had met Kim Semper, but there were good reasons for not calling them for more information. After all, I wanted to keep my letter buried to preserve my plausible deniability. And Cooper's letter writer had already been contacted once about Kim Semper. If I called again and grilled him, he might resent it, and I could use up his good will before I even knew what questions to ask. Also, he might get the impression that the Coordinating Administration for Productivity didn't have its act together, and who knew where that could lead? I didn't want a citizen complaining to his congressional rep.

What I needed was another source, but there wasn't one.

Or was there?

I arranged the personnel files on the floor to look like an organizational hierarchy. If someone were to send a letter praising an employee of the CAP, where might that letter go?

To the top, of course. That was Cooper.

And to the Director of Personnel. That was me.

But what about the space between these two? What about the Assistant Administrator and her Deputy? That is, what about Susana and Tom?

Outside of Susana's office, her administrative assistant, Peter, was preparing to feed a black cat on the fire escape. Almost as soon as he opened the window, Peter sneezed.

"Susana in?"

"Yes," Peter said, "but she's unavailable." He set the cat bowl down and closed the window. Then he sneezed again.

"If you're so allergic," I said, "how come you're feeding the kitty?"

"Oh, I like cats, even if they do make my eyes swell shut." He laughed. "Anyway, feeding Dust is the corporate culture around here, right? When in Rome . . ."

From the other side of Susana's door, I could hear the steady beat of music.

I watched the stray cat as it ate. "I'm surprised, with all the cats on our fire escapes, that it isn't just one continuous cat fight out there."

"They're smart animals," Peter said. "Once they have a routine, they stay out of each other's way."

I nodded, but I wasn't really paying attention. Over the beat of the music, I could hear a female voice that wasn't Susana's counting
one-and-two-and-three-and—

I went to her door and put my hand on the knob.

"I told you," Peter said. "Susana's unavailable. If you want to make an appointment . . ."

"This can't wait," I said. I opened the door.

Susana was in a leotard, and I caught her in the middle of a leg lift. She froze while the three women on the workout tape kept on exercising and counting without her.

"I told Peter I wasn't to be disturbed," she said, still holding her leg up like some varicolored flamingo.

"This won't take but a minute," I said. "In fact, you can go right on with your important government business while we talk."

She stopped the tape and glared at me. "What do you want?"

"To get to the bottom of this Kim Semper thing. And if that's what you really want too, then you can't be throwing me curve balls."

"What are you talking about?" She pushed the audiovisual cart between two file cabinets and threw a dust cover over it.

"I'm talking, Susana, about sitting on information. Or call it withholding evidence. I want your correspondence file on Kim Semper."

Susana circled behind her desk and sat down. Ordinarily, that would have been a good gesture, a way of reminding me that she was, after all, the assistant admin, and this was her turf I had invaded. But it was a hard move to pull off in a leotard. "Just what makes you think I even have such a file?"

That was practically a confession. I fought down a smile. "I'm on your side," I reminded her. "But we've got to show some progress on this. Cooper is on his last official breath. Dying men are unpredictable. But if we hold all the cards, how dangerous can he be?"

She stared over my head, no doubt thinking the same thoughts I had about my own Kim Semper letter. How would Cooper react to knowing that she'd had these letters in her files all along?

"You've got the file where, Susana? In your desk? In one of those cabinets? If I close my eyes," I said, closing them, "then I'll be able to honestly tell Cooper that I don't know *exactly* where my information came from. It was just sort of dropped into my lap."

It took her a minute of rummaging, and then a folder fell into my hands. I opened my eyes. The three letters ranged from two to ten years old.

"Read them in your own office," she said. "And next time, knock."

On my way out, I noticed that Peter was reading something called *America's Industrial Future: A Report of the Presidential Colloquium on U.S. Manufacturing Productivity for the Year 2020 and Beyond.* A thing like that wouldn't ordinarily stick in my mind, except that Tom's secretary, Janet, was reading the same report. She was also holding a mottled white and tan cat in her lap. I didn't bother to confront her about it— that was Tom's fight, if he wanted to fight it. I just knocked on Tom's door and stepped into his office.

He swept a magazine from his desk and into a drawer, but he wasn't fast enough to keep me from noting the cover feature: THE GIRLS OF THE PAC TEN. "What the hell do you want?" he growled.

"A hell of a lot more than I'm getting," I barked back. "Damn little you've done to help this investigation along, Willis. Enough bullshit. I'm up to here with bullshit. I want your goddam Kim Semper correspondence file."

"Like hell." Tom glowered, but a little quiver of uncertainty ran across his lowered eyebrows. He wasn't used to being on the receiving end of such bluster.

"Cut the crap, Tom. This goddam Semper bullshit will toss us all on our asses if we don't give Cooper something to chew on. So give."

A little timidly, he said, "I don't know what you're . . ."

"Like hell," I said, waving de Vega's letters. "Susana came across, and I'd sure as hell hate to tell Cooper that you're the one stalling his goddam investigation."

He bit his lip and took a file cabinet key from his desk drawer. "Jesus," he said. "I've never seen you like this."

"You better hope like hell you never see it again," I said, which was probably overdoing things, but I was on a roll.

As I read it in my office, the first of Tom's letters cheered me considerably. One was twenty years old, which altered my suspect list quite a bit. From my array of files on the floor, I removed anyone who hadn't been with the CAP for the last two decades. That left just myself, Tom Willis, and Tom's secretary Janet. I picked up Janet's file and smiled. Kim Semper, I thought, you have met your match.

And then I read Tom's other letter, the most recent one of all, excepting Cooper's. It praised Mr. Kim Semper, for *his* dedication to public service.

No, I thought. This can't be right.

Unless there was more than one Kim Semper.

I sat down behind my desk. Hard. And I thought about the cat named Dust, who came in a dozen variations, but who, by long tradition, was always Dust, was always considered to be the same cat, because the ancient memo had allowed for the feeding of a cat named Dust, "and only a cat named Dust."

I picked up the phone and dialed the number of the man who had written to praise Mr. Semper. "Mr. Davis," I said when I had him on the line, "one of our employees is in line for a service award, and I just want to make sure it's going to the right person. You wrote a letter to us about a Mr. Kim Semper. Now, we've got a Kim Semple on our staff, and a Tim Kemper, but no Kim Semper. Could you do me the favor of describing the man who was so helpful?"

As lame stories go, this one worked pretty well. It sounded plausible, and it didn't make the CAP look bad. And it brought results. Davis was only happy to make sure Semper or Semple or Kemper got his due. The description fit Peter to a T.

I tried the next most recent letter, but the number had been disconnected. The next one back from that—I changed Tim Kemper to Lynn—brought me a good description of Roxie. The third call, the one that cinched it, paid off with a description that could only be my own Vera.

That's when I buzzed Vera into my office.

"I want a copy of the cat memo," I told her.

"The cat memo?"

"Don't fence with me. If you don't have a copy of it yourself, you know how to get one. I want it within the hour." Then I lowered my voice conspiratorially. "Vera, I don't have anything against cats. Trust me on that."

She had a copy in my hands in five minutes. When I looked at the date, I whistled. Dust the cat had been on this officially sanctioned meal ticket for more than forty years, much longer than I had supposed. The memo also named the secretary who had first started feeding Dust. After a phone call to OPM, I was on my way to Silver Spring, Maryland.

The house I stopped in front of was modest, but nonetheless stood out from all the other clapboard houses on that street. There were abstract, Oriental-looking sculptures in the garden. The white stones around the plum trees had been raked into tidy rows, and there was a fountain bubbling near the walkway to the front door.

A white-haired woman holding a gravel rake came around the side of the house, moving with a grace that belied her eighty years.

"Mrs. Taida?" I said. She looked up and waved me impatiently into the garden. As I opened the gate, I said, "I'm the one who called you, Mrs. Taida. From the Coordinating Administration for Productivity?"

"Yes, of course," she said. As I approached, she riveted me with her gaze. Her eyes were blue as arctic ice.

"You are Janet Taida, yes?"

"You expected me to look more Japanese," she said. "Taida was my husband's name. Sakutaro Taida. The artist." She waved at the sculptures.

"I see," I said, then reached into my pocket for the photocopied memo. "Mrs. Taida, I want to talk to you about the cat named Dust."

"Of course you do," she said. "Come inside and I'll make some tea."

The house was furnished in the traditional Japanese style, with furniture that was close to the floor. While Mrs. Taida started the water boiling in the kitchen, I looked at the artwork hanging on the walls. There were paintings and drawings that seemed vaguely familiar, somehow, but it wasn't until I saw the big pen and ink on the far wall that I knew what I was looking for.

"There's a drawing like this in the administrator's office," I said when Mrs. Taida came into the room with the teapot.

"A drawing *almost* like that one," Mrs. Taida said. She waved toward a cushion. "Won't you sit down?" she commanded. She poured the tea. "That's a Shinto temple. It has two parts, two buildings. But only one stands at a time. Every twenty years, one is torn down and the other is rebuilt. They are both present, always. But the manifestation changes."

"The drawing at work shows the other phase," I said, "when the other building is standing and this one has been torn down."

Mrs. Taida nodded. A white long-haired cat padded into the room.

"Dust?" I said.

Taking up her teacup, Mrs. Taida shook her head. "No, there's only one Dust."

I laughed. "But like the temple, many manifestations." I unfolded the memo. "This memo, the Dust memo, mentions you by name, Mrs. Taida. You started it, didn't you? You were the administrator's secretary when the secretaries received their sanction to keep caring for, as it says here, 'a cat named Dust.' "

"Once we began to feed one, it was very hard to turn the others away. So I read the memo very carefully."

"Mrs. Taida, cats are one thing, but . . ."

"I know. Cats are one thing, but Kim Semper is far more serious, right?" She lowered her teacup. "Let me explain something to you," she said. "The Coordinating Administration for Productivity was commissioned over fifty years ago. They had a clear wartime purpose, which they completed, and then the agency began to drift. Your tea is getting cold."

She waited until I had picked it up and taken a sip.

"A government agency develops a culture, and it attracts people who are comfortable with that culture. After its wartime years the CAP attracted ostriches."

I opened my mouth, but she held up her hand.

"You can't deny it," she said. "For forty years, the CAP has been managed by men and women who wanted to rule over a quiet little fiefdom where nothing much happened."

She sipped her own tea.

"Do you have any idea what it's like to be a secretary under conditions like that?" She shook her head. "Nothing happens. There's too little to do, and the day just crawls by. You can't have any idea how hard it was, at the end of the war and with a Japanese husband, to get a government job. And then to have to sit on my hands all day, doing nothing . . ."

"Mrs. Taida . . ."

"I am not finished speaking," she said with authority, and I felt my face flush. "As I was saying, working at the CAP was like being a sailor on a rudderless ship. Have some more tea."

I held out my cup, as commanded.

"What endures in a government agency?" she asked as she poured again. "The management? The support staff? Job titles shift. Duties change. But the culture remains. It's like the tradition of a secretary feeding a stray cat at ten in the morning. The secretary may retire, but another will come, and if there's a tradition of feeding the stray cat at ten, then the person who takes the job will likely be someone who likes cats anyway. The cat may die or move on, but another will appear before long. The feeding goes on, even if who is fed and by whom changes over time."

She put the teapot down. "Administrators come and go, but the culture endures. And Kim Semper endures. When a citizen calls the agency for help, he isn't referred to management. No one at that level knows anything. No, the citizen is referred to Kim Semper. And for the pleasure of the work itself, of knowing things and being helpful, the secretaries do the job of the Coordinating Administration for Productivity. And they do a very good job. How many of those people who are helped by Kim Semper bother to write letters, do you suppose? And how many of the letters that are written actually end up in the hands of CAP administrators? Kim Semper provides good answers to hard questions about productivity and legislative action. I gave the CAP a rudder, you see. It operates from the galley, not the bridge."

"There's the question of ethics," I said. "There's the matter of lunches paid for by citizens, of benefit derived by fraud."

She looked at me long and hard. It was a look that said everything there was to say about collecting a GS–13 salary working for an agency where the managers were fuzzy about how they should fill their days. She didn't have to say a word.

"Well, what am I supposed to do then?" I said. "Now that I know the truth, what do I say when the administrator asks for my report?"

"You didn't get to where you are today without knowing how to stall," Mrs. Taida said. "You do what you do best, and let the secretaries do what *they* do best."

"What about *after* Cooper is gone?" I said. "This is a bomb just waiting to go off. This is the kind of thing that can sink a little agency like ours."

"The Coordinating Administration for Productivity is a fifty-year-old bureaucracy," Mrs. Taida said, "with a little secret that no one has discovered for forty years. You're the only one who threatens the status quo." She picked up our teacups and the pot. "If you don't rock the boat, I'm sure the CAP, along with Dust and Kim Semper, will endure for time without end. And now, if you don't mind, I have things to do."

I drove back to the office slowly. I knew what I had to do, but I didn't know exactly how to get it done. At least, not until I got as far as the Department of Agriculture. There, I pulled into the right lane and slowed to a crawl.

Size, I thought. The thing that comforts me about the Department of Agriculture is its size. It is big and white and easy to get lost in. That's what safety is.

I drove back and got right to work. It was a big job. I enlisted Vera and Roxie, along with Janet, Peter, and some of the secretaries from downstairs. I didn't explain in great detail what we were doing or why it was important. They understood. In a week, we had generated the very thing that Bill Cooper had called for.

"Results," I announced, shouldering between Susana and Tom to drop my report onto Cooper's desk. It landed with a thud. Cooper blinked slowly, then opened the heavy white binding to the first page. *A Report on Personnel and Operational Dislocation at the Coordinating Administration for Productivity,* it read. "Everything you need to know about Kim Semper is in there."

Cooper nodded. "It's, ah, impressive. You people really knocked yourselves out."

"Yes, sir," I said. "I can't take all the credit. Susana and Tom were instrumental, really."

Neither of them looked up. They were still staring at the report.

Cooper began to scan the executive summary, but his eyes began to glaze when he got to the paragraph about operational location as a time- and institution-based function not contingent upon the identity of the individual operator. "So can you summarize the contents for me?"

"Well," I said, "it's a bit involved. But you can get the gist of it in the summary that you're reading."

Cooper kept thumbing through the summary. It went on for ninety-three pages.

"To really get a complete sense of the situation," I said, "you'll need to read the complete report. Right, Susana?"

She nodded. "Of course."

"Tom?"

"You bet your ass. It's all there, though. Every damn bit of it." He said it with pride, as though he really had made some contribution.

"It took a thousand pages to get it said, Bill. And it really takes a thousand to make sense of it all. So, you see, I can't just give it to you in a sentence."

"I see," Cooper said, nodding, and he was still nodding, still looking at the four-inch volume, when Susana and Tom and I left the room.

"You're a goddam genius is what you are," Tom said. And Susana told me, "Good work."

And when Cooper cleared out for good, he left the report behind. It's there still, taking up space on his successor's desk. Sometimes when

I see it sitting there, I think to myself that a bomb could go off in that room, and everything would be blown to hell but that plastic-bound, metal-spined, ten-pound volume of unreadable prose. It wouldn't suffer so much as a singed page.

It gives me a safe and solid feeling.

Barbara D'Amato is an accomplished short fiction writer who has appeared in I, P.I., Cat Crimes, and Malice Domestic V. Her mystery tales range from poignant to parsimonious, cozy to chilling, and always leave a reader wanting more. "Freedom of the Press" is a short, snappy story about what one has to do to get ahead in Washington, D.C.

Freedom of the Press

Barbara D'Amato

I walked into the office of Representative Peggy Nicklis at 1:55, for a two o'clock appointment. Then I stopped and stared.

She saw my face and started to laugh. When she was done chuckling, she said, "You're Cat Marsala?"

"Yup. Thank you for seeing me, Ms. Nicklis."

"And you expected a much grander office." She was still half laughing.

"Well, I didn't expect—uh—exposed heat pipes, cracked linoleum, a sloping ceiling, two small rooms—I suppose this outer room is for your secretary?—furniture that looks like it was retired from the Library of Congress, and a window the size of the Elvis stamp." In addition there was a slightly off-center bookcase crammed with books, several reasonably adequate bookcases visible in the inner office, some empty cartons, an old desk in the reception room and an old desk in the inner office. Three phones and an answering machine on each desk. Two very large metal wastebaskets. A plush blue cat bed and a litter box in Nicklis's inner office. And a cat. Everything in both offices was tidy; everything was neat and straight and clean, but the place was definitely shabby. Nicklis watched me, smiling.

"It's a matter of seniority. You get better and better offices the longer you're here. Washington is all about how important you are. This is definitely a starter office. Plus, this isn't the only thing," she said. "The nearest bathroom for women is *seven flights* of stairs away from here."

"Jeez!"

"And not just seven flights," she giggled, "but down three, then *up* two, then down two."

"They weren't prepared for you women."

"Well, it also makes you feel sorry for two hundred years of secretaries, dashing for the far-off watercloset."

I had recognized her right away, of course, from a zillion photographs and television interviews. So she seemed like an old friend. She acted like one too, showing me into her office and sitting down next to me in a corner where she had two overstuffed chairs. The cat came over, swept its body across my ankle and told me it wanted to be stroked precisely twice. Cats know exactly what they want. After graciously accepting this homage he allowed Peggy to scratch his ear, then he stared at each of us in turn, collecting admiration.

I asked, "Who is Mr. Cat?"

What I thought she said was:

"His name is Mugum."

"Mugum?" I looked at the tawny, lithe cat. He went to his big, plush cushion and lay down. He lifted one hind leg in the air to inspect it. Apparently decided it was an excellent leg. He put it down and rolled onto his back.

"Mugum is a very unusual name."

"It's spelled 'MGM.' Pronounced Mugum. He's named that because he looks like the MGM lion. MGM is a ginger tom, aren't you, baby?"

"Did you get him after you moved here—"

"Oh, Lord, no! I've had him all his life. He's seven now. We've moved to D.C. together, haven't we, tough guy? MGM goes everywhere with me."

MGM curled up and went to sleep.

Peggy Nicklis was slender, with dark hair cut blunt. An easy-care style. She wore a suit and flat shoes that would be easy to get around in. My mother would have said, "She doesn't do a lot for herself." Peggy also wasn't what United States culture in the waning days of the twentieth century considered especially beautiful.

Peggy Nicklis certainly wasn't the first woman to serve in the House of Representatives, but she was the first from an extremely conservative district just northwest of Chicago. She had received a considerable amount of media attention because she had won without being particularly flashy in her statements or striking-looking in her photographs. The word for Peggy was businesslike, and she had received the trust of the voters, rather than catching their fancy.

Hal Briskman at *Chicago Today* had said to me:

"What we want is a story about how she's settling in, now that she's been in Washington three weeks. Is D.C. intimidating to her? How does she like her office? Are rents breathtakingly expensive? Does she feel like one of the gang yet?"

"That's not very pithy, Hal."

"We don't want pith. Readers are fed up with pith. Don't talk budget deficit with her, Cat. That's not what we want right now. Don't talk health care. Don't talk education priorities. Do a fluff piece."

"Fluff! I don't do fluff."

"Fluff is good for the soul."

"Not this soul. But I *will* do the interview, if you want."

"And do it the way I want. Keep in mind: you play, we pay."

"Oh, very well."

He said he'd pay for the tickets, meals of course, and two nights at a hotel in D.C., which adds up. And pay for the article, of course. Well, that's the business I'm in. I'm freelance, which is always a precarious way to live. And while some of the stories I've done have been big, and my byline is noticed by an occasional reader, I'm not famous.

Being famous would be nice.

Peggy answered my questions straightforwardly. "Well, yes. Rent here truly does take your breath away. For what you'd pay in Chicago for a medium-sized apartment with a Lake Michigan view, here you get one and a half rooms looking out at a fire escape and the brick wall of the building next door ten feet away."

"You're saying we aren't really keeping our legislators happy?"

She smiled. "I wouldn't think of saying that. Anyway, I'm planning to spend most of my time here in the office. I go home mainly to sleep. That way I figure I'll earn more time back in Chicago, too. My folks and my friends are there."

"How about new friends here?"

"I'm meeting a few people. It's slow, though."

"You probably don't have much time to socialize. You have a lot of work and catching up to do."

"Yes. Still, there are parties galore. The White House had the so-called freshmen, the new guys, to dinner. That was exciting. I've been to several special-interest dinners, and a Democratic Party bash in honor of the newcomers. A couple of embassies. My father's family is Polish, so I got asked to their embassy party, of course."

Peggy's secretary came back from late lunch, stuck her head in the door and waved. Peggy introduced her as Annie Boyd.

Peggy said to me, "Could we continue this tomorrow?" To Annie she said, "It was two o'clock Monday and Tuesday, wasn't it?"

In the outer office, Annie nodded her head, yes, it was Monday and Tuesday at two.

The interviewee is always right. I said, "Sure, and thanks." However, it was supposed to be Monday and Tuesday two to three, and this was only two-thirty. Peggy realized that.

"I know we're stopping early. But let me make up for it tomorrow. I'm still backed up with work and I'm barely unpacked."

Well, who could fault a person for that? The last time I moved, it took three months of my life and three years off my life.

Washington was cold but bright Tuesday, and I spent the morning walking. I strolled the Mall, went into the National Air and Space Museum and the National Gallery, and finally walked up Delaware to eat at one of the fast-food places in the underground mall at Union Station. It was truly fast, served coffee in cups as big as soup bowls, and it let me watch the noon news on an overhead TV. There was trouble in the Middle East, fighting in central Europe, and a newsman for United Press International, Lee Chesterton, whom I knew slightly, had driven off the Frederick Douglass Bridge last night and drowned. It was thought alcohol was involved. He was well known here, and it was a big story with a lot of the usual Washington speculation.

After lunch, the Smithsonian beckoned, but a person needs a week to do it justice. No point right now. I strolled through the National Sculpture Garden instead.

A minute or two before the hour, I arrived at Peggy Nicklis's office. Her secretary Annie simply waved me through. No pomp here. Peggy looked tired and the ginger tom was out of sorts too. He hissed at me, then stalked over to the window, jumped up to the ledge and prowled back and forth.

"I heard about Lee Chesterton's accident on the noon news," I told Peggy. "I'd met him a couple of times when he covered a story in Chicago."

"It's a terrible thing to have happened. He was a nice person."

"Yes, terrible. You dated him a couple of times, didn't you?"

She looked up, surprised. "Two or three times. How did you know that?"

"People think reporters just wing it. That must be why they think the job is all glamour and no work." She gave me a lopsided smile. I said, "I always research people I'm going to interview. You were photographed, I think by the Washington *Post*, at a party with him ten days ago or so."

"Yes. It's a shock."

The cat stared at the back of Peggy's neck. He jumped from the windowsill to the desk, and from there to the floor. Peggy got up and shut the door to the outer office. The farther door to the hall was open and she didn't want the cat to get out. The cat stalked past the bed, sheared away, and prowled around the wastebasket as if it were some sort of prey.

I said, "I'm sorry. It must be especially hard for you, so soon after moving in, losing one of the few friends you've met here."

"It is. Although maybe if I'd known him longer it'd be worse." She said this calmly, but there was a lot of sadness in her eyes.

I felt extremely sorry for her. At the same time, I was excited and tense, which made it harder to look relaxed and in charge of a chatty interview. The ginger tom crouched, then sprang forward and ran under the desk. I felt like a cat myself, waiting to spring at a mouse.

"Apparently the investigators believe he'd been drinking," I said. "They're reporting ethanol in the blood."

"He did drink. I asked him not to once, because he always drove his own car. Not like a lot of Washingtonians, you know. They seem to think being chauffeured is proof that you're a real success. Anyway, he didn't like it when I asked him not to drink too much, and I didn't want to upset him, so I just dropped the subject."

Didn't want to turn him off, probably. Unfortunately, Peggy was not a person who would be surrounded by men asking her out.

She said, "Washingtonians drink too much, almost all of them."

I went on. "They think there was somebody else in the car with him. Several cars on the bridge stopped when they saw the Porsche crash through the guardrail. A witness said two people swam away."

"I heard that."

"It looks like they both got out safely. The car floated for a while, and they crawled through an open window. Whoever was with him could swim. But he was a very weak swimmer."

"Unless she—unless whoever it was drowned too."

"Well, no. There was a call from a pay phone reporting the accident. Asking for help. Almost certainly the passenger. I guess she hoped the rescue people might save him."

"I guess."

"I shouldn't have said 'she hoped.' The caller whispered and the news report said the police didn't know if it was a man or woman."

"Yes, I heard that too."

"She has good reason not to want to be identified."

"Yes. The way it is, she could be anybody."

I was profoundly conscious that this could be the scoop of my career. Carefully, I went on.

"Whoever it was, he or she would be guilty of leaving the scene of an accident."

"And that's a crime," Peggy said, placing her hands together, folding the fingers and squeezing.

"Leaving the scene of a fatal accident. I think it's a felony."

She didn't respond. We sat looking at each other for at least half a minute—a *very* long time in polite social discourse. The ginger tom slipped past me, skirted the blue cushion, jumped to the top of a bookcase, and paced back and forth.

Finally, Peggy said:

"Are you going to report that it was me?"

I hesitated too. From feeling excited, I had gone to feeling sick. Some decision had been made viscerally without my brain being involved. It had to do with how I would feel about this six months from now. What I was about to do was foolish. After all, I had my own career to take care of, didn't I? All right. It was my life. I was free to do what I chose. I was going to be foolish.

I said, "No. You've suffered enough."

"What—?"

I pointed to the cat. "He prowls constantly. He's restless. He won't lie down in that bed."

Peggy wrapped her arms around her chest.

I said, "How else would I have known? MGM went everywhere with you. No wonder you're tired. How many pet stores and animal shelters did you have to go to this morning before you found a tom with exactly that coloring?"